Redemption

Cinderella's Secret Witch Diaries

(Book 4)

Ron Vitale

Copyright © 2018 Ron Vitale
All rights reserved.
This book is a work of fiction. Names, characters, places and incidents are the product of the author's imagination or are used fictitiously. Any resemblance to actual events, locales or persons, living or dead, is coincidental.
Visit Ron Vitale's website at www.RonVitale.com
ISBN: 1986864456
ISBN-13: 978-1986864459

To Karen:

There are no guarantees.

Also by Ron Vitale

Ahab's Daughter: The Werewhale Saga (Book 1)
Found: Cinderella's Secret Witch Diaries (Book 3)
Stolen: Cinderella's Secret Witch Diaries (Book 2)
Lost: Cinderella's Secret Witch Diaries (Book 1)
Faith: The Jovian Gate Chronicles (Book 1)
The Jovian Gate Chronicles: Short Story Collection
Betrayals: A Witch's Coven Novel (Book 2)
Awakenings: A Witch's Coven Novel (Book 1)
Dorothea's Song

Chapter 1

I exhaled slowly seeing the white steam get caught up in the wind and blow away from me. Snow blanketed the ground, fresh from overnight, changing the bleak winter landscape into a faerie land. The sun had not risen yet, and a moon still hung high in the sky, rushing off on its way while a pink and orange glow to the east announced the sun's imminent arrival.

The fresh deer tracks in the snow before me and a small pile of droppings marked the spot that the buck had rested for a moment. I knew I was close. I could sense him near me, ahead in the sparse gathering of tall trees that resembled giant skeletons that wore a coat of white. Their leaves had long blown away by the rough winter.

I stopped and crouched down behind a large fallen tree. The buck's hooves clacked against the rocks of the river's embankment, and now I knew where he headed for certain.

Movement to my right caught my attention, and I glanced over to see Jeremiah pointing in the same direction. He already had his rifle out, but I kept mine slung on my back. I preferred to wait until I was closer to an animal before I shot it. We needed to eat to survive, and hunting, for my part, simply meant food for the table. I took no joy in it.

With impressive precision, Jeremiah moved forward, timing his footfalls with the buck's walking on the riverbed's stones. I followed but chose to head off more to the east to be ready to overshoot him if Jeremiah spooked the deer and he ran off. I plunged my hands deep into the pockets of my heavy coat to stay warm. Even with gloves, the biting temperature nipped at me, and when I bent my fingers, pins and needles shot through them.

I loved the cold, but to a point. American winters were harsher than any I had ever seen.

Jeremiah reached the top of the embankment, slowed his pace, and lay flat on his belly. With his rifle out, he looked down at the riverbed. The wind picked up a bit and whipped my scarf across my face, blowing some light snow into my eyes. I could not see for a few moments and repositioned my scarf to protect my face.

Phoebe had made the scarf for me. Its dark purple and pink pattern pleased me. I did not often like such flashy colors, but the scarf complemented my eyes and hair well.

I trudged forward in the snow and went far enough along so that when I came back to the embankment the buck was drinking from the river. Jeremiah remained still and I slowed my walk, searching for a spot to climb down to the riverbed. To my right, a slope with a fallen tree made a perfect path for me to climb down and remain unseen. At the bottom, I held back in order to not walk on the stones and give away my position. If the buck heard me, then he would charge off in the opposite direction and give Jeremiah little time react. The more effective plan would be for Jeremiah to chase the buck in my direction. Unable to cross the wide river, the deer would run to me, and I would take care of the rest. Dragging him home would be hard, but we brought the sled, our knives, and lots of rope.

The buck glanced in my direction, but he could not see me crouched as I was behind the fallen tree. A tiny break in the tree allowed me to peek through and see him, but unless he knew exactly where to look, I could not be found.

From my vantage point, I could see Jeremiah move into position. He crouched low and climbed down the embankment, timing his steps with care. Hiding behind trees and rocks, he reached the riverbed and waved at me. I did not signal back, knowing the buck would see me, but unslung my rifle and prepared to shoot.

Knowing Jeremiah, he would give me a full minute to get into position, not because I needed the time, but out of respect. He liked to be methodical about his hunting, and precision to him was everything.

A sparrow flew across the river, and I watched it land on a branch close to me. The tiny bird settled and stared out at the buck, ready for what came next.

I had lost count how many times Jeremiah and I had hunted, but we made a good team though he tended to be a bit too precise for my taste. My impatience often bucked up against his measured approach. Yet maybe that was why we worked so well together.

I took a deep breath, held it, and waited. If Jeremiah missed, which he hardly ever did, then the buck would charge toward me, and I would have my shot at it.

Jeremiah creeped out from his spot, balancing his rifle, and aimed. His rifle stayed steady, and I counted down. It would only be moments now until he fired. The gunshot would echo across the riverbank, the sparrow next to me would fly away in fear, and the buck would fall onto its side.

Jeremiah's rifle stayed still, and suddenly he fell backward, as though pulled by something, and his rifle went high with his shot launching into the sky. I heard him cry out in surprise, and without a second thought, I rushed toward him.

***

The ground opened up, and without a sound, Jeremiah fell through the ground. He called for help and reached for a branch above him, but his hands grasped empty air. Fear coursed through him, and he expected a long fall into a hidden crevice. He feared hitting the rocks below, breaking his legs, or even losing his life.

Instead, he touched the smooth surface of a man-made floor, but the material was not wood and too smooth to be naturally occurring outside in the middle of the woods. A blue light, only a pinpoint at first, emanated from a small tunnel to his right. He lay on his stomach but quickly pulled himself to his feet, the light growing stronger all the time, expelling the darkness around him.

"Jeremiah, can you hear me?" Phoebe's words echoed in the chamber around him. The light grew, and as he watched, smoke whooshed past him, and he reached out, trying to touch the ceiling, but he could not.

"Where are we?" His voice fluctuated, reverberating off the walls around him, changing intensity and pitch. He swayed a bit as he reached for the walls as they quickly moved past him.

"I don't have much time and need to be brief." She appeared within a sudden beam of light in front of him.

She looked much older than when he had seen her last night when she went to bed, and her appearance caught him off guard. He reached out to touch her hair, longer that he had ever seen it. "What happened to you?"

She shook her head. "I'm fine." A shimmer of light swirled around them, and a cold breeze blew past his face. Phoebe grabbed his hands and held them, squeezing them lightly. "I call back to you because I need your help. You must go back and…"

The connection broke between them, and the room vanished. Jeremiah held his rifle in his hand and had slipped off the rock he had balanced on and fell to the snowy ground. Ahead of him, Cinderella rushed at him, calling out his name. He shook his head and started to speak, but the world dimmed and vanished.

He stood with Phoebe again, and she swayed in the wind, grasping his hands tight. "I cannot stay here for much longer. You're too far away." Her face grimaced, and she squeezed his hands as hard as she could. "Please, you must help Napoleon escape. He must be set free."

"But why?" Jeremiah took the next curve of motion that rocked him to the right, and he hung on to her to help him from falling over. "He tried to kill you."

"Something worse is coming. A creation from men that has no conscience and is out to destroy everyone." Phoebe looked back over her shoulder, and her look of fear could not be hidden. "Napoleon must escape. Let him try to retake Europe. But then you must find Joseph Nicéphore Niépce and use his camera obscura. It'll help you."

"Where are you?" Jeremiah tried to pull her closer to him but could not. She stayed frozen in place. "Your mother and I will come rescue you. Together, we can help you."

Shaking her head, Phoebe leaned as close to his face as she dared. "Promise me." She squeezed his hands harder. "Promise me that you will not tell my mother that I came to talk to you. Everything depends on it. Everything!"

Jeremiah caught a glimpse of a shimmering metallic sphere behind Phoebe, and she let go of his left hand. She clenched her fist, and a pulse of light encircled her arm, and a beam of light fired out at the sphere. It burst into flame, and he heard a crash as it hit something solid. "What is that?"

Phoebe turned back. "I must leave. They found us." She released his hands and put them together in prayer. "Jeremiah, please, all depends on it. If my mother knows that I'm in the future, she will try to follow me, but she needs to be where you are. The timeline will be broken if she knows. All depends on rescuing Napoleon. Everything!"

A blue pulse shot out from behind her, and the bolt hit the wall hard. Sparks flew and a high-pitched sound echoed throughout the room. "Phoebe, wait. I need to know more. I can't just lie to your mother. She'll know!"

"You know her. If she knows, she'll be reckless. Please, trust me." She turned away. "Trust me."

Phoebe vanished from sight, and a wall of sound hit Jeremiah hard. The winter wind rushed through him, displacing air from his lungs, and the light of the rising sun all came toward him. He gasped and his heart beat fast as he searched for a familiar sight to ground himself in what had happened to him. The world swirled, like a wooden top, tumbling to the left and then the right. He closed his eyes, but that only made his disorientation worse.

Jeremiah clutched at the snow on the ground and tried to stop the spinning in his head, but the intensity only increased. A bird called out to the rising sun, the snow, cold to the touch, numbed his right cheek, and without warning, his world went black.

***

I ran past the buck with my rifle slung on my back. I knew enough to stay far away from the buck so that it would not turn on me and attack. I searched for Jeremiah and watched as he fell behind a large tree.

"Jeremiah!" I yelled as loud as I could. His name echoed in the cold morning air from the tree to the small embankment wall.

No one replied.

I came to the fallen tree where he had fallen and cleared it with ease, searching for a few seconds for him. To my right, I found him. He had slipped off a rock and hit the ground hard. The right side of his face was planted in a mound of snow. His eyes fluttered and he moaned, but I could not tell if it was from pain or something else.

"Speak to me." I slid into the snow by him. Gently I turned him over onto his back and put my hands on his cold cheeks. "Are you hurt?"

His eyes opened and his pupils dilated from small to large black circles. "It's you." He smiled and reached up to touch my face.

Two of the knuckles on his right hand were raw and bloody. "Focus on me." I sat him up and he worked with me.

He leaned against the rock next to him, and he noticed the blood on his right hand. "Ouch. That stings."

"What is your name?" I asked, trying to gauge if he had hit his head.

"My name is Jeremiah." He flexed his fingers and grimaced in pain.

"How many fingers am I holding up?" I held my hand in front of him and waited.

"Four." He closed his eyes and took a slow breath in, held it, and then exhaled.

"How about now?" I put my right hand up beside my left.

"I see six." Jeremiah blinked rapidly a few times and then let out a sigh. "Wow."

"Are you dizzy or seeing double?" I checked his eyes still to see if he was tracking with me.

He kept eye contact with me and put both his hands on mine. "I'm okay. I just had the wind knocked out of me and hit the end of the rock hard."

I pulled away from him and checked out the rest of him, paying most attention to his boots and the back of his legs. But nothing appeared unusual. "From my vantage point, it looked like you were pulled down to the ground. Almost as though you had fallen through a hole."

"Nah, I'm fine." He glanced away toward the rising sun. "I just slipped."

I pulled away from him and put my hand on his chest. "Jeremiah Johnson, are you lying to me?"

He took another deep breath but stared at the brightening horizon. "Of course not." He turned back to face me and smiled. "I feel like an idiot because I fell. I'm embarrassed."

"You did that thing that you do when you lie to me." I leaned in close, looking deep in his brown-colored eyes. The morning light lit them up in a golden-brown hue.

"What did I do now?" He chuckled and rubbed the sides of his temple.

"You glanced away from me." I watched him but he remained focused on me, smiling.

"Why would I lie?" He tried to stand up but needed my help. "You'd see right through me if I tried."

I smiled and eased off him. Turning back toward the river, I searched for the deer we had chased, but he had disappeared up the embankment. Chunks of ice floated past us in the water, and steam came out of my mouth. The sun had fully risen and the snow looked pure and white—a blanket that covered the rocks and hung heavy on tree branches.

"Do you feel up for hunting, or do you want to head back?" I put my wool mittens on to keep my fingers warm.

"Let's head back. I could use some coffee to clear my head and then rest up a bit. I really got banged up and need some time to recover." He slung his rifle on his back and headed back home.

I'd known Jeremiah for years now and had only seen him sick once. He had a high fever and spoke deliriously in his sleep of Queen Mab and of his youth. For three days, I worried that the fever would take him, but it did break after midnight on that third night. He slept peacefully then like a child. I watched him walk and could see he had been rattled. His gait looked off, and I knew something bothered him, but I needed to give him time. Jeremiah did not keep secrets from me. But he often did need time to think of what he wanted to say.

We headed back home, and some light clouds came in from the west. The chill remained in the air, and we saw no other sign of people. I spotted a few small birds, but no animals that we could trap for food. We had plenty in our stores, but the buck I had let go would have helped us keep our supplies through any major snowstorm that might hit us later in the month.

January could be a hard month filled with bitter cold and snow that piled in drifts higher than me. I secretly liked the cold though. Growing up in England, we often had a dreary rain, and when we'd go to the city, the grayness would stretch out far and wide through the streets. Here in America, the land was vast and we had such a different climate.

I stopped when I saw Jeremiah hold up his hand for us to stop. He unslung his rifle from his back and held it at the ready.

I crept up close to him and spoke low. "Are there natives nearby?"

He shook his head. "I'm not that good of a tracker. If it were natives, they'd have us surrounded by now."

I closed my eyes and stretched out my senses. I missed having magic, but that wouldn't change anything. I listened and heard a snap of a twig in the trees in front of us and reached for my rifle.

Jeremiah aimed his rifle and took a defensive posture, and I did the same. The rustle of leaves and snapping of twigs continued until a man walked out from the dense forest, and immediately, I relaxed.

Wearing a heavy black coat with a bright red scarf, he waved at us. "Morning!"

"Charley!" I lowered my rifle and ran toward him.

Jeremiah put his weapon away and followed me.

Mr. Radley opened his arms, and I flung myself at him. He wore a great big grin and swung me around like a child. "I've missed you!" He squeezed me tight and kept me close in his left arm and reached out with his right. "But I have room for you, too, Jeremiah. Come on over!"

Embarrassed, Jeremiah come over and shook Mr. Radley's hand. "How is Ginny and the kids?"

"They're fine. That snowstorm from last night wasn't as bad as we thought, but I hadn't seen you two in quite some time. Winter is always so difficult around here, but I thought that Hunter and I would take a morning stroll and come check up on you." He let me go and pointed back toward our homestead. "Ginny baked some breads, and I brought some honey over. I thought you might want some."

"Thank you." Jeremiah warmed a bit and seemed more himself. "You'll have to tell Ginny how much I love her bread."

"More than mine?" I put my fists at my side, feigning anger.

Jeremiah put his hands up in defense. "No, that's not what I mean. I love yours so much more."

"I see you lovebirds are still in your honeymoon phase." Charley winked and then pointed back to the direction he had come. "I also want to see if you'd mind if I take Phoebe back with me. The girls haven't seen her in a while, and we thought it might be nice for her to come over."

At the mention of Phoebe, a worried look came over Jeremiah. I went to say something to him, but Mr. Radley faced me and said, "Of course, if you two are still arguing if my wife's baking is better than yours, well, then maybe it's better that Phoebe stay home to separate you two."

I shook my head and laughed. "Truth be told, Jeremiah does all the baking in the house. I'm horrible at it. I can cook but for some reason, I never did get the hang of baking."

Glancing over to Jeremiah, I expected him to smile or to chime in, but he appeared preoccupied in his thoughts.

Charley noticed his distraction as well and asked, "Do you hear something coming?"

Snapping out of his reverie, Jeremiah scratched the back of his head. "I had a bad fall right before we met up with you, and I'm still a bit dizzy."

"Do you need my help within anything?" Charley, always the knight in shining armor, stepped forward to stand next to Jeremiah. "I can help. Ginny's not expecting me back for a bit."

"No, no, I'm fine. Just a bit dazed, that's all." Jeremiah headed off back to our home and said, "Let's get back to the house, and we'll give Phoebe the good news."

Charley followed Jeremiah and the two of them eased into a conversation about hunting and the latest news from the east. I trailed behind the two of them, watching Jeremiah in concern. Something had happened to him, and I wouldn't stop until I found out what.

***

Phoebe stood before the floor-length mirror, braiding her hair. Outside the wind howled and she knew it would be cold and she needed to be ready to go or when Mr. Radley returned with her mother and stepfather.

She smiled at the thought.

The door opened downstairs, and she did not expect them to be back so soon. She would have to rush. She threw a brush into her bag and called downstairs. "I'll be right there!"

When no one responded, she froze and turned away from the mirror. "Is anyone there?"

A creak from the steps announced that someone walked upstairs. She rushed across her room to slam the door shut but caught a glimpse of the person coming up the stairs and the darkness hit her. She fell forward into its depths. Struggling to break free, she glanced over her shoulder, and her stomach turned as she dropped as though from a great height. The light faded behind her, a glimmer of hope that was out of reach, and she came to a complete stop on her feet. The world had faded away, and she could only see the staircase in front of her.

In front of her, a person approached from the shadows step by step. Phoebe held out her left hand and lit it with her magic. The light emanated forth, lighting up a small sphere around her. Yet the protective spell did nothing to stop the person from approaching.

Her mind raced and she tried to think of a reason for what she saw, but none came to her. The figure stepped into the light and she saw—herself.

"Hello." Her doppelganger appeared many years older, wearing her hair shorter. Yet she had a smile on her face. "I had almost forgotten how young I used to be."

"But how are you…" Phoebe could not finish the question.

"I am from the future and need your help." She kept smiling and reached out to take Phoebe's hand. "You can trust me. I am not a trick."

Cautious at first, Phoebe reached out and took her older self's hand. A flash of blue energy passed between them, but the world did not change in any other way. "It is you." Phoebe's jaw opened and she smiled. "I mean it's me. How did I get there?"

"I do not have much time to explain everything to you. In a few months, you will travel to the future to save our mother. But before you do that, you must help Jeremiah." Phoebe knew herself well and could see that she wanted to say something more but held back on purpose.

"Help him how?" She let go of her older self's hand and took a step back. "You wouldn't come to see me unless there was something urgent happening. Right?"

The older woman glanced away for a second and then leaned to stare right into Phoebe's eyes. "You must help Jeremiah convince your mother to help him rescue Napoleon from his exile."

Phoebe paused a moment and laughed. "You're kidding, right?"

"You must trust me."

"Trust you? This must be some sort of trick. If I truly came from the future to come back and tell myself something, surely it wouldn't be to let out a crazy man like Napoleon." Phoebe huffed and turned on her older self. "Next you're going to tell me that he's had a change of heart and that we should forgive him for all he's done."

"No, that's not what I'm saying." Her older self hung back, searching for the right words to use.

Phoebe pointed at her older self. "I bear the scar from where he cut me with his knife and still have tortured nightmares of him."

"I know that. I've been through all of that as well." She took a tentative step forward and put her hand out to calm Phoebe. "I 'm not asking you to forgive him but to free him so that we can use him. There's a need for him to be a distraction again in Europe, and that will give you time to help right things."

A loud flash of light came from behind the older Phoebe, and she glanced back in frustration.

"Right what things?" Phoebe sensed a more complicated motive behind all that she was being told. "I need to know more if you want me to do this insane thing."

"I am being pulled back." She grimaced in pain as though something pulled at her hair. She fought to keep her ground but started slipping back. "The automatons are coming. They make faeries look like playthings. You have to stop them. Jeremiah knows. You can trust him. He'll do the right thing. Please, I wouldn't have come back to see you unless…"

A burst of brilliant light blinded Phoebe, and she covered her eyes with her hand. The loud rush of wind overcame her senses, and she fell back away from the light. Swirling around her, the wind pushed her back up the time hole she had fallen into, and in an instant, she stood at the top of the steps. Her right foot balanced in the air, ready to go down the next step.

"Phoebe, we're home." Her mother's voice came from the front of the house. "Come on down and get ready to see us before you head off to the Radleys."

Phoebe grabbed the banister to stop herself from falling forward and took a moment to breathe.

Jeremiah stood at the bottom of the steps, and on seeing her face, he rushed up the stairs to her. "Are you well?"

He kept his voice low and balanced her so that she did not fall forward.

"She told me that she had seen you as well. Is it true?" Phoebe put her hand on his arm.

"Yes." He shook his head. "Your older self told me not to tell your mother anything. Please, keep quiet until we can figure something out."

"Okay, but you know Mother. She'll sense something is wrong. She always knows when either of us lie."

"And we won't lie. You head off to the Radleys', I'll talk to her and we'll see each other tomorrow." Jeremiah waited for Phoebe to respond. "Please."

Phoebe waited a moment and thought it through. "I don't know what else I could do that wouldn't worry her." She headed down the stairs. "Okay, I'll remain quiet for now. But what she asked me to do. It doesn't make sense."

Jeremiah frowned. "I know and I think that's why it's of the utmost importance that we do what we were asked. If we tell your mother, we might inadvertently change history or ruin the plans of your future self. For now, you spend the day with the Radleys, and I'll talk with your mother."

She slung her bag on her shoulder and hugged Jeremiah. "I don't like keeping secrets from my mother. All of this could also be some sort of trick." Phoebe released Jeremiah and rushed down the stairs.

"I know." Speaking mostly to himself, Jeremiah watched Phoebe head into the room with her mother and did his best to hide his worry.

***

I broke off a tiny piece of bread and dipped it into some of the honey that Charley had brought over and then popped it into my mouth. The complex swirl of the savory flavors in the bread and the sweet of the honey mixed well together. "Oh, it's delicious. I wasn't expecting the bit of cloves." I glanced around my kitchen and sighed. "I have nothing of value to return to Ginny."

"That's quite all right. I didn't bring the bread and honey over expecting something in return." Charley heard movement behind him and turned to see Phoebe bouncing into the room.

She wore a bright yellow dress with her leggings on. No longer a child and not quite an adult, she straddled the awkward years well. She kissed Charley on the cheek and then rushed over to the bread. "Is this some of Ginny's freshly baked bread?"

"Yes, and it's all mine." I guarded it with my hands and held back. "But you are my favorite daughter…"

"I'm your only daughter." Phoebe reached forward to break off a piece of the bread.

I relented and let her have some, pushing the jar of honey toward her. "Make sure you put some honey on it. That really does the trick, making it the most delicious bread I have ever had."

"High praise!" Jeremiah walked into the room, carrying an armful of books. "I have to get me some of this delicious bread."

I broke off a generous piece for him and dripped some honey on top. The bread was still warm in the middle, and I wanted to pop the bread right into my mouth. "Here, put those books down and have some."

I watched him as he walked and could detect no sign of him acting strangely. He seemed to have recovered from having fallen while hunting.

"Charley, I want you to give these books to your girls. They can have them as long as they'd like. A proper education is important in today's day." Jeremiah put the books down and accepted the bread from me.

"Thank you. They'll love them, but I expect they'll be happier to see Phoebe." A bark outside reminded Charley that Hunter waited for them. "Speaking of the girls, Phoebe, are you ready to head off? I'd like to get back by mid-morning. I have some work to do on the barn door. The wind from the storm broke it off one of its hinges."

"Let me get my coat." Phoebe finished her bread and licked her fingers. She then wiped her hands on her dress, and I tried to ignore her lack of manners. "Come here, Momma, let me give you a kiss."

She threw her arms around me and held me tight. "Please, be good over there. Don't try to be too much of a bother. I know you like to have the twins follow you around like you're their mother duck and they're the ducklings." I kissed her on the cheek and lowered my voice so that only she could hear. "I'm serious. Be careful—with whatever scheme you have going on. I might be older but I'm not blind."

Caught off guard, Phoebe gave a short laugh and replied, "I'll tell Sarah and Teresa what you said so it doesn't go to their heads when I'm strutting around the house and they follow me like quacking ducks." She released me from her hug and said in a whisper, "I'll be careful. I promise."

Mr. Radley buttoned up his coat and said his goodbyes. He took the books that Jeremiah gave him, put them in a bag, and waved. "If things go as well as I expect today, would you mind if I bring her home in the morning? The girls will want her to sleep over and have breakfast with us in the morning."

Jeremiah looked to me to see what I thought. "That's fine."

Phoebe clapped her hands together and grabbed her coat from the rack. "This is to be a party then. I haven't seen your girls in so long. It'll be fun!"

"Oh, yes, it'll be fun." Charley wrapped his scarf around him tight. "It'll be so noisy that I'm glad that I have work to do in the barn." He slung the bag of books onto his shoulder and waved. "I bet I'll still be able to hear them from there."

"You bet you will!" Phoebe headed out of the kitchen, but I could still hear her. "First, we'll have to pretend that we're having a big ball tonight. I think the girls will really like that. It isn't often that the Sun King is coming to visit, so we'll have to decorate, dress up, and put on the very best…"

Her voice faded away as she walked outside and Jeremiah saw Charley to the door. "Good luck today and tonight."

"Looks like I'm going to need it." Charley shook Jeremiah's hand. "Have a good rest of the day, and I'll bring her back tomorrow."

"See you then." Jeremiah walked Charley outside and hurried back inside from the cold.

I went over to the stove and put on a kettle. I needed a cup of tea. "Would you like some more bread?" I would keep the first bit of our conversation civil.

"If I say yes, would that help stave off what's coming next?" Jeremiah scratched the back of his head.

I broke off another piece of bread for him and handed it to him. "You know me that well, do you?"

"Your tell is that you get to be too nice." Jeremiah bit into the bread and talked with his mouth full. "You're never that nice—even to Charley."

I crossed my arms and took a deep breath. "So, tell me, what's going on?"

"What do you mean?" Jeremiah shifted from his left foot to his right. He would rather be anywhere else than standing right now and talking with me.

"Jeremiah, we have known each other for years now, and even though I no longer have magic, I can see through you like a pane of glass."

"I need to talk with you, and you're not going to like what I have to say." He came toward me and took my hand. "Please, sit down."

I glanced over at the kettle and sat. "I'll need to get up once the water's ready. I have a feeling I'm really going to need that cup of tea to calm my nerves."

He sat down next to me at our table and folded his rough hands together. Dirty from falling outside in the snow, he had calluses from the work he did on our farm. "You were right about what happened to me when we were hunting. I didn't fall. I had a vision…"

"Of what?" I crossed my arms and prepared myself for the worst.

He reached out toward me and said, "We need to help Napoleon escape his exile and aid him in his quest to regain control of France."

The words sunk in and I disbelieved it. There was no way Jeremiah could have spoken those words after what we had overcome together. The stone throne, Phoebe nearly killed, and how I had given everything of myself to defeat Napoleon. We had barely defeated him in Russia, and Jeremiah's words stung deep.

I uncrossed my arms and leaned forward and replied, "No."

Jeremiah measured my response and was unsure how to respond. "I'm not telling you this because I believe Napoleon is innocent. He's a monster and doesn't deserve to set foot off that island. I think his punishment wasn't severe enough." He paused and scratched his forehead. "We need to go free him. It's the only thing that will save all of us."

"And if we don't free him. What will happen then? Will all life die? Seriously, how do you expect me to take this and be so forgiving?" I shook my head in disgust.

"You, forgiving?" Jeremiah retorted. "You hold a grudge for years and categorize people's wrongs by their severity. I wouldn't be surprised if you had a book that lists, in order of importance, all the wrongs I have ever done to you since we first met. You are impossible sometimes!"

His bluntness shocked me. I had not seen him so fired up in a long time. "I don't hold grudges like that. I forgive and move on."

"Do you? Truly?" Jeremiah laughed. "If I make a mistake, you'll carry that to your grave."

His forcefulness hit me, and I could see that I had wounded him dearly with my words. I lowered my voice and softened my tone. "That's not true."

"Really?" Jeremiah leaned onto the table. "I have come to you, asking you to trust me with a vision I had, and the first thing you do is to doubt me. I have fought by your side, given my strength and all that I am for you, but your first instinct is to distrust."

His anger stoked my own. "When I first met you, you were a witch hunter. You had tracked me down to drag me back into Europe's problems. For good old England's king and queen." I had lost the thread of my defense and changed tactics. "I have had many betray me over the years. My mother, father, the Silver Fox pretending to be my faerie godmother… All of those people betraying me have left a mark."

"Exactly." Jeremiah leaned back in his chair with a satisfying smirk on his face. "Now we get to the truth. You admit that maybe you are hard on people and refuse to forgive and forget."

I shook my head and caught steam coming out of the kettle. "I will never forget. That's one thing that I cannot do."

"And that is why you will never regain your magic." He released the words at me, and they stung like he had spit at my feet. After he spoke the words, a startled look crossed his face. "I'm sorry. I did not mean that."

I went to the stove and poured myself a cup of tea. I needed time to think. The anger welled up within me, and he knew my deepest fear—that I would never regain the powers I once had. I had sacrificed much to save Phoebe and to defeat Napoleon.

"Would you like some tea?" The emotionless words came from my lips, but inside my head swirled with anger, frustration, and fear.

"No, thank you." His consolatory tone would not sway me.

I came to the table and focused. "I need to know the truth from you. Tell me what your vision was. If you want me to change my mind and to forgive a monster who has invaded all of Europe, causing hundreds of thousands of people to die, then I need to know the full truth."

Jeremiah squirmed in his seat. He took a deep breath and looked up at me as I sat down at the head of the table. I had moved one seat away from him, needing the space to contain my anger. He thought for a moment and then said, "I cannot."

I leaned forward and asked, "Why?"

"I need you to trust me. Please, all depends on it." Jeremiah folded his hands together and pleaded.

"You want me to simply leave our home and put the world at risk again by releasing Napoleon. Is that correct?" I had a difficult time containing the sarcasm in my tone.

"No, I am asking you to trust the man you love. The man who reached out to you on the stone throne and convinced you to get up and continue fighting. I have traveled from here to Russia and back with you, seeing the pain you have suffered and fully understanding why this choice will be so hard for you." He stood up and knelt beside me, pleading. "I beg you, please, do not ask any more of me. If I could tell you, I would. I have shared with you what we need to do, and I need you to trust me like you've never trusted anyone before."

I had never seen Jeremiah deface himself so. I put my cup of tea down and fought back tears. "Please, get up. You do not need to grovel to me. I am not a heartless monster."

He got up and sat in the chair next to me. "And I never said that you were. I'm sorry for what I said earlier."

I cut him off before he could say more. "But you think it's true, don't you?"

He did not flinch or look away from me but held my gaze. "Yes, I do. If you could learn to let go more, I believe your magic would return."

"And this journey that you beg me to go on, what is meant to happen by freeing Napoleon."

"We're going to save the world." He said the words with no emotion.

"From what?"

He took a deep breath and said, "From the future."

He did not turn from me, and from his expression, I knew that he was never more serious in his life. I kept quiet a moment, holding my thoughts together so that the insanity of my next words could be contained and staved off—even if just for a moment. "I'll go with you."

Jeremiah put his hand on mine. "Thank you for trusting me."

I nodded and took his hand in mine, squeezing it tight. "You have a point, and I'm not too proud to admit it. I do need to trust more. You have never given me any reason not to. Your word is good enough for me."

"And the same goes for me. We are a team, you and I." He leaned toward me and gave me an enduring kiss on the lips.

The spark from his kiss woke me and offered just enough energy that I needed to bury the tiny voice of doubt within. Today it would sleep, but I knew that in time that doubt would awake again. I knew myself well enough to know that—as did Jeremiah. For today, we would both pretend that all was well and we would be all right, but deep down both of us knew the real truth—I would bring up my distrust and doubt in the future—no matter how much I tried, we both knew I would.

Chapter 2

Phoebe held the stick in her hand and shook it. Hunter barked as she pretended to play fetch with him. He turned to run off ahead on the trail but stopped and barked again at her. "Okay, okay. I won't play with you anymore. Here you go!" She threw the stick far ahead, and it landed into a small snowdrift.

Charley pointed and said, "Go ahead, Hunter. Go fetch!"

At his master's command, Hunter took off to get the stick.

"He loves this game, doesn't he?" Phoebe rubbed her hands together to stay warm and took in the beautiful countryside. Covered in a heavy snow, the tree branches hung low. She took care to not walk under one that could drop snow on her head.

"Even though my girls play with him every day, he still doesn't get tired of the game." Charley bent over and picked up a large branch, using it to make certain the way was clear in front of them as they walked. "Thank you for coming back to the house with me. I figured it might be good to give your mother and stepdad some time together."

Phoebe looked away and the wind whipped at her face. She covered her face up more with her scarf to protect herself from the cold. "Is it that noticeable that there's been tension between them?"

"It was Ginny's idea that I come over here today. I'm not too knowledgeable about these sorts of things. In our household, there's so many people that there isn't much time to argue. We have to come together to get work on the farm done." Hunter had found the stick and came running back toward them. His brown and white fur was covered in snow.

"When we first came back from defeating Napoleon, things were good. Mom was happy, but I knew that over time she would start to feel the loss of her magic." Phoebe turned to Charley and opened up to him a bit more. "There are times when I hide my own magic from her. It's not that she's jealous of me, but I can see the longing in her face."

"It must be hard to lose that gift. I can only imagine how she must feel." Charley patted his thigh, calling Hunter over to him. The dog dropped the stick at his feet and barked.

Picking the stick up, he winded his arm back and threw it as far as he could out into the field. Hunter paused a moment, unsure where it had gone, and then rushed off to fetch it.

"I tried to convince her to talk to some witches in our state, but she's refused to do so. She's kept everything all bottled up inside, and I think it's starting to come out in ways she didn't intend." Phoebe paused a moment and thought over what she had said. "I mean, it's not that she's outwardly angry all the time, but her patience is less these days. I can't quite explain it, but there's a difference in her."

Charley listened and did not answer at first. He turned away to look at the horizon and lowered his voice. "After Mary passed on, Ginny and I went through a rough time. It was like we lost a part of ourselves. Our eldest daughter died in front of us, and there was nothing we could do to stop it from happening. We were powerless. That affected both of us deeply. I think we both blamed each other for not being able to save our Mary."

Phoebe walked closer to him and put her hand on his shoulder. "I remember that day. I don't think I'll ever forget that." She risked a question and asked, "How did you and Ginny ever recover from your loss?"

He shook his head, and she could see the raw hurt still in his expression. "Some days I don't think we ever have recovered. But what helps is that we're honest with each other. We've suffered a lot and are blessed with the other girls, thanking God for all we now have. It took a long time though to get to where we are, and we didn't do it alone. Our friends and family all helped."

"And that's what I think my mom could use a bit more of—help. She really doesn't do well with admitting that she needs anyone's help. She's very stubborn that way." Phoebe glanced over to their left at Hunter who still searched for the stick. "Maybe if she admitted that she was finding it difficult to get over losing her magic, it would make things easier."

"It probably would. But your mother is a proud woman. And I don't mean that she's like royalty, but she's had to get by on her own, and I think that's really important to her." Charley turned to Phoebe and said, "Maybe if you tell her that, she might listen to you."

"Me? I still think part of her is a bit jealous of the magic I have." Phoebe shrugged. "Well, it's not jealousy so much, but I see this longing in her eye when she catches me practicing. And if I hide it from her, she's uncomfortable around me because she knows that I know what she's feeling about it all."

Charley laughed. "Right there, that's way more complicated than things need to be. She's your mother. Just tell her how you feel." Phoebe went to interrupt him, but he went on. "If you're honest with her, she'll be open with you as well. It might be a difficult talk, but you'll both know where the other is coming from and get through it all. Healing's not going to happen until everything is out in the open."

"You should give yourself more credit. I think that's really smart." Phoebe hugged him.

Charley blushed and returned the hug. "I may not be that smart, but I've learned a thing or two over the years."

A yelp from Hunter distracted both of them. The dog vanished into a mound of snow, and a puff of white shot into the air where he had been.

Charley called over to him. "Come on, Hunter, are you okay?"

A rush of wind blew past Phoebe and nearly knocked her over. She bent her knees and braced herself, and for her, the world went dark. The sun vanished from the sky, and the stars shone forth with a moon high overhead.

Just as soon as the wind had come, the strange blustery weather vanished from sight. In front of her and to her right, a crashing sound distracted her. "Charley!"

She called out to him, and then the world changed again. The ground shook and she reached out her hand in an impulsive response. Her left hand lit up like the whiteness of a high summer full moon.

"What's happening?" Charley turned away from Hunter coming out of the snowdrift and stared up at the suddenly dark sky.

The ground rumbled, and from deep in the forest, trees tore apart, sounding as though hundreds of saws sliced through branch, leaf, and trunk.

"I don't know, but we have to get out of here." Phoebe concentrated and stirred up the magic within her blood. Without much practice, her need drove her more than experience. "I'm going to open the dreamline. When the portal opens, just run through. Whatever it is, we don't have much time."

Charley pulled his rifle off his shoulder, quickly loaded it, and aimed at the massive destructive sound that churned toward them. "I'll be ready. Just whatever you're going to do, you better hurry up!"

Closing her eyes to focus, Phoebe reached out and made contact with the ground. She imagined seeing threads hanging before her, and like the threads were a curtain, she reached out, pulling the threads away until she could see more to what lie beyond. An afternoon sun, cloudy sky, and the bushes of a familiar park first came to mind.

"It's too late, there it is!" Charley steadied his arm and tried to remain calm. Hunter came by his side and barked.

An oversized creature, bright ruby red in color and more than eight feet in height, burst through the trees. A spherical vortex of tiny shards that resembled a sandstorm swirled around the beast. Two glowing red balls hovered over its shoulders and pulsed in rhythm to its breathing. Their eerie light cast an odd pall in the sudden night sky. The creature's two massive arms swung at its side as it pushed down a tree with ease. A human-like face opened its mouth and roared a challenge. As it moved forward, the swirling storm of shards cut through everything in its path, ripping apart tree branches like paper. On seeing Phoebe and Charley, it raised its right arm and discharged a projectile at them.

A javelin shard shot past them both and deeply embedded itself into a tree behind them. Charley fired his rifle in retaliation. The shot hit the beast squarely in the chest but appeared to have not wounded it. The swirling shield of crystalline shards spun faster around it, and the two globes on its shoulder glowed more intensely.

"Phoebs, whatever you're going to do with that portal thing, now would be the time to finish it!" Charley started to reload his rifle and glanced down at Hunter. "Go home, boy. Let them know where we were. Go!"

Without any further direction, Hunter ran off back toward Phoebe's house. More than a half mile away, it would take too much time for Cinderella and Jeremiah to reach them, but Hunter would be safe.

Phoebe had opened the portal enough for her to see her destination. She heard Charley's call to her and opened her eyes. The creature stepped forward and the ground shook. It raised its other arm and aimed it at her. Before she could act, the beast fired another javelin shard. It whizzed through the air, and Phoebe remained calm. Her heart beat fast, but she needed to remain in control. In her right hand, she held the thread to the dreamline, and she pointed her left hand at the quickly approaching weapon. With a subtle twist of her wrist, she nudged the javelin shard off course, and it went past them harmlessly.

Stomping its feet down in frustration, the shard creature pulled itself up to its full height, lowered its head, and rushed forward at its full speed, intending to crash through them like a battering ram. Phoebe turned her attention back to the dreamline and grabbed the last two remaining threads. The portal opened and she yelled over the loud noise to Charley, "Go, now!"

He obeyed and rushed past her into the oval light. Once he cleared the horizon of the dreamline, he vanished and Phoebe rushed forward quickly after him. She caught sight of the creature's face and could not sense intelligence there but just pure anger at its prey escaping. The dreamline enveloped her and she let the threads go. With a snap, the portal closed, and she dropped through the earth like a rock from a high waterfall. Her stomach gave way as though she had fallen from a great height. Below her she could see a light fast approaching, and without much understanding of what she needed to do, she braced herself for the ground.

A pop sounded in her ears and she suddenly found herself standing on the grass of a well-maintained park. With a snap and a burst of air, the dreamline closed behind her. Charley had fallen to the ground, and he looked at her in awe. His rifle still in his hand, he put the weapon down on the ground and swore.

Phoebe smiled and glanced back over her shoulder. "We made it!"

"Barely, but we did. Where did you bring us?" Charley pulled himself to his feet and slung his rifle on his back. At least in the immediate area, he saw no one near them.

"If I did things right, we should be in Paris." Phoebe shivered and wrapped her arms around her. "Unfortunately, it's winter here as well."

"Paris. Do you think you can get us back in time for dinner?" Charley laughed and then pointed back to the spot where they came through the dreamline. "That thing that attacked us. Do you think it'll go after your mom and Jeremiah?"

"I don't know…" Phoebe dusted off her dress and stared up at the sun that tried to peek out behind several large gray clouds. "My mom doesn't have her powers any longer, so I can't reach out to her with my magic and warn her.

"We should get inside. We'll look like fools standing around in the middle of a park in winter. We're lucky no one saw us come out of the dreamline." Charley tried to get a sense of his surroundings but could not see over the hedges that lined the park.

"I wouldn't say that no one noticed how you arrived." Seemingly out of nowhere, a tall man dressed in bright yellow and white, wearing a boutonnière on his jacket, hair all styled slightly out of fashion for the day, came out from behind the hedges and walked toward them. He had his face half hidden with a hat.

Phoebe took a step back and raised her left hand. "Who are you?"

"I've been waiting for you both." He tipped up his hat and flashed a brilliant smile at them. "What took you so long to get here?"

Charley sighed noticeably and relaxed, taking his hand off his rifle. "Oh, it's you!"

"Yes, c'est moi. The Golden Fox has come to your rescue!" He took a step forward, crossing his right foot over his left, and bowed lowed.

"You're still golden and didn't revert back to being silver, right?" Phoebe still stood at the ready to defend herself and Charley.

He took on a more serious expression and stood back with his right hand holding his hat propped up against his waist. "No, I have not changed back into the wily Silver Fox. I'm golden now. I've put my past behind me for good and I've matured a bit." He smiled at them again.

"Can you help us get out of here?" Charley asked.

"I can bring you both back to my home." The Golden Fox pointed back the way he had come through the topiary garden. "It's a bit of a walk, but once inside, we can have more of a regular chat."

"How did you know that we would be here?" Phoebe still stood her ground not trusting him yet.

"The Cryshada came after you, did it not?" He shook his head impatiently. "Well, it did, didn't it?"

"You mean the big ogre-like beast with the swirling shards all around it?" She took a step closer toward the Golden Fox and lowered her voice. "What was that thing? It nearly killed us."

"It's from the faerie world." He started to say more and glanced around him. "This type of talk should take place inside. Please, let's go back to my home."

Phoebe glanced over at Charley who shrugged. "Okay, we'll come with you."

He held out his hand and pointed at Charley's rifle. "We have to hide that thing. You can't walk through the streets of Paris with a weapon on your back. The gendarmes will pick you right up and throw you in jail."

"I'm not going to just throw it in a bush. I might need this." Charley took a step back and looked to Phoebe. "I'm not leaving my rifle after that crystal creature almost ripped us to shreds."

"I'm not saying that you need to toss the rifle away." The Golden Fox came toward him and reached out for the gun. "Give it to me and I'll keep it safe."

Charley took the rifle off his back and started to hand it to him, but stopped. "What are you going to do with it?"

With a simple tug, the Golden Fox easily pulled the weapon out of Charley's hands and then slid it into the hat in his hand. Like a magician completing his trick on stage, the Golden Fox finished putting the rifle into the hat and then tipped the hat back onto his head. "*Voilà!*"

Phoebe clapped her hands. "Nice trick. I'm impressed."

"I have many more like that up my sleeve, but now isn't the time for me to put on a magic show. We should get inside before someone else discovers that you're out here having just stepped through the dreamline." The Golden Fox turned back the way he had come and waved at them to follow him. "Come."

Charley walked on and followed in step with Phoebe. He spoke low and leaned over to her. "Should we trust him?"

"I don't see why not. And it's better than standing out here in the cold without any money or a place to go." She shivered and pulled her coat up to cover her exposed neck.

"I heard that and I don't want you both to be afraid. I've outgrown all my past deeds of torture, psychological violence, and mayhem."

Charley and Phoebe exchanged a troubled look.

"I kid you!" The Golden Fox turned around, watching them with his one eyebrow raised. "Well, I kid about all the torture and mayhem. I have outgrown all of that." He paused a moment and scratched his temple. "But in all honestly, I did do some rather not nice things back in the day. Yet still, I have reformed and grown out of them. You shall see. Let us go to my house, get some tea, though these dreaded French don't know how to make tea for the life of them, and we can all thaw out a bit and have a good chat. Allons-y!"

He sped up and led them out of the topiary park, heading toward the center of Paris. Far off in the distance, down a large hill and on the other side of the Seine, they could see Notre-Dame de Paris. The large cathedral stood as a beacon among all the houses and businesses in the tightly packed streets.

"Is that where we're going?" Phoebe asked.

"You shall see. My house is a modest one, but it will do for now." The Golden Fox sped up and turned a corner leading them fully out of the park. "Come on now. We have a ways to go!"

Charley followed Phoebe and crossed his arms. "I hope we don't regret this."

"Me too." She said.

"I still heard that!" The Golden Fox called back at them.

Phoebe turned back, looking at the way they had come, and hoped that they made the right choice.

***

I missed Phoebe already. I held my cup of tea in my hand and stared out the window. A gust of wind blew some of the fresh snow across the path in front of our house, and the trees shook from it. The truth that I had hidden for a long time had crawled out from deep inside.

"What are you thinking about?" Jeremiah asked. He had come into the kitchen all dressed for the cold.

"Nothing." I lied. I took a sip of tea, and the warm liquid soothed me as it went down.

"I may not be able to read minds, but you look like you just lost your best friend." Jeremiah came close to me, went to hug me, but hung back. "She only went to the Radleys' for the day. She'll be back soon."

I should let him know the truth. He had never lied to me. "I realized that with Phoebe gone there's no one to act as a buffer between the two of us. I'm just stuck here with all my thoughts, and I feel like there's a great rift between us." I turned around to look at him. His wild hair, long and still a bit unkempt, had some gray in it now. He had lines around his eyes, and yet his hands were still strong. "I'm tired of pretending that everything's okay. That I have to be fine with all that we've been through, and now I have to get sucked back into the maelstrom once again. Haven't I given enough? I nearly lost Phoebe last time, and I did lose my magic. I lost a part of me that was precious and dear. I just don't want to be involved any longer."

Jeremiah hung his head down. He shifted his weight onto his right leg and looked back up. I could see the passion in his eyes. "I didn't ask for any of this either. I didn't. But if there's something that I can do to help save people, then I'm going to do it. I only have a twinge of magic in me, and that's all I ever had. I've been able to hold it and become an instrument through it, but that's never stopped me. I have to work with what I have and who I am. If you want to stay here and pine away about the past and your lost powers, then go ahead and do so. I'm leaving to go to the Radleys' and let them know that I'm headed back to Europe."

I shook my head and snuck in a small smile. "That's the one thing I've always admired about you. You just go after whatever you think is right. Doesn't matter if you're afraid, don't know how you're going to get the job done, you just throw yourself into things." My smile faded. "I'm not like that. I have too much doubt in me. I doubt myself and…"

"You doubt others." He finished my sentence for me and I hated that. He took a step closer and put his hand out to me. "I don't know what this journey will entail. I truly don't, but I'm not going to sit here if I've been warned that I can do something about it. Please, come with me and we'll face this together."

A hurricane force gust of wind shook the house. Instead of quickly subsiding, the wind increased, and a shutter ripped off and flew away. I went to the window and looked outside. The trees swayed and snow swirled around like a storm had started up again. But the sun still shone, bright and unobstructed, outside.

"What's going on?" I went closer to the window and then jumped in surprise when a small branch hit the flapping shutter.

"I don't know. It's a clear day. I don't know what would be causing a wind like this." Jeremiah stood beside me and watched the chaos outside.

And then we heard it. First, a pounding shook the ground as though a small earthquake hit the area. The house shook, our dishes rattled on the kitchen shelf, and the wind abruptly stopped. As though suspended in air, twigs, branches, and bramble all dropped from the sky, hitting the house, the path, and everything within eyesight.

A calm descended on the area. My heart beat fast and out of habit I clenched my left fist, trying to prepare my magic. But nothing came to me.

Caught by surprise, I heard the crash on the porch first as though a large weight had dropped from a great height. A loud roar quickly followed and the door to our house blew inward into a thousand pieces. The debris exploded, flying in all directions. The force of the blast caused me to fall backward, and Jeremiah wrapped his arm around me, pulling me away from the noise.

I caught a glimpse of a bright, pulsing red ball of light attached to the shoulder of something crystalline and gigantic.

"What the hell is that?" I tried to get a closer look, but Jeremiah pulled me out of the kitchen toward the back of our house.

"It's a Cryshada." He spoke and his explanation meant nothing to me. He pointed toward the back door. "Head to the barn. We'll get on two horses and head out of here as fast as we can."

I nodded and ran. From behind us, the beast ripped through the house, and I glanced back to see the kitchen being blown apart. Thousands of tiny crystal shards shot through the air, shredding anything in its path. I caught a quick glimpse of the Cryshada's face. Since it was made entirely of a red ruby crystal, I knew it not to be of this world. I'd never seen anything like it. Two large teeth jutted out from its jaw, and its large flat nose gave it a semblance of an ogre from childhood stories.

Jeremiah pulled me onward, and I ran faster to keep up. The creature caught a glimpse of me as well and raised its arm. We turned the corner and bolted out the back down, down the stairs to the right of us as a crystal javelin burst through the wall of our home, like the wood were paper, and the weapon embedded itself deep into the large oak tree by the barn.

"Run!" Jeremiah ran into the barn and went to the nearest stall. The horses neighed and fought to get out, and as quickly as he could, he opened all the stalls. I ran past him and unlocked the back door of the barn, kicking it open so the horses could escape.

I grabbed and leaped onto the nearest horse as it came out of its stall, nearly falling off. I held tight on to the horse's mane and locked my legs around her body.

Behind me Jeremiah fiddled with a knot for a rope that stretched across the one corner of the barn.

I called after him, "Hurry up and get on a horse. That thing will be here any second."

He ignored me and finished his task, running over to the other side of the barn to work on another knot. I pulled at my horse's mane and dug into her side with my heels forcing her to stop. She did so reluctantly and I turned her around.

I urged her back to the barn, hoping to grab Jeremiah before the creature broke in. With a mighty crash, the whole wall of the barn exploded. Debris flew in every direction, and I caught my first good glimpse of the Cryshada. Two glowing globes, like rubies on fire, floated over each shoulder, pulsing in time with its breathing. I watched, frozen in fear, as the creature stepped forward and the swirling crystal storm that surrounded it ripped through the rafters, sending hay everywhere.

My horse refused to move and I fought to keep it calm. Jeremiah waved me back and he yelled something at me, but I could not make it out above the din. He finished whatever he worked on and ran toward me at his top speed. The Cryshada bent over and rushed forward, the ground shaking with each step it took. Jeremiah came beside me and jumped up, and with my help, positioned himself behind me on the horse.

He wrapped his arms around my waist and leaned in close to my ear, saying, "Let's go."

Patting my horse's side and tugging lightly on her mane, she turned the direction that I wanted her to go. The Cryshada took another step forward and then the ground gave way. It tumbled forward and a bright yellow light shot out from the ground. The two ropes that Jeremiah had been working on let loose, and a large tarp from the ceiling fell down on top of the creature in the pit that swallowed it whole. I heard its roar of anger fade away as though it fell a great distance. The yellow light intensified, and I shielded my eyes from it until we were clear and away.

The light intensified even more, and then a rush of wind pulled at us until the noise vanished. The sudden silence caught me off guard.

Jeremiah squeezed me tight and shouted, "Yes!"

"What did you do back there?" I kept our horse galloping at full speed away from the barn.

Jeremiah put his hands on mine, and together we slowed the horse down. "It's okay, my trap worked."

I glanced back over my shoulder and looked at the remains of our barn. All was deathly quiet. "Are you sure it worked?"

Jeremiah looked back and said, "If there's one thing that I'm really good at, it's traps."

"You have them all set up around the farm, don't you?" I hugged him and turned our horse around so that we could see the remains of the barn. "Pretty crafty. I'm impressed."

"I don't take any chances. I used to be a witch hunter, and if anyone ever tried to come after you or Phoebe, well, let's just say I'm prepared." Jeremiah smirked and then kissed me on the cheek.

"Where did you get the magic to set the traps?" I tried to keep calm, but Jeremiah would read between the lines and understand what I truly meant.

"Curious about that, aren't you?" Jeremiah scratched the back of his head. "Over the years, I've acquired a few items that have magic imbued in them. And, in a pinch, you've seen me be a conductor of magic. I can't initiate it on my own, but it can flow through me." He watched me intently and said, "After you lost your magic, I've kept all of this hidden because I didn't want to get you upset. I see how much you miss having your magic, and I wanted to be mindful of that."

"Just like how Phoebe hides her use of magic from me." I took a deep breath and sighed. "Everyone's walking on eggshells around me, afraid that I'm broken up over having lost my magic." I paused and sat with that thought for a moment.

"Well, aren't you?" Jeremiah chided me and then put his arm around my waist.

I slid down off the horse and started walking toward the Radleys'. "Yes, I am. I just don't like the world to know."

"The world?" Jeremiah laughed. "It's Phoebe and I. We're hardly the world. We know you as best as anyone can." He dismounted and pulled the horse around to follow me. "You don't make it easy on anyone, you know. If you'd let more people in, then we could help you."

"But help me with what? I lost my magic. It's gone, for good. Most of my life, I never knew I even had the ability, then I had it, and now it's gone. End of story." I changed the subject because I knew we would just get into another argument, and I really didn't want that. "What was the name of that creature again?"

"It's called a Cryshada." Jeremiah said the foreign name, and it meant nothing to me.

"But how did you know about it?" I thought I knew the answer, but I wanted to be sure.

"It's from the faerie land. It's one of the creatures that defends the faerie royals."

"You mean Queen Mab." I turned back to see his reaction.

"Yes, she taught me about them."

"Had you ever seen them before today?" I asked.

"Yes, I have." He looked away and I knew that I had brought up a sore subject. "Mab and I went on a bunch of travels together. On one trip, we came across one of the creatures."

I thought a moment and asked, "But why would one of these things come now, after all this time, to our house? Mab has been gone for years as has the Golden Fox."

"Maybe all this has something to do with the vision that I had about Napoleon? I don't know. It's not all adding up, but I don't think we should stick around here in case any more come here." Jeremiah sped up and walked beside me. "We should get to the Radleys' as soon as we can and then then let Phoebe know that we're headed off on our journey together."

I kept silent and kept on walking.

Jeremiah fumed and his frustration got the best of him. "Now what?"

"I'm just in a mood today." I replied. I withdrew in my thoughts but then fought against that and let him in. "Part of me just wants to be left alone. I'm tired and I don't want to go on this adventure to save Napoleon. I really want to just scoop up Phoebe and for she and I to head off somewhere safe."

"If that's what you want to do, then you should go do that." Jeremiah's anger bubbled up, and I knew I had pushed his patience too far. "I'm headed to the Radleys' to say my goodbyes, and then I'm headed off to Europe."

"And you're just going to take a horse in the winter, go all the way back to the East Coast and get on a boat to head on over to Europe?" The winter had been a hard one so far, and I expected it to only get worse with the more than half of winter left.

"Sure, I could do that if I wanted to take weeks upon weeks for me to get back to Europe." He adjusted his coat to protect his neck from the cold. "But did you forget that I used to be a witch hunter. I have my ways."

"Look, I don't mean to be so distant today. I'm just going through a rough patch. I'm trying to work this all out, but I'm having a difficult time settling down. Not having my magic has affected me more than I had thought it would." I put my head down and stared at the snow in front of me. "It's been a lot harder than I had expected. And seeing Phoebe use her magic—I'm not jealous, well, I just miss it. I feel like there's an ache in my heart that won't go away. I sometimes wake up from a dream and realize that the magic I had been using was only in my head."

Jeremiah gave me my space and kept quiet. He watched me closely and stayed by me as we walked.

"I used to travel the dreamline, going through time and great distances." I smiled. "I could have just transported us right to Europe if I wanted to. In fact, I could have brought us to Europe yesterday so that we would have arrived before we had even left." The old ache came upon me then, and I held up my left hand. It no longer glowed, and I felt no power there.

I let my words drift off and dropped my hand back at my side. A gust of frigid wind picked up and blew some snow around us. Covering my eyes, I stopped walking and bent over to protect myself from the wind. When the gust passed, I looked up and Jeremiah stood in front of me. He had let our horse continue onward on the path.

Taking me in his arms, he pulled me close and put his right hand on the back of my head. "I can't imagine how difficult all of this is for you. I never had power like you did." He pulled back and looked me in the eyes. "But I tell you that I would not have agreed to go to rescue Napoleon unless it were something that we had to do. I know it makes no sense, and now the Cryshada are after us, and that makes even less sense, but through it all, I will stay with you—if you want me to."

I interrupted him. "I just feel damaged. I'm not myself and part of me feels broken."

"So, what are you going to do about it?" he asked.

I considered his question and didn't reply right away. I could run away and hide as I had done in the past, but that only worked for so long. Eventually, I would need to come back and face my problems. I had to face it. Accept it. I no longer had magic. I closed my eyes and then opened myself up to my fear. "I'm going to come with you to rescue Napoleon. We're going to figure out together why the Cryshada are after us, and when this is all over, I'm going to take a nice long vacation. But in the meantime, I'm with you."

Jeremiah leaned in and kissed me full on the mouth. We held the kiss, and then he slowly pulled away and broke contact. The kiss lingered between us, and we stared at each other. He smiled and replied, "And I'm with you as well. Remember, together, nothing can stop us."

I laughed at his use of our private joke. "No, nothing can stop us."

We said the words together, disengaged from our hug, and started walking to the Radleys'. An odd feeling surged through me. I might not have my magic any longer, but I still could sense when Phoebe was in danger. My nose itched and I rubbed it a bit, hoping that it was just a coincidence, but I feared the truth. If a magical faerie creature tried to kill Jeremiah and I, neither of us had any magic left in our blood. But Phoebe did. It was only a guess, but maybe the Cryshada had meant to find her and stumbled upon us by accident.

I kept my thoughts to myself—Jeremiah and I had done enough talking for the morning. Better to enjoy the winter weather and keep listening rather than jump to conclusions. But to be honest, I had never been wrong to date. I knew that she and Charley would only be minutes ahead of us on the road, but deep down I sensed that something had happened to them. I didn't know what, but once we arrived at the Radleys' house, I'd be able to put all these nonsense thoughts out of my head for good.

Jeremiah directed our horse toward me and said, "You ready?" He had bent down and cupped his hands so that I could mount. "I've seen that face of yours a hundred times to know that you're worried about Phoebe. Am I right?"

"Yes, you are." I stepped into his hands, and he vaulted me up so that I could slide across the horse's back.

He quickly followed and jumped up behind me. "I've never known your premonitions to be wrong, so let's go."

In unison, we kicked lightly the horse's ribs, and we headed off toward the Radleys' as fast as our horse could gallop. I only hoped that I was wrong and that Phoebe was okay. I shook off my concern, but the feeling stayed heavy with me. Something had happened to her. I just didn't know what.

Chapter 3

Phoebe entered the small dwelling and took in the sights. Piles of books lined the entire right-hand side of the room. The nearest stack came to her waist and had a cup and saucer placed on it.

The Golden Fox waved his hand to show off the dark and dank place. "It's not much, but then again, I don't need much and am often not here." He picked up a book off a chair nearest to him and hugged it. "If I'm perfectly honest, this place is more for the books than for me."

Charley closed the door behind him, and it took him a few seconds for his eyes to adjust to the low light. "This is definitely not what I expected." He stepped over a few books piled on the floor and tried to find an open spot to sit down.

"I know it's a bit dingy, but it has a certain charm to it. Well, it does to me at least." He picked up a stack of leather-bound books and moved them to the floor. "Come, sit down. I'll get some tea for both of you, and we can talk."

He left the room and started humming to himself, the sound of clanging pots and pans nearly drowning him out.

"Why is it that we always seem to get mixed up in the weirdest of situations?" Phoebe kept her voice low and shook her head.

"Well, at least he's still in his golden form." Charley motioned over to an empty chair. "Do you want to sit?"

Phoebe walked over to the chair and sat down, careful to not knock over the books in the surrounding area. If she stayed still, she would be fine. "I wish I could send my mom a message to let her know that we're all right."

"I already took care of that for you. Don't worry about that." The Golden Fox strode into the room with a large silver tray, carrying a tea set, a sliced baguette, and a sizeable chunk of cheese. He offered the tea to Phoebe first.

She accepted the cup and saucer, pausing for a moment so that she did not spill the tea. "Where should I put it? I don't want to ruin any of your books."

The Golden Fox motioned with his chin. "Just stick it over there on that pile to the right. It's a steady stack and you won't have to worry about the books toppling over."

Phoebe did as instructed and then took a small plate with some bread and cheese.

"I forgot milk and sugar." He shook his head in admonishment. "Do either of you take that in your tea? I prefer a lightly brewed tea with nothing in it."

Charley took a cup of tea and sat down on a chair nearest Phoebe. "I'm fine without." He took a sip and smiled. "It's the perfect temperature."

"I'm fine, too. I prefer my tea with nothing in it as well." Phoebe took a sip, balancing her small plate of food on her lap. "It is delicious."

"Thank you. I'm very particular about my tea and get it from the source." Placing the tray down on a table on the far side of the room, the Golden Fox pointed at the fireplace and a small fire ignited. "There we go. It's a little cold in here, and I think it'll make it cozier for all of us once we start talking about what we need to do."

Phoebe swallowed her mouthful of tea and then coughed into her hand. "Excuse me?"

"See, this is the part that I'm never really good at. We faeries can do the small talk right, and I've been working on getting better with remembering to serve food to guests. Obviously, you can see that I don't have the keeping a room clean down yet, but I think I've done well in all the other areas."

Charley cut him off and put his tea down. "Can you just tell us what you meant by 'what we need to do'?"

"Oh, yes, you're right. The transitions are hard. Before, when I was the Silver Fox, it didn't matter to me because I just did whatever I wanted or said anything—usually to provoke someone into an anger."

"Fox, please?" Phoebe chided him to focus.

"Well, then, I guess I better just say it." The Golden Fox took a seat closest to them and then took a sip of tea. He placed the cup down and said, "The Earth is going to be destroyed and I need your help to stop it."

Charley glanced over at Phoebe, his look of concern clearly visible. "Destroyed? What do you mean by that?"

"I think I mean vaporized from the best that I can tell. It's hard to predict these things, but this whole world is not going to be here anymore." The Golden Fox took another sip of his tea and waited for the news to sink in.

Phoebe stood up and walked to the door. "I need to get back home then. My mother will know what…"

"You can't do that." The Golden Fox pointed at the door. "If you leave, then things will get worse. She came to talk to you, didn't she?"

"Who came to talk to her?" Charley asked.

"You haven't told him yet? Don't you think that maybe he should know?" The Golden Fox held off from saying more.

"Will someone please tell me what's going on?" Charley got up and knocked over the nearest pile of books. "If Ginny and the kids are in danger, I need to get back to them."

"They're not in immediate danger. It's not like that." The Golden Fox brushed off some unseen dust from his pants. "But I do think she should tell you what happened to her right before you left to go to your house."

Phoebe looked to Charley. "I didn't mean to hide anything from you. We just didn't get a chance to talk, and I didn't want to get you involved. Like you said, there's Ginny and your children. I don't know what I need to do, but it's probably wrapped up with the Golden Fox." She realized that she was rambling and stopped to take a breath. "Let me explain what happened. When I was upstairs in my room, I was visited by an older version of myself. I saw a vision or something. She told me that I need to help Jeremiah convince my mother to go rescue Napoleon."

Charley pounded his fist on his thigh. "I've had enough. I want nothing to do with rescuing that monster. Enough people have died by him, and I don't want anything else to do with him."

The Golden Fox offered more tea to Charley. "See? I thought some tea and a bit of bread and cheese might lighten the mood up a bit."

Charley shook his head in frustration and turned to Phoebe. "Look, I'm sorry. I don't mean to get angry at you. It's not your fault that some faerie creature came after us and tried to kill us. I just don't want to be separated from Ginny and the kids. I had thought that, for once, our lives had settled down and the only problems I had to deal with were wondering how to bring in a better crop of corn next summer." In defeat, he plopped himself down in his chair and crossed his arms.

Phoebe reached out to him and gently touched his arm. "I hear you. I do. I don't want to be involved in all of this as well. But it's hard to ignore or run away from the problem when you're visited by an older version of yourself. She was very persuasive."

The Golden Fox leaned in closer to them both. "We are all part of a great struggle that's taking place across the stars. There are powers beyond what you can comprehend, and if we play our little part right, we might be able to stop a great catastrophe from happening." Charley shifted in his seat and he changed tactics. "But I have already offered some help to you both. I have left a note with Ginny that she is to give to Cinderella and Jeremiah when they arrive at your house. It's not much, but it will at least give her some security that you are well."

"Why don't we just pop back and I can see Ginny or let me talk with her through some water mirror or something? There has to be some easier way to communicate across the miles? You both have great magical powers. Can't you do something like that?" Charley looked to both of them for a glimmer of hope.

Phoebe shook her head and replied, "I only got us here through blind luck. I don't know if I can get us back. I can try it, but I also don't know if doing that would bring more of the Cryshada after us and to your home. It might not be safe."

"She's right. Going back home would only put those you love at risk." The Golden Fox put his index finger to his lips, thinking. "But I don't see any harm in you sending a message to your wife. I think that would be safe to do."

"But what about my mom? Couldn't I do the same thing with her?" Phoebe asked.

The Golden Fox closed his eyes, and his right hand lit up in a golden light. Swirls of energy encircled his hand, and he reached out as though he saw someone standing before him. When he opened his eyes, they glowed the same color as his hand. "I cannot find her or Jeremiah. They are not in a fixed place. Come, here." He reached out to Phoebe and she took his glowing hand.

"Do you see her?" Phoebe called out to a swirling mass of light that coalesced in front of them. A picture started to form of trees going by quickly. She could see the snow, the sky, blue and filled with the brilliant light of day, but then the scene faded away.

"I cannot get through to her. It's as though she has blocked herself off from all magic." He let his power ebb, and the light before them faded away. "I even tried to reach Jeremiah, but your mother is protecting him as well. It is as though there's a void where she should be, and I cannot get through. She's entirely blocked off from any magic."

"Can we try to reach my wife?" Charley walked over to the Golden Fox and put out his hand. "If you're willing to try, I would appreciate that."

"I'll try." The Golden Fox took Charley's hand in his and called forth his magic once again. The golden swirl of light intensified, and his hand lit up like the fire of the sun. With his other hand, the fox snapped his fingers, and the fire in the far corner of the room increased in intensity. A kettle floated across the room and settled on the fire, and, slowly at first, steam poured out of the spout. The steam wafted over to them, cajoled by the Golden Fox, and formed a cloud above them. "I'm almost there. I can see her. Just give me a few more moments."

A picture formed on the cloud, and Charley could see Ginny setting the table for lunch.

"Ginny, can you hear me?" Charley called out to her. Her reddish hair had a few streaks of gray, more than he had noticed when he had seen her earlier that morning, and she shifted her weight toward the sound of his voice.

"Charley, is that you? Where are you?" She spun around and she looked up to a corner of the room.

"It's me, Ginny. I wanted to let you know that I'm all right and that I'm with Phoebe. When you see Cinderella and Jeremiah, tell them that we're both fine. I need to go help Phoebe, and I'll be home as soon as I can."

Ginny climbed up on a chair and peered into the corner of the ceiling. "Is that you in there? I can see you, but you're so small." She laughed. "Maybe it's a good thing I didn't clean away the cobwebs up there. I can see you in them."

"I can see you too Ginny, and I'll be home as soon as I can. I wanted to let you know that Phoebe and I are safe. Let Cinderella know…"

Ginny cut him off and said, "I haven't seen Cinderella and Jeremiah in months. When are you coming home, Charley?"

The steam began to dissipate, and the Golden Fox poured more of his magic to stabilize the picture. "Hurry, I can't hold the link for much longer."

Phoebe came forward. "Would it help if I poured my magic into you?"

The Golden Fox shook his head. "No, that would just throw me off. Hold still. I can keep it going for a bit more." Sweat broke out on his brow and he clenched his teeth in concentration.

"I don't know when I'm coming home. I have to go rescue…" The picture faded and he called to his wife. "Ginny, are you still there?"

"What did you say?" She came back to him, and her face hung close to his in the steam.

"Just know that I love you. I didn't mean to leave you like this." The guilt in his tone hung heavy.

"This is the second time, Charles Radley, that you have left me like this, and I am a patient woman, but I am also not a fool. You are gallivanting all around the world, and I need help here with the girls. Remember your family and come back to us as soon as you can." She blew him a kiss, and the steam cloud disappeared and the image of Ginny with it.

Charley hung his head low and said more to himself than to his wife, "I'll be back as soon as I can. I promise."

The Golden Fox stayed quiet and backed away, cleaning up his empty cup of tea and brought it to the kitchen.

Phoebe put her hand on Charley's arm to comfort him. "I'm sorry that you're stuck here with me. I truly didn't think you'd be coming along. I had planned on going to your house and then sneaking away in the middle of the night." She twirled her hair with her index finger and looked up at him. "Honestly, I didn't really have a plan all worked out. I didn't know what I was going to do except somehow sneak away. What little plan I had would probably have failed. If it makes you feel any better, I'm happy that you're here to help me. I could use it!"

Charley smiled and a bit of his cheery self emerged. "I am happy to be here with you. Your mother has raised you to be a strong young woman. What are you going on now, fifteen?"

Phoebe shook her head. "I'm sixteen now."

Charley shook his head in disbelief. "Time flies so fast." He looked away back at where the steam cloud had been. "My daughters are growing up so fast. When I'm away like this, I miss them and I worry…"

He let the next words be unspoken fearing that they might come true.

"You are right to be afraid. I am as well. But together, we can find a way to succeed." Phoebe beamed her best smile at him. "What do you say?"

"You don't have to convince me. I've been in with you since that Cryshada creature showed up. And your mother would want someone to look out for you." He caught his mistake a bit too late but corrected himself quickly. "I mean, your mother would want someone to partner with you now that you're all grown up. Not that you need me to rescue you or anything."

"That's better. Much better." Phoebe tapped him on the arm. "Remember those words when you get back to your daughters, and they'll love you forever. They'll respect you more."

Charley nodded and scratched the back of his head. "The world is changing faster than I can catch up. Sometimes I just hang on and hope for the best."

"And that's what we all do at times." The Golden Fox re-entered the room and took a seat by them again. "Have you two finished with your little tête-à-tête?"

"Yes, we have." Phoebe sat back down and sipped more of her tea. "So how do we go and break Napoleon out of prison?"

Charley took a piece of cheese from the plate and then sat back down as well.

"First off, he's not in prison. He's in exile on the island of Elba in the Mediterranean. Second, we're not going to help Napoleon escape from the island."

"But that's what my future self told me that I needed to do." Phoebe sat forward in her chair in frustration. "She told me to help."

"No, the exact words were that you needed to 'convince your mother' for her to help Napoleon escape from exile." The Golden Fox wagged his finger at Phoebe. "You've already done that by coming here. As soon as your mother realizes that you both are gone, she'll think you both came here to Europe to help Napoleon because of the vision that Jeremiah had. She and Jeremiah will then go to Elba and find a way to get him off the island."

"But then we need to find a way to meet her." Phoebe looked down at her hand. "I have my magic and you have yours—together we can get a message to her or Jeremiah. There has to be a way."

Charley stayed quiet, observing the Golden Fox. "But that's not what he has in mind. You have another plan, don't you?"

"For a non-magical human, you can be very perceptive when you want to." The Golden Fox tipped his hat at Charley. "Your friend is right. I do have another plan, and it involves doing something entirely different."

"Are you trying to play some trick on us?" Phoebe looked to Charley to see if he would support her.

"You have been sly in the past, and if you're up to some trickery, we're not going to put up with that." Out of instinct, Charley reached behind him but remembered that he no longer had his rifle.

"Both of you have nothing to fear." The Golden Fox smiled as he bared his white teeth. "Now the old me would have come up with something rather exciting, but I'm older now and more mature. I don't have time for games like tying people up and torturing them."

Phoebe stood up and her hand lit up with white magical fire. "I am not to be trifled with." She took a defensive stance and prepared to unleash her power on him.

"Good, you will need that anger to help you survive when things get tough. But thankfully, that's not for today. I am not here to cause any problems, but we won't be going to Elba because we have another job to do. Jeremiah and your mother can handle getting Napoleon out of his exile. He's basically there walking the island alone, and knowing him, he's already plotted a means to escape. He'll just need some support and a push. And what do you think he'll do first?"

"He'll go back to Paris and try to regain power again." Phoebe lowered her arm and let her magic go out. "He's going to start another war and try to take over Europe again."

"Exactly." The Golden Fox clapped his hands. "That's where the three of us come in. He'll regain control of France, raise his army, and the world goes to hell in a handbasket. We need to have a means to stop him for good."

Charley looked to Phoebe and asked, "But why are we freeing him in the first place if we just need to stop him again?"

"I don't know. None of this makes sense to me. But my future self said it was important." Phoebe looked to the Golden Fox. "Do you know why?"

"Yes, I do. For all the war and suffering he's caused, Napoleon has also instituted various codes throughout all his empire. He instituted a set of laws that were consistent throughout all the countries he controlled and brought order to the world. I don't know everything that is to happen, but I think Napoleon is integral to saving the world in the future. I just don't know why."

"But then where are we going?" Phoebe asked.

"Have either of you heard of Joseph Nicéphore Niépce who lives in Chalon-sur-Saône?"

"Who?" Charley turned to Phoebe to see if she knew the name.

She shrugged and sat back down. "I've never heard of him."

"And you won't until a few more years and only in certain scientific circles." The Golden Fox leaned closer to the both of them and said, "Nicéphore, as he prefers to be called, is experimenting with the camera obscura."

"The camera of what?" Charley's confused expression could not be hidden.

"Both of you, listen to me. We're going to visit the father of photography."

Phoebe turned to Charley, equally confused, and said, "What's photography?"

The Golden Fox smiled and rubbed his hands sinisterly. "It's a scientific process to capture an image."

Charley and Phoebe stared at each other in disbelief.

The Golden Fox rolled his eyes and said, "Trust me. Let's gather some supplies and pack. We have a long way to go."

"I only understood about every third word of what he said." Charley got up and stretched. "What about you?"

Phoebe remained silent for a moment and spoke directly at the Golden Fox. "You just want us to help you get the camera obscura to not only capture Napoleon's picture, but trap his very soul."

"Exactly." The Golden Fox's devious smile chilled both Phoebe and Charley to the bone.

***

I tugged gently on the mare's mane and leaned forward, whispering in her ear. "You can slow down now, girl. We're here."

Jeremiah dismounted and put his hand up. "Would you like some help getting down?"

"Thank you." My hands were red from the cold.

He helped me down and then started leading our horse to the Radleys' barn. "I'll be right there. You go on ahead."

He knew me well enough that I had only one thing on my mind. Phoebe's safety. I ran on ahead to the front of the house and heard no children playing outside. The sun had only been up around two hours, but I expected a bustle of activity inside the Radley house. Chores, breakfast, and lots of movement. But from the outside, I could see no movement inside.

I looked back over my shoulder and saw that Jeremiah had reached the barn. He entered and disappeared from view. I heard a few birds chirping as they flitted around a bird feeder that hung on the porch. The tiny sparrows took turns eating the seed and then would fly enough to allow one of the birds to have a chance to eat.

The wind buffeted me, and I braced myself from the bitter cold blast, bending my head over to try to stay warm. When I knocked on the door, I heard no response, and after a few seconds, I knocked harder.

After another few moments, I caught a glimpse of someone coming to the door. She fumbled with the lock and opened the door.

"Cinder!" Martha pulled me inside. "It's so cold out there. Come inside."

She had grown much since I had last seen her. "Are Phoebe and your dad here yet?"

She shook her head. "He went to go to your house early this morning, saying that he'd ask her to come back. We're going to work with her and put on a play, using some of my sisters' dolls. Everything is all set for later. It's been so long since we've had a day of fun with her."

I tried to capture all that she said, but she spoke too rapidly for me to catch it all. I looked past Martha and asked, "Is your mom home?"

She turned around and shouted as loud as she could, "Mom, Cinder is here!" Then she spoke normally to me. "I think she's finishing up on breakfast. Is everything okay?"

I started to respond when I heard Ginny's voice from the back. "What do you want?"

Martha went to shout another reply, and I put my hand on her arm. "It's okay. I'll go see your mom in the kitchen. I can hear her."

"Oh, Jeremiah's here too! Is there going to be a party today?" Martha left my side and greeted Jeremiah as he came rushing inside. He shut the door behind him and then rubbed his hands together to stay warm.

I left the two of them and rushed into the kitchen. Ginny stood at the stove cooking. The smell of bacon and freshly baked bread permeated the air with a homey and comforting smell. "Ginny, it's me."

She spun around with a spatula in her hand. She took in my expression in a second and asked mother to mother, "What's wrong?"

"Has Charley arrived yet with Phoebe?" I expected I knew the answer because I would have heard my daughter by now.

"No, he went to your house. You look worried. What happened?" She put the spatula down on the counter and came over to me and put her hands on my mine.

"Jeremiah and I were attacked by this creature." I didn't know how best to describe the Cryshada and stuck to the basics. "Charley and Phoebe were on the road, but we didn't see them on the way over here. I'm worried that something may have happened to them."

Having seen enough magic in her day, Ginny remained calm and focused on being a mother first. "You found no evidence of foul play on the road over here, right?"

"No, we saw nothing unusual, and I don't know for sure if the magical creature had even found them. I just thought that they'd be here by now."

From the back of the house, they both heard barking. Ginny yelled, "Martha, can you get Hunter? He went out with your father this morning."

Martha ran past the kitchen toward the back door. "Okay, Mom."

A bewildered Jeremiah entered the kitchen and read my expression. "No news?"

"They're not back yet." I tried to calm down, but I had lost Phoebe before, and I did not want to lose her again.

From upstairs, I heard the other Radley children running through the house. Ruth, Sarah, and Teresa came bounding down the stairs. Ginny pointed at Ruth and scolded her. "I told you to look after your little sister. Go back upstairs and get her now before she hurts herself and falls down the stairs. Go!"

Ruth waved at me and flew back up the stairs, pounding the stairs with her heavy shoes.

Sarah and Teresa came to my side and I took a step back. "Nice to see you girls."

Ginny pulled the girls back from me. "Give her some room to breathe. She just got here. You both know better than that."

"Is Phoebe coming over today?" asked Sarah.

Teresa looked to her mother. "We've done all our chores for the past week like you asked without any complaining. You promised that you'd see if Phoebe could stay over our house tonight. Is she on her way over?"

Ginny took a deep breath, and I wondered where her patience came from. I had enough of a time raising one child let alone the entire Radley household. Five girls were a lot of mouths to cook for and hurt feelings to soothe.

"Girls, go in the other room so that I can talk with Cinder for a bit." She gave them her most concerned motherly stare, raising one eyebrow, and pointed to the far room.

Sarah curtsied to me and her sister followed. "We'll be in the other room." Teresa waved to me. "Bye!"

Jeremiah put his arm around me, but I moved away from him to be closer with Ginny. "He should have been back now, and if Hunter's arrived, then something may have happened to them."

Martha came running into the kitchen with Hunter in her arms. The dog tried to squirm away, but she did a good job of calming him and keeping him still. "He's a bit wet from the snow but he's not injured."

Hunter kept barking even as Martha petted him and spoke to him in a soft voice.

Jeremiah checked Hunter for any notes or hidden messages in his collar, but found nothing. "He seems overly excited, but that might just be from all the commotion."

Ginny looked to Martha and said, "Let him down. It's okay. He'll need some time to settle himself."

"I think we should go out on the road and start searching." I did not want to waste a moment.

Jeremiah buttoned his coat. "I think that's a good idea."

A loud knock on the front door startled all of us.

Sarah ran to get the door, shouting, "I'll see who it is!"

"Wait, Sarah!" Ginny tried to stop her daughter, but it was too late.

Sarah had already run out of the kitchen, laughing, and Teresa then chased after her. Jeremiah picked up on Ginny's concern and rushed after the two girls.

Martha, oblivious to her mother's concern, put Hunter down on the floor and knelt down to hug the dog. "You're such a good boy. I bet it was cold out there for you, wasn't it?"

I glanced back toward the front of the house and heard the girls open the front door amid their banter. In moments, Sarah rushed back into the room with a large square envelope in her hands.

She handed it to her mother. "There wasn't anyone there. We just found this envelope. It was like someone had placed it on the porch with magic!" She overexaggerated her movements and whistled while waving her hands in the air.

Jeremiah came back into the kitchen, and I made eye contact with him. He shrugged and put up his empty hands. I looked to Ginny and she had already ripped open the letter to see what was inside.

The girls talked over each other, and I did my best to remain patient, but at that moment, I would have preferred if the children had left the room. Too much was at stake, and I only wanted to know if the letter had anything to do with Phoebe.

Ginny read the letter to herself and then looked to me. "They're safe and with the Golden Fox over in Paris. Here."

She handed me the letter, and I went to read it, but the words on the paper faded away. I tried to take in as much as I could, but the fancy script took a moment to read, and by then it was too late. All the ink had vanished, leaving only a blank parchment. I handed the letter back to Ginny, hoping that when she touched it that the words would come back, but they did not.

"What else was written in the letter?" I stepped closer to Ginny and hoped she could repeat every word back to me.

Sarah grabbed at the parchment in her mother's hand, and Ginny had had enough. She raised herself to her full height. "Girls, all of you, go to the back room now!"

Even Jeremiah took a step back from her stern tone. Sarah, Teresa, and Martha withered from her gaze and rushed out of the room without a peep. From the stairs, Ruth came down with her little sister, and Ginny pointed at them both. "Ruth, take your sister in the back now. I'll be with you all soon, but I need to talk with Cinder and Jeremiah. Please, go."

Ruth followed her mother's request and quickly headed off to the back of the house with her sister. Ginny looked to me and said, "I apologize for all the noise. In the wintertime, my girls don't get out much, and they are overly excited to see you both." She held the parchment up but it remained blank. "The note was short. Charley and Phoebe were mentioned by name and that they were both safe and in Paris. They would be headed on an adventure and that I need not worry. And you were mentioned as well. The last line was: "Tell Cinderella that I need her help and that she should go to Elba the quickest way she knows how."

Jeremiah reached for the letter and asked, "And that was it?" He held the parchment in his hand but could see no markings or magical notations.

"The letter was signed 'Yours, The Golden Fox.'" Ginny put her hands in the pockets of her apron. "It's in jest, right? How can Charley and Phoebe be in Paris? They were just at your house only an hour or two ago."

I did not know how I could answer Ginny's question. The Silver Fox would joke and liked riddles, but I expected that, in his way, the now reformed Golden Fox told the absolute truth. "Powerful magic is involved here."

Ginny crossed herself. "I thought unnatural powers would be out of our lives for good. Nothing good ever comes from that. Never!"

Her response gave me enough evidence that I needed that Phoebe had kept secret her powers from Ginny and the rest of the Radley household. I had no power of my own. All of it gone, and now, when I needed it the most, I felt powerless.

"There is nothing we can do here." Jeremiah handed the letter back to Ginny. "We must take the Golden Fox at his word." He put his arm around me and I relaxed a bit. "As much as we don't know his intentions, we should trust that he has no reason to lie to us."

A heavy weight fell on me when I thought about what we would need to do. "But Elba is off of Italy. We're so far from there. How are we ever to get there in time?"

Ever practical, Jeremiah replied, "I already had a plan on how to get to Europe quickly to find Napoleon. We'll pack up and head off tomorrow to head back east. I'll find my contact in Philadelphia, and then we'll find a witch or wizard who could send us through a portal to get to Europe."

"No, that's not what the letter said." Ginny kept her voice low and leaned in toward us both. "The Golden Fox told you to go to Elba the quickest way that you know."

"That would be through the dreamline, but I can't do that anymore. I don't have the power to do that." In exasperation, I looked to Jeremiah. "By wagon, boat, and foot is the only way we can go until we find a portal back east."

Ginny lowered her voice. "You need to speak to Jessica."

Jeremiah looked to me, saw my bewilderment, and then turned back to Ginny. "Who?"

"Jessica. She lives a few miles to the north. She's a witch. Phoebe is her friend." Ginny raised her eyebrow at seeing our confused faces. "Phoebe's never mentioned her to you?"

"No." There was no other answer I could give. My one-word answer spoke volumes to what Phoebe had chosen to hide from me. My lack of magic and how I suffered from that had affected her more than I had known. My daughter had kept secrets from me.

"I also haven't heard of Jessica." Jeremiah noticed my concerned look and asked, "Does Phoebe go there often?"

"At least once or twice a week. She'll come here for a bit and then heads out to be with her friend. Jessica might be the quickest way for you to get to Elba. Like the Golden Fox said." A loud stream of giggles came from the backroom. Ginny took my arm and squeezed. "You're both welcome to stay for breakfast, but I expect you'll want to head right out. Don't fret too much. They're both safe and we need to trust in that."

"You're right. I worry too much sometimes." I hugged Ginny and looked to Jeremiah. "I'd prefer to get right on the road."

Jeremiah smiled. "I hoped you'd say that." He said his goodbyes to Ginny and then headed out of the kitchen. "Mind if we borrow two horses?"

"No, that's fine." Ginny waved after him. "Jeremiah!"

He stopped running and turned back.

"Bring my husband home safe."

"I will." He bowed his head to her and put his hand on his heart. "I promise."

Jeremiah rushed out of the room, and in seconds, he was gone. I took Ginny's hands in mine and pulled her close for a farewell hug.

"I feel like I need to apologize to you for getting Charley wrapped up in all this mess."

She hugged me back and replied, "It's not your fault." Releasing me, she paused and held my hand as I turned to go. "Cinder, be easy on her. She is a good young woman and looks to learn more about who she is. There's no malice in her actions on hiding Jessica from you. If anything, she probably only wanted to protect your feelings."

"You're right." I waved to Ginny. "We will get Charley back safe to you and the girls. I promise you."

"Thank you." Ginny waved and then headed out of the kitchen before her emotions overcame her. She wiped a tear from her eye and left the kitchen, calling after the kids in the other room.

When I left the house, a rush of excitement washed over me, but also one of fear. Somehow, I was being wrapped back into world events, but this time, I had no way to protect myself, and for the first time in a long, long time, I felt helpless. And, truth be told, I didn't like that feeling.

Chapter 4

Phoebe pulled the blanket up to her chin and shivered. The tiny carriage they rode in shook as it hit a bump on the road. All three of them were wet, tired, and cold. She looked at the small window of the carriage, but condensation had fogged it up. With the side of her hand, she cleared the window but could not see much more than the dull gray sky and trees that lined the road.

"Are we almost there yet?" The Golden Fox stretched his arms to the carriage's roof and yawned.

"You are leading this merry adventure. How are we to know?" Charley turned to him, wearing a scowl.

The carriage hit another hole in the road, and they all were jostled to the right. Phoebe's nose hit the carriage's side and she sighed. "I've lost count of the time. It's been weeks now and we're still on the road. Why couldn't we have just used our magic to go there?"

Tired of giving the same answer, the Golden Fox ignored her question.

Charley rubbed his hands together to keep warm and replied, "Because you've never been to Chalon-sur-Saône or know someone who has. The dreamline can't be opened to a place you've never been."

"That's not necessarily true." The Golden Fox perked up. "Think about it for a minute. If Phoebe is somehow in the future, how did she get there? Someone had to send her there, she found some sort of magical portal, or she went there herself. We don't know for sure if she won't be able to travel through the dreamline in the future by going to places she can intuit or imagine."

"I tried." She spoke low, knowing that what she shared would not be popular with the two of them, especially Charley. "I'm not quite certain how to pull the threads together for places I've not been. If I had a bit more information, I think I could do it…"

"But you might also exit the dreamline and be stuck in a wall of a house or lost in the in-between." The Golden Fox glanced longingly out the window. "I miss the Other side. I haven't seen my faerie cousins for a long time. Maybe, after this adventure, I'll go on a little vacation. I could use some time to relax and see the old sights of my home."

"Why did you stay here in France? You could have gone anywhere." Phoebe sat up and braced herself as the carriage jostled all of them again.

"After I last saw you, I did go off. I needed time to recharge and rest. But after a while, I missed being here." He thought for a moment and then chose to be fully open. "I sensed that trouble was coming, and I felt that I owed it to your mother to come back and help her."

"Can you see into the future and know what's going to happen with Napoleon?" Charley had wanted to ask the question for days, but there had not been time to do so without the question seeming off base.

"Sometimes." The Golden Fox lit up his hand and waved it slowly in front of him. "You know how you sometimes have intense dreams that you'll remember for years? Well, that's how things are for me. I sometimes dream the future. Other times I get a premonition and can intuit that something is going to happen. It's not something that I can directly control."

Phoebe kept her eye on his hand, watching the golden light. "You always know more than you tell us though. I can see it in your eyes. There's more there than you want us to see." She tucked the blanket around her and shifted her legs in order to curl up on her side of the carriage. "I think you often try to weigh what we should and shouldn't know. And I can understand that…"

"You are perceptive. It's not easy to sometimes know what might happen. I can't see everything, but I also have been known to be wrong. Sometimes my dreams are just dreams. I don't have all the future clearly laid out in front of me. I wouldn't want that even if that were possible."

"Is there anything else that you can tell us?" Charley asked.

The Golden Fox stared deep into the light in his hand. He appeared not to hear what Charley had said and was lost in thought. The silence stretched on for a few uncomfortable seconds, and then he closed off his magic. The light from his hand went out, and he turned to Charley and replied, "One day this planet is going to be destroyed. I've seen that. It will be the end of everything we know. The sky, the flowers, even the little tiny ladybugs that I like so much. All of it will vanish and disappear like a rainbow after a thunderstorm…"

Startled, Phoebe leaned forward and put her hands on the Golden Fox's. "Do you tell the truth?"

"Why would I lie?" The Golden Fox smiled at her and leaned in closer to her. "I've seen many futures. One possible future is that the sun will grow and turn red in hue, destroying all life on this planet. Another is of the Earth being ripped in pieces by an asteroid. All of these possibilities swirl around in my head like bees around their hive. But lately, a recurring dream comes to me more and more often. There is a cadence to the progression of the dream, and I cannot stop having it. I see a future with flying automatons and buildings taller than the highest cathedrals. There is so much color and light but also a loneliness and darkness in people's souls. Despair has rotted many and there is great poverty, war, and sickness. Those spirits are still around and are enjoying their time in the future. But then I see a point of light, it comes from the sun, and minutes later, everyone on the Earth is wiped away like dew from the morning sun."

Charley sat back against the pillow behind him and asked, "Do you know when this happens?"

"I do not." The Golden Fox leaned back and sighed. "I think it's a long way off in the future, but I'm linked to that moment, and I don't know why. I've never visited the future. I haven't the power to do that. I can go to the Other side and visit my fellow faerie folk, but the future is a barrier that I cannot cross. Only a chronicler can do that."

"Like me." Phoebe let go of the Golden Fox's hands and turned to look away. "You want me to learn how to do that, don't you?"

"Yes." The Golden Fox kept his voice low. "I do want that."

"And?" Charley prodded him.

"I think I'm the one who helps Phoebe go into the future, but I'm worried that she gets stuck there and can't get back." He let the words out and turned to face Phoebe. "It might be my fault that you're there. I don't understand everything about my dreams yet. Some of it isn't making sense."

"Like Napoleon, right?" Phoebe asked. "You didn't mention him at all."

"Exactly. I have no idea why your future self would tell you that your mother has to help him escape Elba. And that's why we're headed to see Nicéphore Niépce. I want to use his camera obscura so that we can use it not only to put a binding spell on Napoleon, but also to see if we can use it to trap light." He shook his head and furrowed his brow. "That's not the right word to use, but there's light that travels fast, and I want to see if we can capture that light in an image. If you can speak again to your future self, we might be able to trap some of her presence here through the obscura. That might just be enough to help her hone in on being able to come home."

"All of what you say sounds half crazy to me, but then again, I just stepped through the dreamline a few weeks ago with Charley and traveled across the Atlantic. Maybe there are powers greater than either of us know."

An idea popped into Charley's head and he just spoke the words. "Or maybe it's not the magic that's greater, but it's the inventions of men. What if we unleash inventions that we can't control and they get out?"

The Golden Fox patted Charley's arm. "You are right. This camera obscura might not work as I expect, and maybe it doesn't trap the soul. Maybe it creates a copy of one's spirit and then can inhabit others like a ghost. I'll be honest with you both. I really don't know. I'm just trying to do the best I can and only know that Nicéphore Niépce will be the best chance we have of finding out if this invention can help us tame Napoleon."

"When I was a child, I used to dream up wild stories of princes and princesses fighting with the demons of the dark." Phoebe pulled her hair back and then tied it up. "Even my most creative imaginings are nothing like what truly exists."

"Real life is always stranger than fiction. It's just that fiction helps us escape the hardship of our lives sometimes. But with real problems, that's not true. They're not going to go away unless we face them." The Golden Fox stopped talking abruptly and sniffed at the air. He froze and pulled Charley and Phoebe toward the floor. "Get down."

They obeyed and a sudden volley of rifle shots ripped through the air. Several stray shots pierced through the carriage, and from outside they heard their driver fall to the ground, crying out in surprise as he did so. The gunshots continued for a few moments more, killing the horses, and then they heard shouting for the attack to cease.

Phoebe's heart beat fast and her hand shook. She kept low on the ground and whispered, "Are you hurt?"

Charley shook his head but kept his arm over her. He tapped the Golden Fox on the shoulder and asked, "What should we do?"

"Surrender!" The Golden Fox sat up and tried to peek out a window without being seen. "They killed the horses and Michael. We can't just run away."

Charley grabbed his right hand and shook it. "Can't you use that magic of yours to make a weapon for me so that we can fight?"

Phoebe knelt and put her arm on Charley. "He's right. If we surrender, we'll have a better chance of escaping later. We don't know how many men are out there now, and if we try to fight, we'll probably die."

A loud knock on the front of the carriage startled them. They all quieted and held their breaths.

"Come out of the carriage now!" A deep masculine voice barked the command.

Phoebe tried to see who spoke, but whomever it was, he stood away from the windows.

"Yes, yes. We're coming out now." The Golden Fox put his hand on the door to open it and said, "You two only follow me out once you know it's safe."

Charley positioned himself in front of Phoebe to ensure that he would face anyone before she would.

"I can fight for myself. You don't need to defend me." Phoebe tried to push him out of the way, but Charley stayed firm.

"Your mother would never forgive me if I didn't try and protect you." Charley held up his finger when Phoebe went to interrupt him. "If you were my daughter, I'd want someone to try and protect her as well. There's not much I can do. Please, let me help in this."

Phoebe acquiesced and remained quiet. She clenched her left hand and prepared a spell of protection. Closing her eyes, she took in a slow and deep breath, held it, and imagined a hard shell of rock that would encircle her and protect them all from harm. The spell hung in her mind, and she waited to release it when needed.

The Golden Fox exited the carriage and held his hands up in the air. He counted a dozen soldiers, dressed in French military uniforms, forming a semicircle around the carriage.

To his right, an officer of the French army aimed his rifle at the Golden Fox. Of middle age, with wispy blond hair, and of average height, he said, "Tell the others to come out."

"Yes, of course." The Golden Fox turned back around and called into the carriage. "You're being summoned by a very nice man with a really long rifle. I would recommend that you both come outside now and join me in the fun I'm having."

Phoebe caught a glimpse of the man pointing his rifle at the Golden Fox and was tempted to release a spell. She could harm him, but she still could not see how many other men waited for them. She dropped the idea and pushed Charley forward. "Let's just go and get this over with. The sooner we surrender, the sooner we'll find out what they want."

"They might just want us dead." Charley held his position for a moment.

"We would be dead already if they wanted to kill us. Let's go." Phoebe nudged Charley forward.

He stepped out of the carriage onto the metal step and jumped down to the ground. Keeping his arms in the air, he turned back to help Phoebe down.

"Thank you for joining me with our gracious hosts." The Golden Fox kept his hands in the air but could not resist a jab at their soldiers.

"Silence!" The middle-aged man poked the Golden Fox in the stomach with his rifle.

He stumbled back into the wheel of the carriage. "Okay, I get it. You're the guy with the gun, and I should follow what you say."

The French officer went to hit the Golden Fox with his rifle but held for a moment and then stepped back, holding his rifle at him. "My name is Jacques MacDonald. I've been sent by His Majesty Louis XVIII of France to stop you."

Charley leaned over to Phoebe. "How am I understanding him? I don't know French."

Jacques turned his attention to Charley and shouted, "I will not ask again. If you do not remain quiet, I'll have you tied up. Understand?"

The Golden Fox leaned over to Charley and replied, "I've cast a spell on you. You now know French!"

He gave a little smile and turned back just in time to receive the butt of the rifle pressed into his cheek. Three men came over to hold each of them still. "This is no game that a dandy like you might play on a Sunday afternoon. You will tell me your plans, and if I'm not satisfied with your answers, then I might need to get creative."

Phoebe had her spell ready. She only needed to wait a moment or two more to ensure that she could incapacitate Jacques and the three soldiers. The nearest one came to her, and if he touched her, then she would release her spell.

The Golden Fox dropped his smile and bowed his head. "I apologize. I didn't mean to offend. I will tell you our plans."

He glanced over at Charley and Phoebe, giving a little sigh.

"Speak!" Jacques pushed the rifle butt up hard against the Golden Fox's cheek and then withdrew, preparing to smash his face with his rifle.

"Okay, I'll tell you." The Golden Fox looked up to Jacques and said, "We're headed to see a friend in Chalon-sur-Saône."

"Who is this friend of yours?" Jacques held his rifle back, ready to strike at any moment.

"Well, he's not exactly a friend." The Golden Fox smiled, trying to disarm Jacques with his charm. Jacques flinched, pretending to strike, and the Golden Fox quickly continued, "His name is Nicéphore Niépce."

Jacques held still and asked, "Who is he?"

Phoebe had only a few moments left before the nearest soldier reached her. If she wanted to act, she would have to do it soon.

The Golden Fox leaned forward and flashed his brilliant smile at Jacques. "We're just going to visit him because…"

Phoebe let the word out of her mind and a blinding pulse of light shot forth from her left hand. She raised her arms up and the ground rose with her. Mud and rocks flew up, blinding Jacques and the three soldiers. She pushed her hands outward and grimaced from the effort. The ground shook and a wall of earth surrounded them.

Jacques rushed forward and hit the Golden Fox hard in the face. He fell back against the carriage, blood coming out of his mouth.

Charley bent down low and rushed forward, knocking Jacques into the wall of mud. Phoebe redirected her spell and the mud rippled and surrounded them in a sphere with only a small opening up above.

"Charley, come back." Phoebe yelled over the din, pushing outward as far as she could to keep them safe from the soldiers. On hearing the first gunshots, she shifted her hand and changed the mud to rock. A bullet whizzed by her, and the next shots hit the solid wall of moving earth that surrounded them.

Charley fell back into the Golden Fox and quickly turned around to help him. "We have to get out of here. Do some of your faerie magic and help us." More rifle shots could be heard above the pulsating wall of earth that surrounded them.

Wiping the blood from his mouth, the Golden Fox opened his eyes and released his spell. Golden light lit up the left wall of rock. "Go, now!" He struggled and grimaced in pain. "I can't hold it open long."

Charley grabbed Phoebe and together they rushed into the open gateway. They vanished and the Golden Fox went to follow them, but an arm coming out of the hardened mud wall grabbed him. Forcing himself the rest of the way through the now crumbling caked mud, Jacques pulled at the Golden Fox and his spell broke. With a grunt, Jacques knocked the Golden Fox down and then punched him several times in the face.

"Stay down." He straddled the Golden Fox and held both his hands down. "I've got you, faerie lord." He pulled a thin chain out of his pocket and wrapped it around the Golden Fox's hand.

Startled from the blow and being knocked to the ground, he tried to push Jacques off him. Gathering his strength, he let loose his magic, but nothing came. The chain around his hand glowed faintly and then the light faded.

"Silver does wonders, doesn't it?" Jacques punched the Golden Fox again in the face.

His head turned to the side and he spit out blood. "I surrender." The Golden Fox tried to shift Jacques off him but received another solid punch in the face.

"Stay down." Jacques wrapped up the Golden Fox's free hand, tying them both together with the silver chain. "Now you'll tell me what you're up to."

Spitting out saliva and more blood, the Golden Fox stared up at Jacques and asked, "Who the hell are you?"

"I'm Jacques MacDonald, Marshall of France, but to you, I'm a witch hunter, and you're going to tell me where you sent the witch and her friend."

The Golden Fox tried to call forth his magic, but the silver drained it from him, and his last conscious thought was hoping that where he sent Phoebe and Charley wouldn't be as bad as he thought.

***

I pulled the reins to slow down my horse, giving him some time to relax. Jeremiah and I had ridden hard on the open field, but now we entered a small clump of trees. The bitter cold still nipped at us, and the steam rushed out of our horses' mouths. Jeremiah slowed next to me and sat up straight in his saddle.

"What are you going to say to Jessica when you meet her?" He brought his mount to a slow walk.

"I'm not quite sure yet." I turned all around and heard nothing except for the breathing of our horses and the wind. "What if one of those crystal creatures comes after us again?"

"Then we'll get away as fast as we can." Jeremiah patted down the neck of his horse, and I could see that he wanted to say something more but held back.

"Tell me, what's on your mind?" We were about halfway through the trees. I held the reins tight in my hands, ready to start up at a fast gallop at a moment's notice.

"You know me that well?" Jeremiah smiled and a dimple formed on his right cheek.

"You're often not subtle when you want to get something off your chest." I didn't smile in return, more concerned about a surprise visitor popping up at any time.

Jeremiah cleared the trees first, and up ahead we both saw the twisting path that led to a small house. The farm lands that surrounded it stretched far past the boundaries of the house. Someone had spent a lot of time clearing the land and tending crops.

"No, subtlety isn't my way. I prefer to be much more direct." He pointed down at the house ahead and said, "Be easy on her. Jessica isn't your enemy, and she's not trying to take Phoebe away from you."

We just weren't going to have a good day today. My temper flared and I had difficulty in remaining calm. "I know that. I'm not going to blame her for…" I stopped talking and realized what Jeremiah had done.

"Realize what?" He prodded me and his smile had faded. He, too, could be extremely serious in the moment.

I hesitated to respond and then glanced away a moment, but I did turn back to face him. "I realize that Phoebe has had to hide Jessica from me because she probably thinks that I wouldn't approve, or even worse, that I might be jealous." I said the words from my heart, and I instantly felt better.

"It'll be good to remember that. I love you dearly…" He paused a moment, searching for the right words.

"But?" I prompted him to say more, giving me the ammunition I would need to fight back.

"There is no 'but.' I do love you and I want to make certain that you're kind to yourself and to Phoebe. It isn't anyone's fault that you no longer have your magic. And that's okay. You're still you." He said the words and they probably made him feel good, but not me.

I held up my left hand and didn't even try to call on any magic. I had tried daily for so long that the failure had built a heavy weight on my heart. Better to let it be and move on. "I know all of that. I do, but I would be lying if I didn't admit that I still miss it. And now that Phoebe is older and I could teach her, that's when I am now lost without it. I'm still angry over it."

"And that's what I'm saying. Be aware of your anger. It's not Jessica's fault. Let's get to know her, and maybe she could help us find a way to Europe faster?" Jeremiah adjusted the rifle on his back and I stayed next to him. He matched my horse's gait and then remained quiet.

"I sometimes wish that all of this would go away." I said the words more for myself than for him. "I waited so long to find happiness and I've worked hard to get where I am today, but it's still hard for me to accept all that I've been through. I'm angry, frustrated, and feel alone."

"But you're never alone. You have me. Our friends and Phoebe." Jeremiah reached his hand out to me and touched my gloved hand.

"That still doesn't take the pain away. I feel lost and sometimes I just wish that I would get over my loss faster." I squeezed his hand and then let go. "All of this is a lot more difficult than I had ever expected. I really thought I would adapt in time and that I would move on now that we're back in America." I glanced around the beautiful snow-filled landscape and took all of the scene in. "But that's not true. I'm still hurting and I'm beginning to think that I'll always have this burden on me. It's a weight on my chest, and I just want it all to be taken from me."

"Then just let it go." Jeremiah spoke softly

"You make it seem that it's so easy to do. That one simply just does it." I shook my head and fumed.

"That is exactly what I'm saying. Don't overthink it. Just let it go." Jeremiah pushed me and I hated it when he did that.

"Listen, we're different people. What works for you doesn't for me. And that's just the way it is." I glanced down at the small house and watched the white smoke coming out of its chimney.

"If you were more open to change, then maybe it wouldn't be so hard for you." He started to say more but knew enough that he stood on unsafe ground.

"You're trying to incite me, and I'm not going to fall into your trap." I didn't look over at him but focused on the idyllic scene ahead.

"There's no trap. It's all pretty simple. Just let yourself off the hook and accept that you're angry. Say it, own up to it, and then let it go." Jeremiah's smugness hung all over his words.

"Maybe I don't want to let it all go. Maybe the anger and frustration is all I have left, and I want to remember even the tiniest hope of what having lost my magic really means to me. If I were to let it all go, I'd have to move on, and I'm not ready for that yet. I'm just not. Can you understand that?" I faced him and I left a full range of emotion come out in my voice and body language.

"You're the hardest working person I know." He reached for me but I steered my horse away. "But you're also the one person that makes things so much more difficult for yourself than they need to be. Things don't have to be this hard. You're making it harder for yourself. Don't you see that?"

I took his words in and knew that if I answered that we would spiral into an argument, and I wasn't in the mood for that. "Let's drop this now. We're almost there and I'm upset enough that Phoebe and Charley aren't around. I know that you think I could be making things easier on myself, but from where I sit, I'm doing the best that I can. I can't go any faster, and it's been hard for me. Can we just accept that as it is and let it go for now?"

A word formed on his lips, but he turned away and said, "Sure. I can do that. I'm just worried about you." He faced me and reached out again.

I took his gloved hand in mine, and that represented well how our marriage had been for the last year—muffled in protective gear. "Thank you."

We rode on in silence for the next few minutes, and that gave me time to clear my head. Jeremiah led the way and I hung back, watching the brilliant blue sky and the bright sun. Yet still, the frigid weather bit at both of us, and I knew that I had to find a way to let go of my loss. I had to accept it, but I wasn't quite ready to do that yet. Part of me thought there still might be a way to regain my powers, and Jeremiah seemed to think that if I just let everything go that I'd be able to heal and move on.

None of that worked for me though because the ache, hurt, and loss of a part of me remained a fresh wound. I had lost friends, family and my magic. What else did I have to lose? I already felt broken and despondent half the time. And yet I knew I was being too hard on myself and on Jeremiah. He had been patient, understanding, but I now knew that he wanted me to speed things up and get over my loss. He wanted to move onward, and I just wasn't ready to let it go yet.

I thought of Phoebe, could see her smiling at something funny that I said to her, and I hoped and prayed that she was safe.

"We'll tie our horses up front and give her plenty of time to see us." Jeremiah urged his horse on the last bit toward the house. "I definitely don't want her to think we're trying to sneak up on her. Messing with a witch isn't my idea of a good time."

I laughed and then covered my ears from a bitter blast of wind. "You're probably right. Though Ginny didn't give us the full story on what type of witch Jessica is. Maybe she only makes potions and helps the kids in the area when they're sick."

Jeremiah shrugged in his saddle. "You could be right. She might not have any magical abilities at all. I guess we'll soon see."

He stopped his horse and hopped off easily, started to tie up his mount, and then stopped. "Let's just head our horses inside her barn. They can't stay outside in weather like this."

I didn't disagree and remained quiet until we made it to the barn. I kept my eye on the house but could see no movement in any of the windows. The only sign of life was the gray smoke coming out of the chimney. I dismounted and Charley opened the barn door. We hurried inside, tied up our horses, and took a few moments to warm up.

Jeremiah rubbed his hands together and then exhaled into his palms. From behind him, a cow mooed in a stall. Startled, he jumped forward a step, and said, "Well, excuse me."

He put his gloves back on and asked, "Ready?"

I went up to him and kissed him on the lips.

Startled, he smiled and wrapped his arms around me. "What's that for?"

"I just wanted you to know that I love you." I shivered and hugged him back. "I know it's not been easy lately between us. I just wanted you to know that I appreciate your support."

He kissed me back and we lingered for a few moments until the cow mooed again. Jeremiah looked over his shoulder and said, "Okay, okay, I'll leave now."

I led him out of the barn, holding his hand, and we quickly walked toward the house. Snowdrifts had piled to the right-hand side of the door, and a fierce wind blew the snow toward us. I bowed, shielding my eyes with my hand, and we hurried up the steps to the front door of the house.

Two old wooden rocking chairs were covered in snow on the wraparound porch. Snow swirled from the wind, but someone had cleared a pathway toward the front door.

I rapped hard on the door and waited a few moments. Jeremiah came close to me and tried to shield me from the wind. Peering into the window, I could not see much inside, and after a few more seconds, I knocked harder.

Jeremiah looked inside. "I don't see anything. Do you?"

"No, I didn't either. Maybe she's not home?" I asked.

As if the house heard us, the door swung open inward, and I caught a blast of warm air, coming from inside.

Jeremiah took a step back. "Looks like we're being invited inside. Should we go in?"

I couldn't see anyone in the room ahead. "Might as well." I walked through the entrance, and a myriad of exotic smells assaulted my senses. In the corner of the tiny room, a small wood-burning stove caught my attention. A large pot filled with canned tomatoes bubbled slowly. A wooden spoon, probably used to stir the sauce, rested on the counter. Empty jars to be used for canning were placed on a small kitchen table.

"Anyone home?" Jeremiah called out, and in response, a tabby cat came out of the shadows and rubbed its head against his leg. He bent down and petted the cat, evoking from it a low purr. "Friendly little guy."

A door to the left of the kitchen opened, and an older woman walked in. She carried several more glass jars in her arms and stopped. Obviously surprised to see us in her house, she stopped and asked, "What do you want?"

"Here, let me help you with that." I took two jars from her and put them on the kitchen table. "I'm Phoebe's mother and we're hoping you might be able to help us."

At the mention of Phoebe, the woman relaxed a bit and smiled. "You have such an intelligent daughter. She's always so pleasant to have over." She put down the remaining jars she carried and added, "And what a quick learner she is. What do you need help with? Is everything all right with her?"

"That's why we're here. She and Mr. Radley had to run from—" I stopped, unsure of how to continue.

Jeremiah came to my side and finished. "Mrs. Radley was kind enough to let us know that Phoebe used to come visit you often, and we thought that maybe you might be willing to help us."

The woman, probably in her late fifties by my best guess, stood up straight, and her entire demeanor changed. Her gray hair was pulled back in a bun. She no longer hunched over, and she beamed a confident smile at me. "She told you I'm a witch, didn't she?"

"Is that a problem?" I replied, waiting to see what she would do next. I glanced quickly over to Jeremiah, and he still seemed relaxed.

"It's only a problem if you don't like witches." She came up to me and put her hand on my shoulder. "I'm Jessica. When I was younger, I used to go by Jessica of the Summer Wind. It never quite caught on, but I liked it."

"Will you help us then?"

She motioned for us to sit at her table and I did so. The wooden chair scraped across the floor, and after I was seated, Jeremiah sat beside me. Jessica cleared the jars from in front of us and sat across from me. "I will if I can. But first, I need to know what has happened."

"A faerie creature came to hunt her down, and she and Mr. Radley have disappeared. We were hoping that you might have magic or a spell to help us get to Europe quickly." I tried to not sound so desperate but failed. Time wasn't on our side and we needed help fast.

"I am good with potions that heal, cause love to grow, or even the occasional revenge salve that will cause your enemy to regret what they've done to you, but travel spells aren't my specialty. I can't help you there."

I tried to hide my disappointment on my face, failing miserably. "I had hoped that maybe you could help us." I went to get up and looked to Jeremiah. "I apologize for barging into your home and taking up your time."

Jessica shook her head. "You have not bothered me. I don't get too many visitors out here these days. When the weather warms, I'll sell my sauce at the local market, but in the winter, it's just my cats and I."

As if reminded of something, she held up her hand. "But do not discourage so easily. I may not be able to help you, but I can take you to a place that might."

"Tell me more." I leaned forward, eager to be on our way. Every second that passed, Phoebe and Charley could be more at risk.

"Do you not know of the World Tree?" Jessica leaned back in her chair, taking in my response.

"Should I know of this?" I crossed my arms and waited for her to reply.

"Phoebe loved going to the World Tree. I sometimes think that she came to visit me only because of that." Seeing that neither Jeremiah and I knew of what she spoke, Jessica stopped her banter and got straight to the point. "The World Tree is a sacred place for witches. There are only a few left now. When I was young, there were many more, but over time, they died or were destroyed by the hunters."

She stared directly at Jeremiah in an accusatory way. He looked right at her and then replied, "I haven't been a hunter now for years."

Jessica shook her head and pounded her fist on the table. "I did not mean that you personally destroyed the World Trees. But it was your brethren who came from across the ocean, hunting down the magic they sought. They stripped the land bare and brought the power back to England to help strengthen the isle against Napoleon." She then paused a moment and seemed to speak only to herself. "And it seems that they succeeded. Napoleon never did set foot on the British islands. The magic held, but at a great cost. Now only a few trees are left."

"And what do these trees do?" I asked, half-guessing the answer.

"They're connected, of course. Not everyone can travel through the dreamline like Phoebe or how you used to. For everyday witches like me, the World Tree gave me a chance to explore the world and bring back some of the most exotic of herbs."

Her words stung and I tried to ignore them. How I used to. I had fought my private war long enough, and to deal with my grief, I clenched my left fist, took a slow, deliberate deep breath, and then exhaled.

Seeing me visibly upset, Jeremiah went to put his arm around me, but I moved away. "It seems that you know a lot more about me than I you."

Jessica bit her lip and glanced away. "I apologize if I offended you. Phoebe told me…"

I did not want to hear any more. "It seems that Phoebe shared with you much of my personal struggles, and I'd rather not go into the details of my private life with you right now."

"It was not my intention to bring up an uncomfortable topic for you. I want to help." Jessica pointed out the window to her right. "The World Tree will get you to where you want to go. And it's not that far. You can get there on foot. I can take care of your horses until you get back."

The wind howled and snow from a drift on the porch swirled and piled up against the window. Jeremiah put his hands on his hips and asked, "How far is this tree?"

"Less than a mile. I head out there almost every day. I can take you if you want." Jessica crossed the room and took a heavy coat off a chair and slipped into it. "I'll take you to the World Tree, show you how to get inside, and then you both can be on your way. And I'm willing to help you more if you'd like."

Her tone bothered me, but, to be honest, I wasn't at my best. Losing Phoebe and being chased by a faerie creature that destroyed my house had put me in a foul mood. "How much could you really help me?"

Jessica smiled and she turned away, heading to the door. "If you have the courage to ask, I might be of much more help than you think. You take me for a washed-up witch, but in my prime, I led the largest coven on the East Coast."

Jeremiah put his hands in his pockets and said, "I'll go feed the horses and meet you outside."

"Thank you." I kissed him on the cheek as he passed. I knew I had offended him by turning him away earlier and would need to talk with him. His patience with my emotional depression had been admirable. I needed help. I knew that. But I did not know where to turn.

Jessica watched Jeremiah leave, and she shut the door behind him. "He's a good man."

"I know that. But we're not here to talk about him. You want to know about me." I sighed and fidgeted with a lock of my hair. "How can you help me?"

"What do you truly desire?" Jessica asked back.

"You know that. Come on." I did not feel like playing games.

"Then say it. Speak the words and release them from having power over you." Jessica crossed the room and took my hands in hers.

I closed my eyes and the words came to me like a strong gust of wind. I spoke quickly, out of breath, expelling the words from me. "I want my powers back."

When I opened my eyes, Jessica nodded. "I know that. But why?"

I hadn't thought to ask that question before. I paused a moment and said, "I want to be able to protect Phoebe and Jeremiah. I want to be able to keep safe those I love. I want..." The thought came to me, and the words caught in my throat.

"Yes?" Jessica urged me on.

Tears welled up in my eyes and I pushed onward. "I don't ever want to be abandoned and lost again. My magic protected me and kept me safe."

She pulled me close and embraced me like a mother would. It had been too long since my own mother had held me. She had left me to go with the Silver Fox in the faerie world and I lost her. My father had traveled the seas, leaving me to the whims of my stepmother and her daughters.

Jessica whispered in my ear. "You still feel lost and alone, don't you?"

"Yes, I do." Uncomfortable from her hug, I pulled back and gathered myself together. "I want to feel whole again. My magic is gone." I put my hand over my heart. "It's like there's a wound there that never heals. I feel so hurt and alone. Everything that I thought I had found is gone. My world has been changed, and I'm just adrift in it."

"Just like me." Jessica showed me her hands. "I, too, lost my magic once."

"But you're a witch. My daughter comes to see you, and I assumed you've been teaching her." I stopped talking, looking incredulous.

"Once a witch, always a witch. It is in my blood. I am who I am." She pointed at me and touched my chest with her index finger. "Just like you. You are a witch as well."

"But I don't want to just mix potions together and help the sick. I want..." I realized that my words might offend her. "I'm sorry. I didn't mean to insult you."

"It is fine." Jessica pulled herself up to her full height. "There are no words that you can say that can harm me. I know who I am and am comfortable with that. And that's what I can teach you."

"But I don't want to just settle. I want to find a way to gain my powers back. I want to feel alive again and travel the dreamline, to see the stars, the earth, and the power all around us. I want all of that again."

"And you can have that, if you are patient." Jessica turned to go, paused, and looked back over her shoulder. "Trust me."

She left and a blast of cold wind rushed in and chilled me. I stood there alone in the house. I had a decision to make. I could stay put or I could take the first few steps out the door, on a new journey, to somewhere that I did not know. I might never find my powers again. If I didn't, I would need to learn how to live without them and be happy. Yes, I had a chance of finding my magic, but if I couldn't regain that, then I needed to find a way to heal myself. And sitting still and not taking Jessica's offer of help would only keep me stuck. For Phoebe, Jeremiah, and most of all myself, I needed to try.

With one step forward, I headed to the door, paused a moment, and crossed the threshold. Better to try and fail than to give up. A blast of cold air hit me. I bundled up against the cold and headed outside.

Chapter 5

Phoebe opened her eyes and took a moment to orient herself. She lay on her back in a forest clearing. The grass, soft and lush, acted as a nice cushion. In the sky, the moon shone bright, blocking out most of the stars. A cricket chirped near her, singing its night song with a consistency that calmed her. Gone was the cold temperatures of winter, and in its stead, humidity and warmth enveloped her.

"Charley, are you here?" She sat up and called out as loud as she dared.

A groan from off to her right in the bushes answered her.

"Charley?" She rushed over to the spot and found Charley bent over a fallen tree.

"Yeah, I'm here." He slid down to the forest floor and checked that he had all his extremities. "What happened to us?"

Phoebe looked around the forest. "The Golden Fox sent us somewhere." A toad off to the right started croaking. "Where he sent us, I'm not so sure."

"My stomach feels like it's done a flip." He got to his knees and shook his head. "And my head doesn't feel much better. This travel by magic isn't as easy as you witches make it sound."

"We should try to find some shelter so that we can rest for the night. It's been a long day for us, and we should get some sleep." She spun around in a circle with her hands on her hips. "Any ideas?"

"I wouldn't mind something to eat as well. I'm hungry." Charley looked up at the moon and pointed. "Hey, look at that!"

Phoebe followed where he pointed and started at the near full moon. "What do you see?"

"It's different. Look!" Charley closed his right eye, looked at the left of the moon, and said, "The face is gone. You know, the man in the moon."

Phoebe looked for the familiar spots on the moon and nodded. "That's not good."

"What do you think it means?" Charley asked.

"My mom told me about this once a long time ago." Cupping her hands around her eyes, Phoebe stared for a few moments and said, "I think I know where we're at."

After she remained quieted for a bit longer, Charley prompted her to speak. "And?"

She frowned and replied, "We're on the Other side." When he didn't react from her words, she added, "Faerie land."

Charley came closer to Phoebe and spoke in a low voice. "That's not good, right?"

"Well, it depends where in faerie land we are." Phoebe pointed at the edge of the clearing. "If we're not careful, we might fall into a faerie trap or worse."

"Or maybe you're already in a trap and it's too late!" A tall thin man, dressed all in white, came out of the clearing behind them.

Phoebe spun around with her left hand aglow in magical fire, ready to release a spell. "Who are you?"

Charley put up his fists and knew he looked silly, but the need to protect himself and Phoebe was too strong to ignore. He moved closer to her and scanned the area for another sort of weapon but came up short.

"Relax, I'm not here to harm you." The tall man brushed his shoulder and smiled at them, showing all his teeth. "My name is Ignatius. You can say that I'm a cousin of the Golden Fox's."

Phoebe and Charley exchanged glances and Phoebe asked, "Where exactly are we?"

Ignatius crossed the distance between them and folded his hands in front of him. "You are correct that you are on the Other side." He pointed up at the moon. "It's always a dead giveaway. Back on your home, you never get to see this side of things. You only see the one face of our dear moon, but here on the Other side, well, we see lots of things."

Charley lowered his fists, and Phoebe let her magic ebb and dissipate. "Are you able to help us rescue the Golden Fox?"

"He doesn't need any helping. He'll be fine. I wouldn't worry about him at all." Ignatius looked back over his shoulder. "Maybe you might want to think about why he sent you here."

Phoebe came up close to Ignatius and pointed her finger at him. "Listen, I know that you faerie types enjoy riddles and toying with mortals like us, but we're traveling in the dead of winter to find Joseph

Nicéphore Niépce and were even chased by some Cryshada creature…"

Ignatius interrupted her and knocked her finger away. "First, don't you ever point your finger at me." He took a step back and quickly followed up with "Second, tell me more about the Cryshada."

Phoebe bit back her anger and replied, "It was an ogre-like creature. Big, with a swirl of shards all around it, and it tried to kill us."

"I know what they look like, but what I want to know is why it came after you." Ignatius brushed back his long blond hair from his face and stared off in the distance. "I wonder…"

"What do you wonder?" Phoebe pressed her point again and took a step closer to him. "Look, we nearly died a few minutes ago, and neither of us are in the mood to have a long philosophical discussion about the details. It would be nice if you could take us to a place of safety where we can eat some food, rest, and then we can have a nice long chat with you."

Ignatius turned back to her as if seeing her for the first time. "Oh, you are right. My manners are not what they used to be. I've been alone here a long, long time, and I think I have become stuck in my ways."

"Where are the rest of your kind?" Charley continued to scan the surrounding area for any other sign of life.

"Most of my kind have moved on. There are only a few of us left." Ignatius headed off out of the clearing. "Come, follow me and I'll take you to my home. You'll get to rest, have some food, and then we can talk some more."

"We would appreciate that." Phoebe glanced back at Charley and he nodded. "Lead the way and we'll follow you."

Ignatius left the clearing and stopped a few yards in the forest. "I should remind you not to touch anything no matter how friendly it might seem." He pointed at several fireflies that flitted off in the distance. "Especially those little creatures. They're known for setting things on fire when they get angry."

Charley paused a moment and asked, "Are you serious?"

Ignatius shook his head and laughed. "The Golden Fox was right. You mortals are so easy to fool."

Charley clenched his fists and strode forward, but Phoebe put out her arm and stopped him from advancing. She lit her hand up with magic and changed the subject. "I find that my powers are stronger here. Do you know why?"

Ignatius started off again and answered her in a loud voice. Any other being, within miles, would know of their location. "You're closer to the source of your power. Weren't you taught that as a witch?"

"My training hasn't been as regular as I would have liked." Phoebe said no more on the subject and kept walking.

"Ah, the Golden Fox did tell me about your mother. Powerful witch she was, but now that she's lost her magic, she's also lost her way." Ignatius spotted a dirt trail and turned right to head down a slight embankment. "Where we are headed, your magic will only become stronger. My home is by the Shard Chimes of Forget-me-not. There's strong magic there, and if we have time, I will show you the source."

"The source of all magic?" Charley tried to keep up in the conversation but he had been lost since it started.

"No, the source of power on this plane. The Other side is linked to your world with the moon as our prism." He glanced back and saw Phoebe's and Charley's confused expressions. Stopping, he pulled a piece of rolled-up parchment from his pocket. "Imagine that this side of the parchment is the Other side. Now imagine the moon in the center. When you go through the moon, you then cross back over to your world." He turned over the paper and said, "Voilà! Understand?"

"So, you're telling us that the Golden Fox sent us through the moon to get here to the Other side?" Charley glanced up at the sky and tried to grasp the distance they had traveled.

"Yes, you got it!" Ignatius started up again and this time walked faster.

Phoebe stared up at the sky, through the tops of the trees, into the starry night. The moon hung high in the air, its unfamiliar face beaming down on them. "How are we going to get back home?"

She said the words low and to herself, but Charley came up to her and put his arm around her. "Don't worry. We'll get back. For now, let's just keep up with him."

As if he heard them, Ignatius called out ahead of them. "Come, come. Keep up. We're almost at the crossing!"

Charley pulled Phoebe close, giving her a solid hug, and said, "I promised your mother a long time ago that I would look out for you. I may not have magic, and you might think you're old enough to take care of yourself, but I'll be by your side to help you as best I can and will do my best to bring you back safe." He let her out of his bear hug and shrugged. "Even if you go to hell and back, I'll be by your side."

Phoebe threw her arms around his neck and hugged him tightly. "Thank you." She disengaged herself from him and headed off and went down the embankment, following Ignatius.

The dirt path opened up, and they saw him waiting for them. He had his arms crossed, and he tapped his foot on the ground. "Are you both done talking now? We only have a little bit more to go and then we'll be safe."

"You mean we're not safe now?" Charley glanced back over his shoulder but saw nothing but trees and bushes in the moonlight.

Ignatius pointed back the way they had come. "I wouldn't want you both to stay here the rest of the night. Some creature from the deep might come right up underneath your feet and feed on you. It's a bit of a nightmare place for mortals if you don't know where to go." He turned back around and headed off the dirt path. "Just keep following me, and whatever you do, don't go stepping on any small pool of water."

Phoebe looked down and couldn't see water anywhere near her. "Umm, okay. Any reason why?"

"Well, it's usually the tear duct of the Chlorisis." His voice sounded suddenly far away. "It's a big creature with huge eyes that likes to hide under the ground."

Phoebe walked in between two trees and slowed down, seeing that Ignatius had climbed down a steep embankment. "You're certain that we're almost there."

Charley followed close behind her and grabbed onto a tree branch to balance himself. "It feels like we're climbing down the side of a mountain. How did it get so steep so fast?"

"Watch out for this next part. Just keep walking no matter what," Ignatius called back to them.

Phoebe thought she caught a glimpse of an open area up ahead but couldn't be certain. She slid down the next few yards, careful to hang onto a branch, and the ground opened up suddenly beneath her. Instead of a gradual downward climb, the only path forward was a narrow log placed across a crevice. Up ahead Ignatius walked across the log with ease. He glanced down below and pointed. "You definitely don't want to fall down there. I think your squishy insides wouldn't take kindly to that."

"What did he say?" Charley asked. He grunted in stopping himself from sliding too far forward. "Did he say something about how far we have yet?" On seeing the sudden cliff and the solitary log ahead, he stopped. "He's fooling us, right?"

"No, we have to get across, and he warned us not to fall." Phoebe had stepped up on the log and held onto a long branch to an evergreen tree. "Let's just do this quickly."

"Wait a second!" Charley repositioned himself to be closer to her. "Is there some sort of rope or vine we can tie onto each other?"

Phoebe walked across the log, made it about a third of the way, and stopped. "Just don't look down. I should have never looked down."

Charley edged forward and glanced down. In the moonlight, the distance to the ground would be plenty enough to kill them from the fall. "Just be careful!"

"I got that part down." Phoebe edged forward and used her arms to balance herself. Just out of reach, another large evergreen branch hung out over the crevice. "Let me just grab that and I'll be fine." She took two steps forward, wobbled a bit, and grabbed a fistful of pine needles. "Damn."

"Take it easy. No need to go too fast." Charley had his one foot up on the log and had half a mind to run up and chase across to help her, but he thought that might only make things worse.

Ignatius waited for them at the end, and he had his arm out to Phoebe. "You're almost there. Just a few more feet and I got you."

"I'm not really fond of heights. In fact, I'd rather be anywhere right now except balancing high up on a log over a fall that would break me in two." Phoebe waved her left hand and it lit up. "And I know all sorts of magic spells, but nothing that would help me from falling."

Charley took another step onto the log and reached above for the evergreen branch. "Just keep going on ahead. You're almost there."

A gust of wind blew hard at them, and Phoebe closed her eyes and held on tight to the branch above her. "I know I can do this. I know I can." She opened her eyes, checked her footing, and then walked the rest of the few feet across without a problem.

Ignatius grabbed her hand and pulled her safely down off the log. "See, you made it!"

Charley took a few steps forward on the log and balanced. "If Ginny and the kids could only see me now." He took a few steps, stopped to catch his balance, and waved his arms in the air like he was a bird. "Oh, boy. You're right. Never look down. Just don't look down."

Phoebe put her hand out to him. "Charley, it's not that bad. You're almost there."

"Liar!" He grabbed the evergreen branch and took a deep breath. "Okay, here goes." He took a few more steps forward, made it halfway, and then turned sideways, balancing again as he had a moment of instability. "Just a few more steps."

Charley grabbed the closest evergreen branch and took the next step, and his right foot slipped off the log. He reached out and grabbed on tight to the branch above him with both hands, stabilizing himself on the log so he didn't fall.

Phoebe reached out to him in desperation, but he was still a few feet out of her reach. "Charley!" Her call out to him echoed into the chasm below.

Ignatius leaned against a tree, looking at his nails. He made no gesture to help and rolled his eyes upward.

"Don't come after me. You're safe and I just need a few moments to gather myself." His shirt sleeves fell up, and the muscles of his forearms flexed as he pulled himself up. Balancing on one leg, with his right still off the log, he grunted and used his upper body strength to right himself until he had both feet back on the log.

Phoebe climbed back up on the log to head after him, and Ignatius came over to her and held her back. "You'll only make it more difficult for him, and you'll put yourself in danger."

She gave him an icy stare but came back down and made room for Charley to walk the rest of the way.

"Trust me, he'll be fine. He has a firm grasp of the branches above, and he'll be able to make it the last few feet." Ignatius pointed at Charley who had started moving again. "Look, he's almost across."

Phoebe pulled away from Ignatius and reached out toward Charley. "Come on, you're almost there."

Charley stopped and took a moment to reposition his right foot on the log and tested the strength of the branches above him. He tried not to look down, but he caught a glimpse of a bird flying far below him. How far down the ground was he did not know and didn't want to find out. "Okay, that's enough of that. Just a few more steps and then I'll be there."

He moved his left foot, followed quickly with his right, and shimmied the last few feet until he could reach Phoebe's hand. She grasped his hand firmly and then pulled him off the log. He stumbled off but quickly caught himself and collapsed onto the ground.

"Phew, made it." Charley sat up and wiped the sweat from his forehead. "For a moment there, I thought I had taken my last step and was going to fall."

Phoebe turned on Ignatius with both hands clenched at her side. "Why did you do nothing to help him? You could have done something. Even just helping me reach out and pull him across."

Ignatius brushed a lock of hair from his eyes and sighed. "I didn't want to help him. It was that simple. If I did, yes, I could have used my magic and lifted him across. I'm actually quite gifted in several spells like that."

"You mean you could have helped both of us across but chose not to?" Phoebe rushed forward and punched him in the chest. "How dare you put both of our lives at risk and not help!"

Ignatius looked to Charley who had pulled himself up off the ground and came to Phoebe's side. "Should I do everything and be your faerie godfather, helping you with all of your little problems?"

"We could have died, and you had the ability to save us and didn't!" Phoebe pushed him away and then turned fuming.

"Yes, I could have saved you, but if I did that, then what would you both learn?" Ignatius pointed back at the log. "I didn't even use my own magic to help myself. I walked across it just fine. And you know why?"

"I've heard enough of you. Come on, Charley, let's go." Phoebe started to storm off in anger.

"Just like your mother. Looking for someone to swoop in and save you. I remember hearing her pleas all those years ago. I just ignored them. But the Golden Fox, well, he was silver at the time, wasn't he? The Silver Fox did get involved and went to help your mother, and you know how that all turned out, don't you?" Ignatius put out his hands, showing them his palms. "I don't have an endless supply of magic. I only have so much to use each day. I like to save it for a true emergency, like, for when, maybe, some Cryshada might stumble upon us and then try to impale us with their crystal javelins. I'd rather have a spell ready to defend against them than wasting it because you and your friend here can't walk across a simple log."

Charley stepped between the two of them and put his arms out. Phoebe had stopped and spun around, ready to let out her anger at Ignatius. "Stop. Both of you. I'm tired, was a bit scared, but I really just want to find a place where I can get some food and relax. How about you both call it a truce and we move on?"

"You're taking his side in this?" Phoebe shouted. Her neck was covered in blotchy marks from her anger. Her body temperature had risen, and her temper could not be dissuaded.

"I'm not taking anyone's side. I'm just saying that we're not going to get anywhere standing here yelling at each other. Instead, why don't we all cool off a bit and work together." Charley turned to Ignatius. "How does that sound to you?"

"Just peachy." Ignatius crossed his arms and sulked.

"Phoebe, please. I know you're upset, but we need to work together. You're probably tired and hungry too." He lowered his voice and took a few steps toward her. "Plus, he's a faerie and they're always a bit out there, aren't they?"

She smiled in spite of her anger, and Ignatius said, "I heard that."

Charley came up to him and said, "Good, I wanted you to. I understand that you didn't want to waste your magic on us. I get that, but you could learn a thing or two about common decency and not being so stuck up."

"What do you mean by that?" Ignatius took a step back from Charley in surprise. "I thought you understood me."

"I understand that you're a selfish and lonely faerie and that most of your kind has moved on and you're one of the very few that are left. And that probably makes you a bit stuck up and lonely, doesn't it?" Charley showed Ignatius his closed fist. "I don't mind if you don't save me with your magic, but if there's ever a chance that Phoebe needs help and you refuse to do so. Well, I'll do everything in my power to make sure you regret that. Understand?"

Ignatius cleared his throat and nodded. "I get it. I haven't been a good host. Have I?" He didn't wait for an answer. "We are truly close to my home. Let's go and get settled in for the rest of the night. You'll both get some rest, and I'll cook you both some breakfast. I rather like that meal."

He turned away from Charley and headed off through the trees.

Phoebe walked after him and said to Charley, "Thanks for trying. I appreciate it."

"You're welcome." Speaking more to himself than her, he said, "I guess some people you can never really change."

The moon hung high overhead, and they picked up their pace following Ignatius as best they could.

***

Jeremiah stopped walking and bent low. His long hair blew in the wind, and he covered his neck as best he could. "Are we almost there?"

I wrapped my scarf around my head, covering my mouth, and braced myself from a strong gust of wind and glanced over at Jessica. She had dressed in layers with the outermost being a reddish-colored shawl that she had pulled tightly around her. "Yes, right through this patch and you'll see the World Tree."

We walked on for a few more minutes in silence. I passed the time, thinking of Phoebe. Wondering if she and Charley were well. The cold wind continued to whip at us in bursts, blowing snow off tree limbs that blinded us each time for a few moments. The forest looked desolate with no leaves on most of the trees and the few dried-up ones were covered in snow.

At the top of a small hill, Jessica pointed at the World Tree only yards away. "You should see her in the summer when she's covered in luscious green leaves and all the birds from the surrounding area make nests in her branches."

Jeremiah brushed some snow out of his beard. He turned back the way we had come and watched the horizon.

"Do you see something?" I reached out and touched his arm.

"I'm not sure. I just get the sense that we're being followed, but it might be nothing." He continued to scan the horizon but saw no sign of anyone, or thing, following us.

Jessica led the way down the hill and carefully picked a path through the snow. "Let's hurry up then if you think something might be coming."

I reached the bottom after her with Jeremiah right behind me. She touched a low-hanging tree branch and then rested her forehead against the trunk of the tree. Oversized compared to any tree in the area, I guessed it to be a large oak. From its branches and trunk, I could not discern any sign that the tree was different or unusual in any way. To me, it simply looked like a normal tree.

"Is there a way to get inside?" I asked.

Jessica did not respond, lost in her communing with the tree, but Jeremiah reached for his pistol.

A brilliant globe of red light appeared at the top of the hill behind us. The globe expanded, and a crashing wave of sound, like that of a giant rock cracking in two, echoed throughout the area. One of the Cryshada creatures pulled itself from a giant crack in the sky, and with a crash, the portal vanished.

The creature raised itself to its full height, and the two pulsing red globes over its shoulders exuded crystal shards that swirled around the creature like a globe. The circling shards crashed into each other and sounded like a massive sleet storm hitting the windows of our house.

First to react, Jeremiah aimed his pistol and fired. His shot hit the left globe over the Cryshada's shoulder. The globe blinked and then exploded, shooting tiny crystal shards in all directions. I spun around as did Jeremiah, and our coats protected us from the pieces that flew past us.

The creature stumbled and cried out in fury. It then pushed itself up using its large hands and fired a crystalline javelin at us. The shot went wide, embedding itself deep into the trunk of a tree by us. I shook Jessica, who appeared lost in a trance, and said, "Whatever we're supposed to be doing here, well, we better get going fast!"

She opened her eyes and for a moment was disoriented. Her gaze looked past me as though she saw something that I could not. "Go into the trunk. She's ready for us."

Jeremiah pulled out his second pistol and fired. This time his shot sunk into the forearm of the Cryshada and appeared to do no damage to it. He put his pistols away and rushed over to us. "Time to go!"

The Cryshada roared again and ran down the hill at its full speed. We had only moments before it reached us.

I put my hand on the trunk and felt an opening with my hand. "I think I found it. Let's go." I ran around the circumference of the trunk and found a large opening that I had not seen only moments before.

I ducked down and went inside, and the sound from outside faded away. I stood in a large cave. Phosphorescent lichen lit up the area, and up ahead I could see a faint white light. Jessica and Jeremiah appeared beside me, but I could not hear the Cryshada.

"Can that thing follow us here?" Jeremiah looked back around, and as if in answer, the cave shook, and a rush of wind from outside hit us with its coldness.

The sound of shredding wood drowned out my voice. I tugged at Jessica's sleeve and pointed at the far end of the cave. "Is that where we need to go?"

"Yes." She nodded and pulled both of us in that direction and started running. Careful not to trip on a rock, Jessica led us toward the light that slowly started to grow in intensity.

Behind us, the glowing red light from the Cryshada announced its arrival. How it had fit through the hole in the tree's trunk I did not know, but it stood at its full height and still did not touch the ceiling or the sides of the cave.

We did not stop and ran faster toward the now glowing white light. Jessica reached it first and said, "Go inside now. We have to go. Quickly!"

Jeremiah grabbed my hand and together we jumped inside. The Cryshada rushed at us like a bull, and instead of horns, it had its fists balled ready to strike us.

Jessica followed us and the light grew, pulling us down through the ground into the warmth. I could not make out the sides of the cave or its ceiling. We fell but then, unexpectedly, changed direction, falling sideways through rock, mud, and earth. I closed my eyes and prayed that we would survive as the course of our journey changed in intensity.

Mud covered my face, and I held my breath as I suddenly emerged in a thick wetness I couldn't see through. Out of instinct, I kicked and broke free of the mud, and with a loud pop, I was flung out of the earth and birthed into a warm body of water. I opened my eyes and looked down at my hands. In the dimness, I could only see them covered in mud that had begun to dissolve. Someone touched me from behind, and I pulled away in fear only to see Jessica. Her hair floated around her like a tangled mess.

She pointed upward, and far away I could see light. She swam and I followed her, searching for Jeremiah and fearing for his safety. I held the air tight within my lungs and scanned around for him, looking, hoping, and even praying for my husband's safety. From behind me, a loud rumble grew in volume, and I kicked forward faster, desperately trying to reach the surface.

My lungs burned, needing air, but I could not swim fast enough. The current pulled at me and I fought against it, struggling to rise upward, always upward, never giving in to the pull of the deep. I could no longer see Jessica, and I fought onward, wanting to survive. The need for air became a craving that I could not resist. Spots formed in front of my eyes, and I could hear the pounding of my heart reverberating within me. I needed air, light, and freedom. I needed to break free of the water and had to survive. I must.

I kicked onward, ignoring the burning in my chest and the fear in my heart, and at the last moment that I thought I could remain conscious, my hand broke through to the surface, and I came up fast, gasping for breath. I coughed and turned on my back, floating so that I could take in as much air as I needed. Jessica swam close to me, and she barely seemed phased by what we had just experienced.

"The first time is always the hardest." She put her hands under me to keep me afloat and remained quiet while I coughed some more.

"Jeremiah?" It's the only word I could speak. I coughed again and grabbed Jessica in desperation.

Water erupted all around me, and Jeremiah came out of the water like a seal. He exhaled loudly and then gasped for air. When he splashed back into the water, he swam over to me, kicking furiously. "We have to—" A coughing spasm caught him mid-sentence, but he kept swimming toward shore.

I turned over in the water and followed him toward land. The moon shone high overhead, and darkness enveloped all else. I could make out trees and bushes on the shore, and fireflies lit up the forest like faerie lights.

Jeremiah pushed me onward and increased his speed. "Go, go!"

Jessica reached land first, and she helped pull me to shore. My legs were weak and I stumbled onto the sand. My wet winter clothes dragged me down. Warm and muggy, the night air was heavy around us, reminding me of a late summer night back home.

I stood back up and felt Jeremiah's arms around me. He dragged me out of the water as quickly as he could and Jessica helped.

"It followed us." His few words told me all that I needed to know.

Jeremiah pulled his pistols out and shook the water out of them. He eyed them for a moment and then in disgust threw them onto the sandy beach.

A loud splash startled me and I turned back around to see the Cryshada break through the water and roar up as the creature's crystalline body sparkled in the moonlight. When it hit the water again, its remaining globe over its shoulder pulsed. Shards shot out from the globe and surrounded it with an atmosphere of tiny crystal particles. The creature wheezed, taking in the fine air laced with particles, and then it noticed us on the beach. It roared a challenge and thrust its large arms into the water, propelling itself forward as though it would ram us.

Jeremiah looked around in desperation. "We need a weapon."

He went to run but I grabbed him. "No."

Jessica also had started to run and asked, "What are you doing?"

"I'm tired of running." I faced the Cryshada and planted both my feet firmly into the sand. I would become a wall and the creature would not pass me. I was a wall, high and wide, unpassable. I could see the spell in front of me and reached out with my hands, and surprised beyond belief, I saw my left hand glowed a brilliant cobalt blue. The wall would grow and I would become it. I closed my eyes, and the rush of magic came up through the ground into my boots, my socks, touching my skin, electrifying me with the glory of energy that I had not felt coursing through me in too long a time.

I reached out and a brilliant blue beam of light shot forth from the palm of my hand, and the wall became a translucent obstacle between us. The Cryshada crashed into it, and startled, it bounced back unable to break through. It pounded both its fists against the barrier, and I took in the energy around me, allowing myself to be its instrument.

As I closed my fist, the wall bent to my will and I folded the height and width of the spell around the Cryshada, pushing it back down beneath the water. I forced it back, and the blue energy from my hand intensified, cutting back the water, sand, and earth until the Cryshada went back through the portal we had passed, and with a swirl of my hand, I closed the loop. The portal shut with a pop, water splashed up high into the air, and I ended the spell.

The blue light from my hand faded immediately, and I stood strong on the beach with a great smile on my face.

"What the hell was that?" Jeremiah slapped his hand on his thigh. He rushed me and gave me a great big hug.

Startled, I snapped to attention and hugged him close. "I don't know. I just reached inside and felt the magic again."

He kissed me and I kissed him back.

Pushing him away, I held up my left hand and called forth my magic. With no hesitation, my hand lit up again in a brilliant cobalt blue. Magic tendrils of power swirled around my palm.

Jessica put her hand on my shoulder with her eyes opened wide, startled at what she saw. "I hadn't seen this coming."

Jeremiah stared at my hand. "How do you feel?"

"I feel fine." I laughed and a tremendous rush of joy came up over me. "I feel like it's the most natural thing in the world." I pointed at the ground and let up my magic. The blue tendrils of light surged across the beach, twirling together like living vines, and then surrounded me in a dress made of pure energy.

I closed my fist and willed the power to shut off and it did.

Jeremiah embraced me and stood back from me. "Maybe going through the portal triggered some sort of change within you?"

Jessica took my hand in hers, turned it over, and studied my palm with great intensity. "I think it's this place. We're not where I expected us to be."

"And where was that?" Jeremiah picked up his water-logged pistols, shook the last remaining bit of water out of them, and then put them away.

"I had hoped the World Tree would take us to Europe but instead…" Jessica looked up at the moon, staring at its different face.

"We've gone to the Other side, haven't we?" I looked out at the dense forest around us and took in the hundreds of fireflies twinkling in the night. The moon overhead hung full with a face different than I had ever seen.

"Yes, it appears so to me." Jessica turned away from the water. "We should leave here in case the Cryshada finds a way to come back or something else comes, thinking we're its dinner."

"We need to find a way back home." I couldn't see far due to the thick number of trees around us. "I could use my magic and…"

Jessica cut me off before I could say more. "Let's try and stay low for a while until we can find out where we are and how to get to safety. We should leave here quickly before someone or something comes to see what the light show was all about."

I squeezed Jessica's hand and asked, "What about you? Has your magic returned as well?"

"I don't know if—" She fell silent and pulled her hand away.

Jeremiah turned away to give us some privacy and headed toward the first few forest trees to scout around a bit.

"Don't be afraid. Just try." I squeezed her hand again and smiled.

"But if I fail." Jessica pulled her hand away and hid it behind her. "It's been so long since I could call the magic to me. I don't know if I remember how."

I reached for her hand and held it in mine. Closing my eyes, I imagined standing on a hilltop that looked down at the sea. The waves crashed against the beach and I could see a seagull drifting in the wind. My hand lit up again, and I shared my vision with her. "Just try."

Jessica gasped and followed my lead. "I can see the beach, feel the wind on my face, and smell the ocean. It's beautiful." She closed her eyes and took in a deep breath.

"Now it's your turn. Show me where you want to be." I peeked open my right eye. Jessica had tilted up her head, had both eyes firmly closed, and slowly took in a deep breath.

Her right hand flinched at first and then purple flickers of light coursed over it. Unaware of what was happening to her hand, Jessica kept her eyes closed and said, "I can see something."

"What is it that you see?" I asked, watching her small smile grow into a large grin.

"I'm standing on a hill by a lighthouse. There's a steep cliff in front of me, and I'm looking out over the ocean. I can see a dolphin in the water. And down on the beach, a young girl is pointing out at the water."

She laughed and relaxed even more. "It's me. I'm remembering this now. I remember being on the beach with my mother and looking out at the ocean as a little girl."

I closed both eyes again and let my magic course through her, sharing with her the memory. I pulled back all my magic but still held her hand firmly. In response, Jessica's hand lit up in a brilliant purple light. The energy pulsed and grew in its intensity.

"The dolphin came to me and…" She remained quiet for a moment and laughed again. "I remember now. It spoke to me and I could understand it."

Jessica opened her eyes and was taken aback upon seeing her hand glowing. I spied Jeremiah looking back at us, but he still kept his distance.

"Remember this moment. You have the magic within you. It's powerful just like it's within me. I don't know why or how we got our magic back, and maybe it's only while we're here in the Other side. I really don't know…" I hugged Jessica and then took a step back. "Are you ready to go on now?"

"Yes." Jessica lit up her hand and let out her magic. The purple wisps of energy flitted off into the night sky. "I just need a moment. I've not been able to wield magic for longer than I can remember, but it's all coming back to me."

Jeremiah waved at me to come to him, and I touched Jessica on the shoulder. "I'll be right back."

I walked over to Jeremiah and he spoke to me in a low voice. "We should go. I sense there's something out there that's watching us, but I don't know what it is."

"Is it another Cryshada?" I asked, looking around for any telltale sign of one of the creatures.

"No, we would have heard it by now." He leaned close to me and whispered, "I'm not sure what it is, but we should go."

I looked into the dark forest, but I could see nothing besides a few lightning bugs twinkling in the night. "Go where?"

"Let's just head on the clearest path away from this lake and get to some sort of safety or shelter." He paused a moment and held his finger to his lips.

Keeping my voice to the barest whisper, I asked, "What?"

"I thought I heard something." He stood close to me, and we both waited a moment, but the feeling passed.

Jessica came to stand next to us and asked, "Ready to go?"

Jeremiah hesitated a moment longer but then turned around. "Yes, let's get out of here before any other Cryshada come after us."

"Which way are we going?" Jessica glanced up at the moon in the sky and then spun around.

I headed out on the closest path and waved them both along. "Come, let's go this way."

Jeremiah followed without a word but kept his attention on the trees to the left.

Jessica hesitated a moment and asked, "Why that way?"

"West is best." I said the words and smiled at her. On seeing that she didn't understand, I waited until she caught up. "When Phoebe was little, I used to joke with her all the time about that. This goes back to before I even met Jeremiah. Anytime there was an issue, instead of heading back east, we'd always pick up and head west."

I lost my train of thought, and at the mention of Phoebe, I worried about her.

Jessica put her arm around me. "We'll find her. You have to believe that."

I faked a smile and nodded. "I know. It's just sometimes it's harder than others."

We headed off to the west into the forest, and I wished and prayed that wherever she was that my Phoebe was safe.

Chapter 6

Charley sat down on a large rock in front of a large cave opening and shook his head. "Are you serious?"

Ignatius shrugged and pointed at the opening. "What?"

Phoebe raised an eyebrow and asked, "You live in that cave?"

"Yes, I do. What's wrong with that?" He helped Charley up off the rock and shepherded him to the threshold. "I've lived here for years and it's a beautiful spot. It's close to the Shard Chimes of Forget-me-not, and a little farther down the road over there is a nice hot spring."

"Well, let's just get inside so I can sit down and relax. I've been walking since early this morning, and I don't know what time it is. All I know is that I feel like it's been weeks since I've had a chance to rest." Charley scratched the back of his head and then rubbed his lower back. "And I'm not getting any younger, you know. I can't go around adventuring like I used to when I was in my twenties."

Phoebe followed him and it took a few moments for her eyes to adjust to the darkness within the cave. On the wall she noticed etchings of animals and painted primitive stick figures. "What's with the artwork on the walls?"

Ignatius led the way and called back to her. "A long time ago people lived here and made some of the first cave drawings. I don't know what happened to them though. When I found this place, the art came with it."

He led them into a large hollowed-out portion of the cave that stretched up dozens of feet above them. A walkway of stone was carved in the walls and encircled the dwelling. Plush rugs covered the ground, a beautifully carved set of furniture took up most of the room, and bookcases lined the wall on the left.

"This is my merry little home." Ignatius smiled and spun around, pointing all the way up to the top. "Up there is my bedroom, a study, and a gorgeous bathroom. I have hot water from the local spring, and I had the best marble put in. Took me decades to get it right, but it's one of a kind. You'll not find any dwelling here in the

Other side that integrates so perfectly with the local environment and modern tastes."

Charley stood in the center of the large cave with his hands on his hips and tilted his head back. "Wow, you're not kidding. Your place is amazing."

"Yes, it's a bit unusual, but I rather like that." Ignatius motioned to a comfortable sofa filled with soft pillows in bright colors. "Please, sit down and you both can rest."

Phoebe sat down and placed a pillow in her lap, resting for the first time in a long while. "Did you do all this work yourself?"

"I've had help over the years. Several craftsmen from your world came over to help me. Most just wanted to come here for the visit. It's not often that you get to see the Other side." Ignatius carried over a tray of cheeses, crackers, and some dried meats. "Then again, I guess they didn't expect that they'd lose their memory of the whole visit. Still, they enjoy themselves while they're here."

Charley was about to sit down next to Phoebe, and he stopped himself. "You're not going to do the same thing to us, are you?" He asked half-jokingly but wanted to gauge Ignatius' reaction.

"Of course not. Do you think I want to incur Cinderella's wrath? I might do some stupid things from time to time, but I'm not that dumb." Ignatius placed the tray on a coffee table in front of them and went to go fetch two golden chalices. Changing the topic, he asked, "What would you both like to drink?"

"Water for me would be fine." Phoebe nibbled on a piece of cheese. "Thank you."

"Water's fine for me as well." Charley popped a cracker into his mouth. "How long have you been here?"

Ignatius placed their drinks in front of them and then sat down across from them in a finely ornate chair. The carved legs bore the most intricate design of entwined vines. Folding his hands on his lap, he sighed. "At least a hundred years. Maybe two. I don't keep track as well as I should, but time here in the Other side goes a bit differently then back at your home."

"Speaking of which. How soon can you get us back there?" Phoebe popped a cracker in her mouth and leaned forward. "I'd like to see my mother soon."

"It'll be soon enough. Don't rush things. Have some food, take a little rest, and in the morning, I'll have you on your way to see your mother." Ignatius pulled out a pocket watch, stared at it for a moment, and then put it away. "Trust me, you'll see her soon."

Charley reached for a piece of cheese, took a small bite, and then picked up the small chalice. "It's all delicious. Thank you. It feels good to stop and relax a bit." He took a small sip from the chalice, put it down, and immediately fell back on the sofa with his eyes closed.

"Charley, what's wrong?" Phoebe grabbed him and shook him.

"Don't worry about it. He's just sleeping." Ignatius crossed his legs and sat back in his chair. "Finally, we get a chance for the two of us to talk."

Phoebe stood up and raised her hand. Lit with magical fire she pointed at Ignatius, ready to release a spell on him. "Undo whatever you did to him, or you'll have to face me."

"You're so much like your mother." Ignatius pulled his pocket watch back out and flipped it open. "We don't have much time, and you have a long way to go. Now you can argue with me all you like, but I'm telling you the truth when I say that your friend there hasn't been harmed. I just put a sleeping draught in his drink. He'll sleep a few hours and feel refreshed when he wakes."

"What do you want from me?" Phoebe stood in a defensive posture, ready to pounce on him.

"Relax, I don't want to harm you." He uncrossed his legs and leaned in toward her. "I'm actually here to help you."

"What about Charley? Is he really going to be okay?" Phoebe asked. She kept her hand up, lit with magic, and was ready to strike him. The words to a flame spell were on her tongue.

"Yes, he'll be fine." Ignatius stood up and beckoned her to follow him. "Now you have to decide if you're ready or not."

"Ready for what?" She stood firm unwilling to move.

"Your test, of course." Ignatius shook his head. "Don't they teach you modern witches anything where you come from?"

"I haven't had much of an upbringing in the ways of witchcraft. I'm pretty much self-taught, and I've learned a few things from my mother before she…" Phoebe quieted and lowered her hand. The magic went out and she became lost in thought.

"Before she lost her magic?" Ignatius completed the sentence for her. "Come on. Stop standing there like a troubled little thing who needs to be rescued. Get up and follow me!"

Phoebe hesitated a moment, but then against her better judgment, she followed the faerie to the mouth of the cave. She stood next to him, and together they stood there looking out at the night sky.

"It'll be sunrise soon so you don't have much time." He pointed toward the horizon. "That's where the sun will rise. Due west."

Phoebe went to correct him and caught herself. "Oh, yes, we're on the Other side. Backwards is forwards and all of that, right?"

"Not really, but you have the concept down, so let's just leave it at that." Ignatius moved his arm a bit to the right and focused on a path through the forest. "That's where you have to go."

"And what will I find there?" Phoebe asked.

"Your test, of course." Ignatius took a step back and gently pushed Phoebe forward. "You don't have much time, so you better get going."

"Suppose I don't go, what will happen to Charley and me?" Phoebe stayed put and waited for Ignatius to answer before she headed off.

"Not much. Charley will wake up a few hours from now feeling refreshed." He glanced down at his nails and brushed some dirt off his hand. "And you, well, how do I put it? You'll be fine too, but you will have missed out on one of the biggest opportunities of your life."

"You're exaggerating." Phoebe crossed her arms and took a step back. "You just want me to do something for you, and I don't understand why yet, but you're just playing this up for me."

"Put it this way: Any witch who had an opportunity to do what you have a chance to do would start running down there this minute." Ignatius turned away and headed back inside his home. "But don't take my word on it. Take your mother's. She would give anything to go where you could be headed."

He left her there to stand alone, and she called back to him. "Is it dangerous?"

He stopped and turned to face her again. "Not any more than life is dangerous. You won't need to fight enemies or anything like that." He came behind her and put his arm around her in a protective embrace and his voice softened. "I wish I could tell you more, but you have to trust yourself. I'll be here with Charley when you return. Trust me."

Ignatius took his hand away and went back inside. Phoebe stood alone staring out at the beautiful night sky. She could see thousands of stars up above her in the firmament of the heavens. The moon hung low now on the eastern horizon, and fireflies still lit the boughs of many trees. Above it all, the warmth of the night air and the humidity called to her along with hundreds of insects singing in the night. The beauty of it all nearly took her breath away.

She had wanted to find out more about her powers and had hidden away most of her questions from her mother. One day they would talk about magic, but not until they had had some distance on the subject. Phoebe could only guess at what her mother felt about no longer having her magic. She turned from thoughts of her mother, acknowledging them but sweeping them away. She needed to think first of herself. And with that decision, the next became easier. She took a step forward and then another. Before she knew it, she had walked far away from the cave and had reached the path through the forest. The night beckoned to her and she went on. Afraid, but ready for whatever the night would bring to her.

Before long the trail widened and the forest thinned until she found herself in a large clearing. An enormous crystal, purple in hue and three times as tall as her, jutted from the ground. Wider than she could stretch out her arms, the crystal reflected the moonlight, causing beams of light from the crystal's various facets to shine out across the surrounding forest.

Phoebe took a cautious step forward and glanced around. "Well, I guess this is the famous Shard Chimes of Forget-me-not." Taking another step, she could only see so far into the darkness beyond the crystal. "I would have preferred to come in the daylight when I could actually see instead of being on a strange plane in the middle of the night. But I guess this will have to do."

She walked a few feet closer and noticed that her footprints glowed for a few moments as she walked onward. Her tracks started at the beginning of the clearing, leading up to her present spot. "Well, that's pretty."

As soon as she spoke, the massive crystal came to life. A deep purple light emanated from the structure, and the clearing lit up in a psychedelic purplish glow. "Did I do that?"

Her words left her and the crystal pulsed in response. "Yes, you did."

Startled, Phoebe spun around. A young boy stood behind her. His skin sparkled in the moonlight, and he wore no clothes that Phoebe could see, but he wasn't naked. His hair blew in the light night wind, and he stood with his hands behind his back.

"Who are you?" Phoebe asked. "You didn't come here to try and hurt me, did you?"

The boy laughed and his voice was slightly off key at a higher pitch. "No, I don't hurt people. I only show them what they want to see."

"Are you part of this test that Ignatius told me about?" Phoebe pointed at the crystal behind her. "He wanted me to come out here as part of my initiation of being a witch. Though I'm not quite sure why I would have to go through all this. I've been using my magic for years now. Seems a bit odd to me."

The boy came closer to her but did not move his legs. It appeared as though some force pulled him across the ground. "You are not the first one to wonder why you were being tested and compared yourself to them. I've seen all sorts of wizards and witches over the years. Most of them don't want to be here. They're afraid."

Phoebe glanced around. "I can understand that. It's in the middle of the night, there's no one else around, and I'm in a strange forest with a giant crystal sticking out of the ground that is pulsing with a magical glow. Definitely, not my favorite place to be. Alone."

"Are you ready for your test?" He stopped moving toward her and waited for her response.

"I'm not sure to be honest." Phoebe rubbed the side of her arms, and her shoulders slumped forward. "I'm afraid that I might fail."

The boy shook his head. "It's not that sort of test. You're not going to be graded or judged or asked to perform certain types of spells. You either know that already or will learn. No, this is a different sort of test. One that is a lot harder than that." He stopped talking and shook his head. "But I forget. First, let me introduce myself. I'm Lapis lazuli. You can call me Lapis."

"Like the gem?" Phoebe asked.

"Well, the gem's like me, more like." His melodic voice echoed through the night. "Before we start, I need to ask if you are here on your own free will. It's important."

"Of course, I am. What would have happened if I said no?"

"I would just send you back home, and you'd lose all memory of our conversation." The boy moved unnaturally again toward her, seemingly floating toward Phoebe. "It actually happens more than you might think."

"Well, I said 'yes' and I'm ready to go. What do you need me to do?" Phoebe looked around for where to go next.

"Take my hand." Lapis reached out to her and waited.

Without hesitation, Phoebe grabbed his hand. Even though it was cold, lifeless, and feeling like crystal, she squeezed his hand. Lapis floated toward the giant crystal. He stopped right in front of the giant structure and said, "Clear your mind of all fear, confusion, and worry. Think of the one thing you want to know. The deepest and most intimate question that you've had about your life. Together, we'll explore that, and then we'll come back to this very spot. You'll be changed and so will I. Together, we'll go on a journey. Ready?"

Phoebe took a slow deep breath and squeezed his hand tight. "I guess this is as ready as I'll ever be." She hesitated a moment. "I'm still scared."

Lapis took both her hands in his. "That's normal. The unknown is always scary, and we don't know what to expect. But I'm here with you and we'll go together."

"Will you be with me the whole time?" Phoebe tried to hide the fear in her voice.

"No, I probably won't. It's hard to explain, but we'll break off and then meet back here. If you choose to come back, that is. Some decide never to return, and others go elsewhere. It's always difficult for me to know who will do what. I can guess, but I might be wrong. Still, there is nothing to be afraid of. Ready?"

Phoebe took a deep breath and exhaled slowly. "Yes, let's go before my courage leaves me."

Lapis took a step toward the giant crystal and vanished into it. He pulled Phoebe with him, and as though she walked through water, she disappeared into the crystal along with him.

Her body passed through the gem, and she became enveloped in sound. Music from the depths of the crystal coursed through her body. The most enchanting of songs. The music reminded her of wind chimes, but richer and fuller in pitch and tone. The music played through her body, and her bones were instruments in an organic orchestra that came alive for her. Sound passed through her, and her last waking thought before she lost consciousness was of her mother.

***

I stopped to rest and sat down on a rock. Jessica came next to me and did not even look winded. "Do you think we've gone far enough away from the lake?"

Jessica nodded. "I do." She turned to Jeremiah and asked, "Would you mind climbing up that tree there and see if you can scout around?"

Jeremiah kept his hands in his pockets and looked up. I could see from how he shrugged his shoulders and had his jaw clenched that something was bothering him. I could sometimes read him like an open page.

"I can do that. What in particular should I be looking for?" He took off his wet jacket and wrung it dry.

"Maybe see if there's a castle somewhere nearby or some village?" I shrugged unsure of what to tell him. "Maybe just look for some place where we could get a change of clothes and rest."

"Got it." He headed off to a tree toward the right and pulled himself up to the first set of branches. In moments, he had scrambled up the trunk and disappeared up through the leaves.

Jessica leaned in toward me and lowered her voice. "It's not my place to say anything, but after you get to be a certain age, most people give you some latitude."

"What?" I crossed my arms and waited for her to say more.

"He's upset with you about something." Jessica turned her head up and tried to find him through the foliage but could not. "He's a good man, but he looks frustrated."

"I don't know if I feel like talking about this now." I turned away and stared at a large black ant that crawled on the rock by my hand.

"Of course, you don't so that's why I'm bringing it up." Jessica leaned closer and whispered, "You two need to talk. You just received your magic back, and I've seen your face. I'm feeling it too."

"I said I don't want to talk about it." I remained firm and turned back to look at her. I wasn't in the mood to deal with all that had happened. I needed some time.

"Well, what would you like to talk about then?" Jessica backed down and put her hands in her lap, resting.

"I want to try something." I stood up and tried my best to wring out water from my clothes. "I want to see if I can find my daughter."

Jessica sat back, watching me, and started to reply but then chose to remain silent.

"What?" I glanced down at her.

"Nothing. I was going to ask if you needed help, but it's probably best if you do this on your own." Jessica sat still and folded her hands together.

"Let me see if I can do this." I closed my eyes and reached out with my left hand. I could feel the warmth arrive, and I peeked a quick look, amazed at seeing my hand lit up in swirling energy of cobalt blue. I would never get tired of seeing that my magic had returned.

Standing firm on both feet, I clenched my fist and then imagined Phoebe. I pictured her the last I saw her. Bundled up in her winter coat, her blonde hair tied back, and her smile. I reached out with my magic and said the words. "Daughter of mine, wherever you are, let me see you."

The magical fire swirled around my hand, and I opened my eyes to see the world from afar. Images flashed around me, and I caught a glimpse of trees rushing past me and the moon up above. I could feel her presence, and then as if a door closed before me, she disappeared.

A rush of emotion came up over me, and a tiny cry escaped my lips. My hand dropped and I extinguished my magic.

Jessica jumped up to help and put her arm around me. "Are you okay?"

I sobbed and could not hold back the tears any longer. "She just left this plane."

She pulled me close and held me tight. "That doesn't mean that she's dead!"

"I know, I know. I lost her once to Napoleon and she nearly died. I've been holding all these feelings back because I want to be strong. I'm just a wreck." I wiped the tears from my eyes and sniffled.

"You are not weak when you show emotion." Jessica hugged me tight and then let me go. She put her hands on my shoulders and looked me right in the eye. "Being vulnerable shows strength. All of us go through difficult times, and you will get through this."

I laughed and sniffled again. "I know. I'm just so tired. I've been fighting so long my feelings of inadequacy, and now I have my magic back. And as soon as I do, Phoebe's gone again. It's just not fair."

Jessica smiled. "Life isn't fair. That's what my mother always used to tell me. She was a hard woman, but she loved me no matter what I did." She cocked her head and laughed heartily. "And I did some pretty stupid things back when I was young, but she stood by me no matter what."

"I just wanted to settle down, relax, and to enjoy my life." I took a deep breath and looked for my handkerchief in my pocket, but everything was drenched from being in the lake.

"Is that really true?" Jessica crossed her arms. "Phoebe would come to me and tell me about how sad you looked. She told me that she didn't want to bother you about her questions about magic because she thought she'd only hurt you if she asked them."

"I..." My words failed me. I didn't know what to say.

"It's true, isn't it?" Jessica prodded me with her index finger. "Say it."

"I didn't want her to come to me about questions about magic. It just hurt me too much, and I couldn't find a way to get through that. I wanted my magic back so badly." I pulled back and shivered. "That was selfish of me. I know it. I just couldn't find a way to get through it."

"When you see Phoebe next, then you can tell her this yourself." Jessica handed me a dry handkerchief and I accepted.

"Where did you get this?" I wiped clean my nose and did the same for the tears on my cheeks.

"Magic." Jessica winked at me and then turned back around, calling up to Jeremiah. "See anything up there?"

A few seconds later, from far up, we heard a crack of a branch and leaves rustling. "I'm almost at the top." Jeremiah's voice was so far away.

I missed him, but so much had changed, and I wondered if he would ever forgive me for how I had treated him. I had locked him out of my heart for fear that any emotion would break me. I needed to steel myself off from the world and be strong. Always strong. And in doing that, I had nearly lost everyone close to me.

Jessica cupped her hands over her mouth and called, "Let us know when you're up there and what you see."

We heard him grunt from exertion, and then he replied, "You'll be the first to know!"

The annoyance in his tone was thick.

I didn't say anything and turned away. I glanced down at my hand and lit it with magical fire. Blue wisps of energy coursed around my fingers, but no heat emanated from it. I stared at my hand and a thought came to me. I could leave here right now. I could travel the dreamline and use my powers as a chronicler to travel in time. I hadn't used my abilities in years, but I betted that I could find out and leave here, go back to when this whole mess started and fix it all. I could be the one to unite and bring peace to everything again. I didn't need a magic faerie or prince on a white horse to save me. I could do it myself.

I lifted my hand up to ignite my power and cast me back to a time when I last remembered using my magic. Back those years ago... I could do it. I formed the place in my mind and concentrated.

"Stop!" Jessica grabbed my hand and I lost my concentration.

"What are you doing?" I pulled away from her.

"Don't do it." She advanced on me and reached for my hand again.

"I was going to try and help us." I held steady and refused to back up another step.

"You were going to travel on the dreamline and use your powers to go save the day. Weren't you?" Jessica put her hands together and pleaded. "Please, you must trust me. That's not going to help right now."

"How did you know that?" The words tumbled out of me.

"One of my powers is that I can sometimes pick up thoughts in people's minds when I'm close to them. Not all the time, but when someone is thinking intensely. I saw what you wanted, and it's not going to help." She sighed and explained, "Going back in time might make things worse. There's no way to know for sure that you could fix what seems broken, and there are forces at work that we don't understand. Let's figure out where we are, how to get some help, and make a plan. Leaving us might not fix anything at all and could make things worse."

I looked up at where Jeremiah was in the tree. "You're right. It wouldn't be fair to desert both of you. But Phoebe's no longer on this plane. I could try to travel where she is. We could go after her together."

Jessica shook her head. "I wouldn't do that. The World Tree brought us here. There's a reason why we need to be here at this time. We don't know what that reason is yet, but if we're patient then we'll be ready."

"But I want to…"

"I know, I know." Jessica grabbed my hands and tried to calm me. "You want to go save the world. You're a rescuer. Phoebe told me that about you. I understand that. I do. But sometimes it's helpful to relax, find out what's around us, and then make a decision once we know more." She pointed up at the night sky. "I have my magic back too and it's a great feeling. But I want to know more before we run off. For all we know, once we leave this area, we might lose our powers again. If you ran off in the dreamline, you might get stuck wherever you go, and then Jeremiah and I wouldn't be able to find you."

"I hadn't thought of that." I put my left hand down and quieted my powers. "I just feel so helpless, and after years of not having my magic… Well, I just want to do something."

"And we are. We'll be fine. Let's work together and figure out where we are and come up with a plan."

"Can you hear me down there?" Jeremiah called from high up in the tree.

"Yes, we can." I raised my voice and yelled louder. "What do you see?"

We heard some rustling of the leaves as he shifted his position and then replied, "It's beautiful. The trees are all lit up with magical lights."

"Do you see anything else?" I asked.

He repositioned himself and we heard him curse as he lost his footing for a moment. "Hold on a second."

We heard him grunt again and a tree branch snapped.

"You okay up there?" I walked right up to the trunk and looked straight up but could not see him.

"Yep, I'm fine. Just lost my footing there for a bit and almost fell to my death, but I'm good." He pulled himself around in another direction and then said, "You're not going to believe this."

Jessica looked to me and I shrugged having no idea what he saw. "What do you see?"

"It's a castle in the clouds." He paused a moment and then started up again. "It's beautiful. And it's moving. There are these lines that look like they're made out of light. Something is pulling the castle toward us."

I turned to Jessica and asked, "Any idea of what that is?"

"I don't know." She looked up and yelled, "Do you think it's a bad thing, trying to chase after us?"

Jeremiah didn't respond for a few moments and then said, "I don't think so. I don't see any weapons on it, and there's no birds or creatures that I can see running from it. Just looks like an enormous castle on an extremely large cloud headed in our direction. It'll be here in a few minutes. It's coming toward us pretty fast."

I put my hands on my hips and faced Jessica. "So, how's your climbing skills?"

She smiled and replied, "Probably better than yours."

She reached up and grabbed the lowest branch and pulled herself up to the next one, balancing on it.

I laughed and shook my head. "You're probably right. I'm not a good climber, and I don't have any spells that can make me fly."

Jeremiah heard us and came down from the very top. I still couldn't see him, but I could hear him better. "There's a few vines that I can use to pull you up. Hold on a bit and I'll be right there."

Jessica had already made her way up to the next set of branches. In another few minutes, she would probably be halfway up. I pulled myself up to the closest branch and made it safely to the first level. I started to climb to the next when the entire area lit up like day.

Night vanished and we heard a loud trumpet rock the area with a tremendously powerful burst of music. It sounded like a hundred men with instruments, blowing out the same note. Just as soon as the music started, it stopped and the light vanished. Darkness returned but it took several moments for my eyes to readjust.

"You both have to see this. It's amazing!"

I had never heard Jeremiah so excited before. Far off in the distance we heard another blast of music. And a few seconds later, we heard a rumble from hundreds of drums banging out the beat of a few notes. The beating went fast, slowed, and then started again until everything went quiet.

"Damn." I cursed after slipping and scratching my shin. I caught myself fine but stopped to rub the scratch.

A vine appeared right in front of me, and I heard Jeremiah call to me. "I got you. Tie it around your body and I will pull you up."

"Don't think that this means that I couldn't beat you climbing up a tree!" I called after Jessica and heard her laughing.

"See you at the top!" she replied and then set to climbing faster.

Swallowing my pride, I tied the vine around my waist and then wrapped it around my arm, holding on with both hands. "Okay, I'm ready."

Jeremiah heaved and I moved a few feet. Bracing my feet against the nearest branches, I helped as best I could and continued climbing up. I wouldn't beat Jessica, but I would get to the top, and that was all that mattered in the end.

Chapter 7

Phoebe awoke with a start. She grabbed at her throat and coughed. When she opened her eyes, Lapis knelt next to her with his hand out.

"We have arrived."

She accepted his hand and blinked rapidly. Everything around her had changed. Nothing looked familiar. The sky had a dark pink hue, and the sun seemed hotter and more orange in color. Made entirely of crystal, the ground bore no plants, leaves, or debris of any kind. Instead she rested on a flat crystal slab.

"Where are we?" She sat up and an invisible bubble of air surrounded her. When she focused her attention on Lapis, she noticed fine particles in the air.

"We traveled to my home on the Crystal plane. We have left the Other side and its companion place that you call home and are out past the normal boundaries of your world." He took a few steps away from her and pointed to an enormous structure several yards away. "We are at the Shard Chimes of Forget-me-not, and your test is to play them."

Phoebe stood up and massaged the back of her neck. "Everything is so big here." She glanced up at the chimes that jutted out of the ground. Pale purple in color, each chime towered over her.

"Yes, my world is much different than yours." He knelt and touched the ground, and the crystal around his hand lit up a brilliant red, fading quickly. "Life is in the crystals here. We don't have water or food like you do. Everything survives from the energy from within or from our sun."

Phoebe walked toward the chimes, easily walking through the fine particles in the air as though she wore rain gear. The invisible force around her protected her by allowing her to breathe air. "I can't stay here long then. I'll need to eat and drink sooner or later."

"You'll not be here long enough, but I will help you with your test. Then you'll return back home a full witch." Lapis followed her as she headed toward the chimes.

"But what if I fail?" Phoebe stopped and glanced over at him. "Will I lose all my magic then?"

"We all fail at some time or another. You misunderstand the purpose of this test. It's not to grade you, but to teach you something."

Phoebe raised an eyebrow and shrugged. "But what am I supposed to actually do?"

"It's simple. Just touch the shards that you want to activate and think of a question that you always wanted answered. The question can be anything, but I would advise you to think first before you make a decision, and then let the chimes know that you made your choice. I'll be waiting here for when you've completed the test."

"That all sounds simple enough." Phoebe took the last remaining steps toward the chimes and stopped. She glanced back and asked, "Do I have to worry about something attacking me? Will one of those Cryshada come for me, and should I be prepared to fight?"

"No, I've already told you that it's not that type of test. You'll be entirely safe. Just relax and I will be here for you when you return. I promise." Lapis waved at her and sat down on a large crystal rock that jutted out of the ground. "Go, I'll be right here."

"Go? Where is it going to take me?" Phoebe hesitated and put her hand to her mouth and bit her fingernail.

Lapis smiled and folded his tiny hands in front of him. "Only where you want it to take you." He thought a moment and added, "This is your chance to be free of the one burning question that has haunted you your entire life. Dig deep, listen to yourself, and embrace what you really want to know."

Confused, Phoebe turned back around and took the last few steps to stand in front of the chimes. She reached out and placed her hand on the nearest crystal piece, expecting it to be cold to the touch, but instead it was warm. The chime changed from its pale purple color to a brilliant yellow and emitted a high-pitched sound.

Phoebe took another step and touched the next chime, and it awoke for her, turning green, and let out a slightly lower in pitch sound. The note held as long as she kept her hand on the crystal and ended immediately once she pulled away.

Closing her eyes, she focused on a question. What would she ask? What did she want to know? The words did not come to her, and she trusted herself by walking forward with her hand gently grazing the crystal chimes. She walked faster hearing the sounds becoming increasingly deeper in tone. She then opened her eyes, and the colors of the crystals changed from yellow to green to blue and then a deep indigo and brilliant violet. The last sound became so deep that she felt the bass in the pit of her stomach.

When she reached the end of the line, she turned to face the crystals and ran back with her hand out, touching each one in succession. The crystals would flare up in their brilliant color, emit their note, and then fade away as soon as she moved on to the next. She stopped where she had started, breathing fast. The last chime faded away and she noticed an opening between the red and orange chimes that she had not seen before.

She glanced back at Lapis, and he had not moved. Still sitting with his hands in his lap, he smiled back at her but gave no other indication on whether she should stay where she was or go forward.

Phoebe clenched her fists, took a deep breath, and then rushed forward. She outstretched her arms and touched both the red and orange chimes. Their sounds were high, clear, and true. The last note stuck with her, and her question came to her unbidden. She let her feelings wash over her, and the words to her question formed in her mind.

As if in response to her, the crystal corridor opened up before her. When she touched the left wall, it glowed a vibrant red. Grazing the right crystal with the tips of her fingers caused the chimes to glow a bright orange.

At the end of the passageway, a bright white light pulsed as though it were the beating of a heart. Lapis stood waiting for her, but his features had changed somewhat.

"Are you ready?" His voice had risen in pitch.

"Are you Lapis? Your hair is longer and you look like a girl."

"I'm his twin sister Lazuli." She twirled her long blonde hair around her index finger. "I've been waiting for you here. Are you ready?"

Phoebe put her hands at her side and said, "I'm nervous. Your brother didn't give me much to go on. He just went on about how I'd be tested and I didn't need to worry."

"He was right about the not worrying part, but he could have helped you by giving you a bit more to go on." Although she looked like a young girl no more than nine in age, she had an ageless quality to her. "What are you nervous about?"

"I'm worried that I'm going to fail the test and I won't become a full-fledged witch." She stopped for a moment to think and said,

"And I don't even know what that even means. I just thought you discovered you had powers and then joined a coven. I wish my…"

She stopped talking and she blushed.

Ignoring her embarrassment, Lazuli pointed to a large crystal that jutted out of the floor. "Let's sit down. Before your test begins, let's talk this through. I want you to be as prepared as you can be."

"Now you have me worried again." Phoebe crossed the room and sat next to Lazuli. She fidgeted with her hands, trying to remain calm.

"You don't have anything to fear. The only thing you really need is your question. What is the one question that you always wanted to have answered? The one true question about who you are, what your purpose is, and your place in all of creation."

"There are a lot of questions that I've been wondering about." Phoebe said but then quieted. She glanced away. "I'm afraid to ask my question."

"Why are you afraid?" Lazuli leaned closer to Phoebe and went to touch her hand but held back.

"I don't know what the answer is going to be." She stared down at the ground. "I don't even know why I'm here. I've run off from some creature that was chasing me, and I don't know what I'm going to do. I just want to have some time to relax. To be free and to not feel like the weight of the world is on my shoulders."

Lazuli smiled and nodded. "I know exactly how that feels." This time she did rest her hand on Phoebe's arm. "Trust me. What is your question?"

Phoebe opened up, let go of her fear, and said, "Did my mother really want to have me?" She folded her arms across her chest. "I'm ashamed to want to know the answer to that."

"Why haven't you asked your mother that?" Lazuli asked.

"I couldn't do that. It wouldn't be fair to her. She's had a hard enough of a life already. Her mother dying when she was young, her father leaving and her stepmother treating her so harshly. And then with what happened with my father…" Phoebe let the words trail off, but a burst of courage came to her. "He led her on and then left her for her best friend while she was pregnant with me. And then she lost her magic because of me."

Lazuli listened and did not interrupt. When Phoebe was finished speaking, she tapped her foot on the crystal ground and asked, "Is that your fault that your mother's life was so difficult?"

"No, but..."

"Let me finish." Lazuli raised her hand. I let you speak and now I have something that I want to say. She pointed to the crystal wall across from her. "Your question is a good one and will get to the heart of what you need to overcome to be a true witch. We can find the answer to your question. It'll not be easy, but we can do it together."

Phoebe glanced over at the crystal wall. "I don't want to confront my mother about this. It's not that I'm afraid. I just don't want to tax her right now with any of this. She's probably upset already because Charley and I have gone missing and she'll need to free Napoleon." She chuckled and shook her head. "I can just about see how upset she is over all of this. My mother doesn't take well to change, and I can imagine that having to find me and then help Napoleon without her magic is going to cause her enough stress. I don't want to add to that."

"And we won't." Lazuli got up and pulled Phoebe with her over to the wall. "We'll go together."

Afraid to ask, Phoebe said in a whisper, "Go where?"

"To see your birth, of course." Lazuli tugged her harder, and they stood before the wall.

"Are you serious?" Incredulous, Phoebe stared at the clear crystal wall in front of her. "We're just going to pop back in time and see my birth."

"It's not quite like that." Lazuli touched the wall and it started to glow pale blue in color. The hue intensified slowly, built up over time, and the wall transformed into a wall of water. "We're only going to use the Shard Chimes of Forget-me-not as a means to remember what happened."

"Okay, I'm ready. What do we need to do?" Phoebe steeled herself for what came next.

"All you need to do is put your hand up to the wall and touch it. That's it." Lazuli shook her head and laughed.

"Oh, I thought we were going to have to jump through some sort of portal or balance on a rope lit on fire. That seems to be the common theme of my life recently." Phoebe let her shoulders rest and raised her hand. "Do you promise that's all I need to do? Just put my hand up and touch the wall. That's it?"

"Yes." Lazuli let her hand touch the watery wall in front of her. As she did so, she grabbed for Phoebe's right hand. "When you're ready, just put your hand up like mine. We'll be in the chimes' memories, and then it'll be like we were actually there. And when you're ready to come back, just wish it to be so, and we'll wake up right here. It truly is that simple."

Lazuli closed her eyes and went into a deep trance. Phoebe took a deep breath, reached out, and hesitated. What if she received an answer to her question and it wasn't the answer she wanted? What if something happened? What if? She shook her head and forced her hand forward into the crystal wall. The crystal felt like warm water, and as she closed her eyes, she heard a sound like one she had never heard before. She slipped away, falling into the water, and concentrated on the sound. In a breath, she opened her eyes.

Her mother grabbed at her large belly and hissed through her teeth. "Renée!"

Phoebe rushed forward to help her mother, but Lazuli held her back. "She can't see you or interact with you. We're only looking back into the folds of time." She waved her hand in the air, and for a brief moment, the scene in front of her wavered.

They could see the crystal walls of the Shard Chimes of Forget-me-not. The illusion reappeared and Phoebe stayed put, watching the scene play out.

Her mother stumbled into the side of the barn, leaning hard into the wall, and bent herself over with her hands on her knees. She took in short breaths and exhaled just as quickly. As soon as the contraction had started, it subsided.

Taking a moment to gather herself, Cinderella slowly stood up straight with her right hand on the small of her back. When she had steadied and calmed herself, she headed back toward the house. "Renée, I need your help! The baby's coming."

Not seeing anyone coming, she walked faster toward the house. Without warning, a warm liquid drizzled down her leg. She redoubled her efforts and made it to the front door.

From behind, Renée put her arm around her. "There you are." She shouldered Cinderella's weight onto her and led her into her bedroom.

"I thought you couldn't hear me. I was starting to get nervous." Cinderella sat a moment on the bed and caught her breath. "What am I supposed to do?"

Renée smiled at her and helped her back up. "Remember what we talked about. We're going to walk around, and when you feel the pain again, you tell me and we'll stop. Then you lean forward and put your hands on my shoulders, and I'll talk you through the contraction. You're going to be fine."

Sweat had broken out on Cinderella's forehead, and she obeyed, walking out of the bedroom into their small kitchen.

Phoebe stood back, like a ghost, watching her birth play out. Her mother looked so young, and a twinge of sorrow passed through her at seeing Renée again. She had been dead many long years now.

"How close are your contractions?" Renée walked right next to Cinderella, poised to catch her if she stumbled.

"They're pretty close together. The last one I had was really strong. And right after that, my water started leaking." She glanced down, seeing wetness in parts of her skirt. "How often should I…"

Her voice trailed off and her stomach spasmed. She reached for Renée's hand and bit her tongue, hissing out the breath she had within her.

Renée positioned herself right in front of Cinderella with her legs firmly planted on the ground. "Listen to me. Lean forward and put your hands on my shoulder. Slowly inhale through your nose, hold a few seconds, and then exhale. I'm right here for you."

Cinderella did as told and took a slow deep breath, held it, and then exhaled through her mouth. When the pain from the contraction didn't subside, Renée took Cinderella's palm in hers and squeezed the fleshy part between her index finger and thumb. "This pressure point is going to help with the pain. Take another deep breath through your nose, hold, and then slowly exhale. Let the pain wash over you. You are by the water, with your feet in the sand, looking upriver with the sun shining high up in the sky."

Renée squeezed harder on the fleshy part of Cinderella's hand. "That feels good."

"Listen to me. Close your eyes, stand with your feet apart, and take another slow breath through your nose. Imagine again that you're standing on the embankment of the lake and it's early summer. The wind is blowing lightly, and each leaf on the tree branches is doing its own little dance. You can see the sun go behind a cloud and the shadow fall across the water. Placid, calm, and relaxed, the lake looks like a tiny pool, but you know that it's connected to a river, moving onward and passing you by." Renée placed her hands on Cinderella's shoulders and helped to brace her. She wobbled a bit and more liquid ran down her leg.

The contraction faded away and slowly Cinderella recovered. "Okay, I'm feeling better. Should we go to the bed now?"

Renée shook her head. "Let's walk some more."

Cinderella looked up through her locks of hair and stood up straight again. "You're hiding something from me. What is it?"

"Just keep walking. Walking is good for you and the baby." Renée took her hands off Cinderella and pointed ahead. "Focus on walking and breathing. That's your job right now."

Stubborn as ever, Cinderella put her hands on her hips. "What aren't you telling me?"

Renée shook her head. "One day I hope you will ease off a bit. Nothing is wrong. Everything is going as planned."

"But?" Cinderella pressed.

"You're going to be at this for hours." Renée started walking away and drew the imagining path out for her friend. "Come on, let's keep you walking."

"How long?" Cinderella asked.

"I can't tell you for certain. I expect your baby will be born when she's ready." Renée stopped and went back to put her hand on Cinderella. "I'm here for you, and we're going to do this together."

"You are here for me, aren't you?" Cinderella took a few steps and let out a whimper. "And he isn't." She began to cry, and when Renée came to comfort her, she held her hand out. "No, I'm not going to let my memories of him get to me." She wiped her nose on her sleeve and cleared away the tears.

"I'm here for you. And you are going to be a great mother. Trust me." Renée took Cinderella's hand and started walking her around the room.

"Do you think so?" Her face looked so young and innocent. "Sometimes I think I'm going to fail at all this. I don't know what I'm doing and I'm afraid."

"That's normal. All new moms feel that way. The ones that don't are just too afraid to admit it." Renée slowed the pace and stopped. She moved her lips and watched Cinderella.

"What are you doing…" Another strong contraction hit Cinderella hard, but this time she was more prepared for it. She bent forward and put her hands on Renée's shoulder, and Renée braced herself for Cinderella's weight.

"Focus on my voice. Close your eyes, take a nice and slow breath in through your nose, and hold it for a few seconds. Then exhale. You are still on the lake embankment, and you see a bird flying overhead to land on a tree branch. The sun is warm on your face and it's a beautiful day. You are happy and free." She leaned forward to better support her friend. "Okay, slowly exhale."

Cinderella followed her orders and pulled her hands off of Renée's shoulders to grab her belly. "I felt her move. She's coming soon."

Lazuli pulled Phoebe away. "How are you feeling?"

Distracted from the scene, Phoebe turned toward Lazuli and fought to hold back a rush of emotion. "It's surreal to see this so lifelike. I didn't know that she went through so much to have me. There's a lot that she never shared with me over the years. I know that she struggled with the Silver Fox before I was born, but she never told me the full story, and she only would say small tidbits about giving birth to me. I could never quite tell if she went through a lot of pain or if she had regretted having me. We just never really talked about it."

"Your mother has gone through much in her life, and yet she has always been there for you. No matter the cost, she has sacrificed herself for you. But it's a different story in hearing all the heroics and myths about what your parent does and then actually seeing how the events played out. Let's go to the bedroom, and we'll speed up time a bit to when you were actually born."

Lazuli walked out of the small main room of the house, and as she did so, Renée and Cinderella faded away. Phoebe paused a moment to watch them, and a pang of sorrow washed over her.

"Come, they are there now." Lazuli headed into the bedroom and Phoebe followed.

Her mother lay in the bed, using the posts of the bed to support her legs. Her hair was fully drenched and her face flushed. She grunted as she bore down, exhaling her breath as she did so.

Renée had rolled up the sleeves to her dress, and she had pulled a small table up against the bed. A large bowl filled with water rested on the table with a stack of towels, a sharp knife, and large bag. "Good, that was a productive push. You are doing amazing."

She reached over on the table, grabbing a small vial, and poured some liquid into her hand.

"I'm tired. I need to rest a moment." Cinderella closed her eyes and breathed in slowly.

Renée rubbed the oil on Cinderella's exposed skin below the vaginal opening. "This olive oil will help your skin stretch and cause less ripping when the baby comes out." She glanced down and could see the baby's head. "I need you to take a good and solid deep breath. I know you're tired, but I am here with you. You are not alone. I will help you through this, and soon you will hold your little girl in your arms. Are you ready?"

Cinderella kept her eyes closed and nodded.

"Okay, take another deep and slow breath, and hold it for a few moments."

She followed Renée's instruction and then grabbed a fistful of the sheets on either side of her.

"Now bear down and push as you exhale. Slow, steady, and strong." Renée held her friend's leg and watched as Cinderella let out the air in her lungs.

She gave a loud grunt and pushed. Renée watched as the baby's head pushed out.

Phoebe hung back mesmerized. She did not want to ruin the moment and knew that neither her mother nor Renée could hear her. She simply wanted to experience her birth, lock it up inside, and treasure it always as she watched how her mother fought to bring her into the world and the force of will it took to push past the fatigue, fear, and doubt.

Renée had her fingers on the baby's face, and Cinderella finished exhaling. "You're almost there. You've done a fantastic job. Another deep breath and then push down hard."

Cinderella laughed and started to cry at the same time. "I can't. I'm so tired."

Renée leaned in closer to Cinderella but kept her hands on the baby. "Listen to me. Take a slow breath in through your nose. Come on, follow what I'm doing." She mimicked the breathing and Cinderella followed along. "Good. Hold the breath and then bear down hard and slowly exhale, building up to push."

Cinderella exhaled and a guttural sound came out of her mouth, and a vein popped out on her neck, and her face was red from her exertion.

The baby's shoulders had passed out, and Renée tugged gently until she appeared to slide the rest of the way out of the birth canal. The umbilical cord came out as well. Holding the baby in one arm, Renée grabbed a damp towel and wiped off bloody mucus and a white film all over the baby's chest and face.

Phoebe watched and saw the baby take in a big breath of air, and when she exhaled, she gave her first cry. Lazuli clapped her hands and beamed in joy. She turned her face upright, and a large smile broke out on her face.

Renée finished cleaning the baby and said, "Here, let me help you." She pulled open Cinderella's nightshirt, exposing her breasts. "Here, let her feel your skin."

Careful to not tangle the umbilical cord, she placed the tiny baby on Cinderella's chest, and her friend pulled her close against her. She gave a deep sigh, and her tears could not be held back. "Hello, little one. Your name is Phoebe, and Mama is right here for you."

Renée pushed Cinderella's wet hair back from her face and then stood back watching mother and daughter.

Coming closer, Phoebe stood on the other side of the bed and watched herself as a tiny baby in her mother's arms. She said nothing but just watched the scene.

"You're my little precious one." Cinderella smiled at seeing her daughter's open eyes for the first time. "I promise you. I will always be there for you. I will never abandon you. I will be at your side no matter who you grow to be, what you want to do—I will always love you no matter what."

She kissed her daughter's forehead and laughed.

Renée leaned close to Cinderella and put her hand on her friend's shoulder.

"She's so beautiful, isn't she?"

"Yes, she is." Renée checked the umbilical cord. "The afterbirth will come soon, and we'll need to prepare for that. It'll be messy but won't hurt." She glanced down at the blood and mucus on the sheets. "You didn't tear too much. Once the afterbirth is out, I'll clean you up so you and Phoebe can rest."

Lazuli put her hand on Phoebe's arm. "It is time for us to go. We need to return."

Phoebe watched her mother's face, taking in her expression of pure joy, and turned to go. Lazuli raised up her hand, but they both heard the request from behind. "Wait."

They both turned around surprised. Phoebe recovered first. "Mother, you can see us?"

Cinderella smiled at her daughter. "I could find you among the stars. You are my light and my love. Never forget that. Never."

Unaware, Renée put down more towels on the bed to catch the afterbirth.

Phoebe waved to her mother and said, "I won't forget that. Thank you."

The world wobbled and faded away until Lazuli and Phoebe stood side by side before the crystal wall. The wall of water in front of them had vanished, and now only the hard crystal wall remained.

"I've never seen that happen before." Lazuli stepped back and relaxed her arms at her side. "Your mother must be a powerful witch."

"She's a chronicler. She can travel through time on the dreamline." Phoebe turned away lost in thought.

"Are you okay?" Lazuli asked, seeing the distant look in Phoebe's eye.

"Yes, I just have a lot to think about, that's all."

"You have your answer now, don't you?" Lazuli reached for Phoebe's hand and took it in hers. "Some never get an answer to their question, but yours was clear, and now you have what you wanted to know."

"But how is that going to help me become a better witch?" Phoebe glanced down at her boots.

"It won't. It'll help you be a better person, and that's all that matters." Lazuli let go of Phoebe's hand and headed toward the entrance to the chimes.

Phoebe watched her go, and Lazuli's words stuck with her.

Chapter 8

"Cinderella, give me your hand." Jeremiah offered his hand to me.

I accepted and he pulled me across the divide. I tried not to stare below, but I knew that if I fell that I would be dead. I balanced on my right leg and then fell forward into his arms safe.

"Come here." He repositioned himself and directed me onto the branch in front of him. "There, you'll have a better view."

Jessica had settled herself on a bough to my right. She had wrapped her arms around parts of the trunk and stared out at the approaching castle in the clouds.

"What do you think that is?" I asked Jeremiah and leaned back into him.

He hesitated a moment before answering. "I don't know, but may we talk?" He lowered his voice and maybe it was best that we couldn't look into each other's eyes. There would be a lot to say, and I didn't know if I was ready for our talk.

"We might not have the type of time that you want to talk. Maybe we should focus on the castle approaching us?"

As if in response, the trumpets flared up again. This time they were louder and hit a higher note. Several birds flew out of the tree closest to the castle and scattered away from it.

"We don't ever have time to talk or we ignore it." He sighed and I heard him take a breath to cover up his telltale sign for when he was angry or frustrated. "I just want you to know that I'm not going anywhere. I understand that finding magic again is what you have wanted for a long time, and I'll back off if you need space. That's all I wanted to say."

"Thank you." A whole host of responses and thoughts came to me, but what bothered me the most rose to the surface. "Right now, I'm only concerned about Phoebe. I want to find her and Charley, make sure they're both okay, and then go find Napoleon and confront him."

"You mean rescue him, right?" Jeremiah chuckled. He knew me well enough that I didn't misspeak.

"No, I'm going to confront him. And if I have magic and he doesn't, well, then we'll have a good talk." I would have said more, but the castle was nearly upon us. I glanced up and could not see through the clouds to what it floated on. Whatever magic supported it, I did not know or understand.

Jessica turned back to us and waved with a big smile on her face. Clearly excited, she pointed up at the approaching castle in exasperation.

"What if it's not friendly? What are we going to do?" I said.

Jeremiah chuckled. "We can't run so I hope that you and Jessica have a plan or we'll be sitting ducks."

Across the clearing, I followed the golden line attached to the bottom of the castle and stretched out to the ground. "What do you think is pulling it?"

"I don't know. There are five of those lines." Jeremiah pointed to the fifth one that I had missed. "That last one is clear and difficult to see. It looks to be ahead of the others."

The trumpets ceased playing, and the drums took up the beat. The pounding started off slow, then built up faster and faster, and from a break in the trees, I spied movement. "Look, did you see that?"

"What did you see?" Jeremiah tried to make out the movement in the trees below.

"I think it's a—"

A loud roar from directly in front of us caused a shift in the air, and an illusion fell away to reveal a giant's face staring down at us. Taller than the tree we were in, he had an enormous beard, and his fists held tight onto the clear line connected to the castle. Unable or unwilling to let go of the line, he roared at us again.

Within his beard, a tiny winged person flew out toward us. She landed on the end of our bough, balancing expertly with a longbow drawn.

"Curious." Her voice was melodic in tone and reasoned. Shorter than me, she had long limbs, a slight golden tint to her skin, and blonde hair cut short.

I held up my left hand and ignited my hand with my magic. Wisps of cobalt blue, like tongues of fire, danced around my fingers. "Who are you?"

"I could ask the same of you." She caught movement out of the corner of her eye and in split second notched another arrow in her bow. One pointed toward me and the other at Jessica. I didn't want to find out how she would be able to fire the arrows in two opposite directions.

"We are not here to harm you. We are visitors who have come far from America." Jessica held her hand high as it glowed in a deep purple hue.

"My name is Snap and I'm the front watch." She motioned upward with her chin but kept her bow pointed at us. "What are you three doing in this tree?"

"We heard the trumpets and drums and wanted to see what approached. Where we come from we've never seen anything like this." Jeremiah held onto me tightly. He had his arms wrapped around my waist. If we fell, we'd fall together.

"I'm not here to harm you. We're just going through this area." Snap lowered her bow. "We need to keep moving forward. Would you like to come up and visit us?"

I glanced back at Jeremiah. "What do you think?"

"Better to be up there than sitting on a tree." He whispered in my ear.

"Jessica, do you agree that we should go up there and see the castle?" I asked.

She lowered her left hand and let her magic fade out. "I'd love to go up there and see it."

"We're in agreement then. Yes, we'll go with you." I lowered my hand as well. "How are we going to get up there?"

Snap slung her bow on her back. "We'll fly, of course."

She put her fingers to her mouth and whistled. In response, she stared up at the cloud above and put her hand over her eyes to shield out the sun that had come out again.

Behind her the giant turned its head and glanced upward as well. An enormous snake-like creature broke forth from the clouds.

It had a large head that resembled that of a dragon from the fairy tales I used to read when young. Letting out a loud roar, the creature flew down from the cloud and then quickly arrived next to us.

"How is it flying? I don't see that it has any wings." I shielded my eyes from the sun's glare.

"The wyrm have the magic of our plane within them, and this one is my favorite." She leaned over the branch that she balanced on and hugged the dragon's body. "Isn't that right, Ruby?"

Ruby nuzzled her head against Snap and purred like a cat.

"Well, she seems friendly enough." Jeremiah said.

Snap nodded. "She won't harm you unless I tell her to or someone tries to hurt her." Pushing herself away from Ruby, she said, "All of you, get on her back. We'll head up to the castle."

I reached out and touched Ruby's skin and was surprised with how smooth it was. Her scales did resemble that of a snake, but they were smoother and larger. I climbed on and found small tufts of hair that I could hold onto. I also locked my legs around the wyrm's body and held on tight.

Jeremiah helped Jessica on, and then he climbed on behind me. Snap fluttered her wings and took flight. Her golden skin glittered in the sun. "Here we go!"

Ruby turned around slowly, mindful that we were on her back, and flew after Snap. She did not fly erratically as she had when we had first seen her. Instead, she was measured in her speed, and I leaned forward and thanked her.

The higher we flew, the more I could see of the surrounding forest and of all its beauty. The trees went on for as far as I could see, but to the east, a large mountain stood on the horizon. Its white cap stood out against the blue sky. The giant that pulled the castle forward faded off in the distance, and from our vantage point, I spied the other giants holding onto their golden lines. They started off again, and a blast from the trumpets came from up in the castle.

I glanced back over my shoulder, and Jeremiah smiled at me and said something, but I couldn't hear him.

"What?"

He leaned closer to me and said louder, "I hope we land soon!"

Taking a deep breath and widening his eyes, he hung on tight, a look of fear on his face. I laughed at his honesty. Behind him Jessica had closed her eyes and turned toward the sun, letting its warmth fall on her face. All trace of night had vanished. Relaxed and at peace, she exuded a calm that I did not feel. How she could let go and be so serene I did not know.

In front of us, Snap led the way. Her wings moved as fast as a hummingbird's, and she flew upward, disappearing from view. Seconds later we entered the clouds, and the sun vanished and all became calm. There was no wind and the trumpets became muffled and sounded like they were far away.

"I can't see the bottom of the castle, can you?" I scanned the sky above but could only see a thick fog.

"Neither can I. These clouds are too thick," Jeremiah said. "It's like we're on a boat and a dense fog had suddenly come upon us."

"I've never seen magic like this." Jessica leaned forward and took her right hand off of Ruby and stretched out. Almost like a swirl of snow, the cloud broke apart at her touch and dissipated only to reform after they had flown through it. "Whatever created this castle has immense magic and power. This isn't some parlor trick but beyond any that I have ever seen."

"I think I see something." I pointed ahead to a light up above us.

Snap flew toward the light, and as we approached, I could make out a drawbridge that had opened on the bottom part of the castle. Two other faeries stood guard on each side of the drawbridge. Two glowing globes lit either side, and Snap headed straight toward them. Ruby followed and then hovered before the opening.

I couldn't hear what Snap said to the two faerie guards, but she whizzed back to us. "This is where you get off." She turned to Ruby and said, "Let them off here, and then you can go back to playing. Thank you for coming to help me."

Ruby let out a controlled roar and then landed on the drawbridge. The wyrm's claws dug into the ground, and it bent down low to make it easier for us to exit. I hopped off her back and then turned around to pet her. "Thank you for being easy on us."

Jeremiah helped Jessica down and Snap landed in front of me. "We're almost there. Come."

She led the way into the belly of the castle, and the two faerie guards stood at attention and did not turn toward us. I wondered what they stood guard against. With a castle so large, a flying dragon, and a faerie army, they appeared to be a formidable force to me.

Snap led the way into the castle, and I stopped once inside. Instead of a dreary subterranean underbelly that I had expected, we walked up a long set of stairs that opened up into a beautiful green field. Trees stretched up high into the sky, and the castle's keep and towers were intermingled with them. The field stretched farther than I could see. Intricate dwellings that resembled elaborate huts surrounded the outskirts of the castle's grounds, with more elaborate buildings rising higher until the castle dominated the central section, stretching up far into the sky. The white stone of the castle shone bright and clean with the topmost portion shimmering in gold. A formidable wall surrounded the entire grounds and kept out any invaders.

"Amazing." I did not know what else to say.

"Who built all of this?" Jeremiah spun around and tried to take in everything all at once. "This is beautiful."

Snap landed on the ground and beamed at her home. "Thank you. Welcome to Dewdrop, home of the remaining faeries on the Other side."

"Remaining?" Jessica asked. "Where have the rest gone?"

"Some have left and many have died from the war." Snap lowered her head and put two fingers over her heart. "And we will never forget them."

Jeremiah looked across the fields to the huts ahead. "How many of your kind are left here?"

Snap's nose bristled and she scowled. "That's not a very polite question to ask your host."

Jessica put her hand on Jeremiah's shoulder, signaling him to back down and said, "And we're thankful that you have taken us in. Can you tell us the name of our host?"

"I can tell you myself."

I spun around, surprised by the faerie who appeared right behind us. He wore a white suit, hat to match, and beamed a teeth-filled smile at us. "And who are you?"

He took his hat off and bowed to us. His mannerisms reminded me of those of the Golden Fox in how stately he moved and in his playing a role. "My name is Ignatius, and I'm the lord and ruler of this castle." He paused a moment, scratched the side of his head, and said, "Come to think of it, I'm the lord of everything in the Other side, considering there's no one left but me and the flower faeries."

"No one?" I raised an eyebrow, skeptical of him.

"Well, yes, it is only me, myself, and I left on the Other side. Everyone else has moved on, leaving me all alone." He sighed and stood back at his full height and put his hat back on.

Jeremiah came closer to him and looked him up and down. "You remind me of someone I met here once. His name is Tristan. Do you know him?"

Ignatius nodded and rolled his eyes. "I never was a fan of that one. He always thought that he had it better than the rest of us. I was glad when he moved on after Baba Yaga left the stone throne. Now it is truly me, myself, and I."

I crossed my arms over my chest and dared to ask him a question. "We're looking for two people. Would you be able to help us?"

Ignatius smacked his hand against his forehead. "Stupid me! I almost forgot. You're looking for Charley and Phoebe, right?"

"Have you seen them?" The words tumbled out of my mouth faster than I could check my excitement.

"Yes, I have." He started to say more, but Snap came up to him and saluted. He turned to face her and asked, "What is it? You look upset."

Snap stood at her tallest and said, "They're coming."

"Now?" Ignatius asked. He stared up at the sky, shielding his eyes with his hand in an attempt to see past the glare of the sun. "Right now?"

Snap nodded and fidgeted with her hands. "There's more than a dozen of them, and this time the prince is with them as well." She glanced back the way they had come and asked, "Do you want me to gather the rest of the faeries to prepare our defenses?"

"Yes, go do that." He grabbed her before she could run off and pulled her close, giving her a fatherly kiss on the forehead. "Be careful. If they breach the defenses, then retreat inside the castle and stay hidden. I do not want you or any of your friends to get hurt or worse."

His tenderness lit her up and she beamed. "Yes, sire!"

Without a glance toward us, she took off and flew down the stairs that we had come.

"Who's coming to attack you?" I asked.

He stared off at the horizon, ignoring me.

Jessica came up to him and gently put her hand on his arm. "We can help. Both of us have magic."

I nodded and clenched my left fist at my side. It had been a long time since I had last let loose my magic without fear that I would lose my powers. I could feel the energy tickling my fingertips.

"The Cryshada are coming. Many of them and their prince. They want to take this castle, destroy me, and then take over all of the Other side." He headed toward the castle and we followed him. "Come with me, we'll go inside and prepare for the approaching battle."

"If you show me where some weapons are, I'm happy to help as well." Jeremiah walked with his hands in his pockets, looking a bit lost without his working guns. "I doubt my bare fists will be of much help."

Ignatius stopped and faced Jeremiah. "Do you know how to use a bow?"

"I've used one for hunting from time to time."

"Good, we can use someone like you who can help us." Ignatius started up again but stopped suddenly. "This is unfortunate."

"What's wrong?" I stood by him and his erratic nature had started to grate on me.

"She's back." Seeing that none of us understood or knew who he was talking about, he said, "Phoebe is back. I thought she would be gone longer. She's come at the worst possible time."

I grabbed his arm and held him from leaving. "Please, tell me where she is. I want to find my daughter."

Ignatius gave me a cold look, staring at my hand on his arm.

I let him go and then put my hands up in the air as a sign that I did not wish to harm him. "Please, we've come so far to find her and Charley."

"You don't understand. It's much more complicated than that." He turned away from me and started up again.

Jeremiah jogged up to Ignatius and kept pace with him as Jessica and I followed behind him. "Tell us how we can help and we will. But we need to understand what we're up against."

"We don't have much time." He stopped running and said, "We have to protect this castle at all costs. If it falls, then the Cryshada will overrun it and we'll all be lost."

"Tell us where to go find Phoebe, and we'll go to her." Jessica stood across from Jeremiah, and the two of them tried reasoning with Ignatius.

But I had had enough talk. I closed my eyes, lit my hand with fiery blue magic, and searched for Phoebe. I found her within seconds. She stood in front of a cave, and Charley ran out to greet her. The two of them talked and then a third person came out of the cave. He came into my field of vision, and I could not believe what I saw. Ignatius left the cave and looked through the veil of the dreamline and addressed me. "You've found my secret. I am here as well."

Startled, I opened my eyes and gasped in surprise.

Ignatius nodded to me and said, "I told you that there's only me, myself, and I left here. Now do you understand?"

I didn't but at least I knew where Phoebe was. I opened a gate into the dreamline, stepped through, and ignored both Jessica and

Jeremiah calling after me. I had to go. Trouble or no, I would not let Phoebe out of my sight again.

***

Charley stood at the edge of the cave, rubbing the back of his neck. "What did you do to me?"

Ignatius sat on a rock whittling away at a piece of wood with a knife. "I put you into a magical sleep. I bet you feel rested now, don't you?"

Balling his fists, Charley rushed Ignatius and took a swing at him. Moving faster than he could see, Ignatius bent, like a ray of light being redirected with a mirror, away from the punch. Missing entirely, Charley stumbled forward. "What did you do with Phoebe?"

"Calm down. She isn't hurt. I sent her on her witch's test." Ignatius put down the knife and piece of wood and put his hands in the air. "I'm telling you the truth. I didn't harm her. She's fine. I promise."

Charley feigned to rush Ignatius to see if he would flinch and he didn't. He hung back in a defensive posture. "Don't play games with me. I promised her mother that I would keep an eye out for her. I have kids of my own, and I know how it feels to lose a child."

Ignatius lowered his hands and his eyes teared up. "I know how that feels as well." He leaned forward with his shoulders slouched and hung his head low. "I truly haven't done anything to harm Phoebe. She needed to go on her own, and I know that you wouldn't have allowed that."

Relaxing a bit, Charley let his guard down and asked, "Where did you send her off to?"

"She went to see the Shard Chimes of Forget-me-not. She'll be tested there and…"

Charley rushed forward as fast as he could but changed direction at the last second, and Ignatius fell for the trap. With both arms, Charley pulled him off the rock and then wrapped his legs around Ignatius'. He held him in a tight wrestling hold, keeping him stationary on the ground.

Ignatius did not fight back and went limp. "Okay, okay, you got me! I'm not going anywhere. Easy on my hair."

Charley wrapped his arms tightly around Ignatius' chest and squeezed him as tightly as he could. Any normal person would have been in pain from the hold. "I want you to take me to her now!"

"I can't do that, you fool. She has to be on her own, and once she's at the chimes, then her experience will be different than yours. I can't just go there and bring you to her. Things just don't work that way." Ignatius shook his head as quickly as he could to fix his long locks of hair. "I'm telling you the truth."

"I don't believe you." Charley bent his body back and squeezed with all his strength to crush Ignatius' ribs. "Bring me to her now!"

"I told you that I can't do that." Ignatius tried to say more but struggled against Charley's hold.

"Did you two miss me?" Phoebe appeared at the edge of the forest and ran over to Charley. "Looks like you both did."

She smiled at Charley and ruffled his hair.

He let Ignatius out of his hold and jumped up to greet Phoebe with a big hug. "You're okay! I was worried that something had happened to you."

"I'm fine. I met two people that helped me with my test and I'm back." She returned Charley's hug.

"Did you pass?" Charley asked.

"It wasn't that type of test. But I guess I could say that I got the answer that I had always wanted and now know more of who I am as a witch." She let go of him and went over to help Ignatius up off the ground.

"Thank you." He dusted off his white clothes, frowning at all the dirt stains on his pants.

"No, I should thank you. The test showed me what I wanted to see, and I know what I need to do now." Phoebe pulled back her hair in a ponytail and used some string to tie it in place.

Charley looked to her and asked, "And what exactly is that?"

"We need to go back and rescue the Golden Fox from the prison that the French army put him in." She looked to Ignatius and said, "Unless you know if he's not there anymore and has escaped."

"I don't keep tabs on my cousin that way, and your guess is as good as anyone's. He sent you both here to help you escape, and when you're ready, I can help you both get back there."

"What about you? Are you going to come with us?" Charley asked.

"No, my place is here on the Other side. There's a matter that I need to attend to soon, and it'll need all of my attention." He looked as though he wanted to say more but abruptly stopped talking and then pointed to the cave entrance. "If you want to leave now, I can help you."

Charley headed toward the cave. "Yes, the sooner we get out of here and back home, the better."

Phoebe hesitated and looked toward the horizon. "She's over there, isn't she?"

"Yes, your mother searches for you. Do you want to go see her?" Ignatius asked.

"I do. Can you send us to her?"

"I can."

Charley shook his head in frustration. "Then why didn't you do that sooner and help us."

"Things have changed in the last few minutes. I now know where Cinderella is." He closed his eyes and mouthed a few words silently to himself.

"Well, now what's happening?" Charley walked over to Phoebe's side and stared at him.

He opened his eyes and said, "Hurry, come with me. They're in danger and need our help."

Phoebe followed without a word, but Charley asked, "Who is in danger? What's going on?"

Ignatius ignored his questions, and they rushed to the back of the cave. A mountain spring bubbled, filling a large pool of water. The steam from the warm water filled the back portion of the cave with its high humidity.

"We'll jump in and when you exit, be prepared to fight." Ignatius jumped in headfirst and vanished beneath the water's surface.

Phoebe lit her hand in the glow of magic and faced Charley. "My mother's in trouble. I can sense it. She's probably with Jeremiah, so they'll both need our help." She closed her eyes and kept her hand out in front of her. "I can feel that something's wrong. Please, let's go!"

Without another word, she jumped into the pool of water feet first and vanished from sight. Charley looked around for someone else to talk to, but he was alone.

"For once, I wish we'd not go gallivanting off into the unknown." He glanced up at the cavern's ceiling and said, "Ginny, wish me luck."

He jumped into the pool of warm water and fell straight down, through the opening there into a crack in the dreamline, and vanished as all went black.

**

I crossed into the dreamline and reached out to Phoebe. I could see her, closer than I had expected, and the swirl of the sky came fast upon me, and I walked onward, fighting past the blur of the darkness of space.

The ground shifted, and I stepped out of the dreamline and stood alone in the forest. Night had descended again, and Phoebe stood alone in front of me. I caught a glimpse of someone near her, but he blinked out of existence before I could recognize him.

"Are you well? And where's Charley?" I ran to her and hugged her close. "I was so afraid that something bad had happened to you."

"Mom, I'm fine. Charley's fine too." She returned my hug and squeezed me tight. "Where are we?"

"I don't know, but I have my magic back and used the dreamline to come find you."

Phoebe laughed and pulled away from me. "I was coming to find you. I saw that you were in trouble and I wanted to help. Something was coming to attack you."

I turned back the way I had come and pointed at a crack in the dreamline. The passage back to the castle fizzled and wavered, but through the wisps of magical light, we could see the castle in the clouds. "The Cryshada are coming to attack. When we return, I'll bring us back to the exact moment I left, and we'll only have minutes before they arrive."

"Before we head back, we need to talk." Phoebe faced me and folded her hands in front of her. "I need to tell you something and it can't wait."

"We have time. I can spend a few minutes here before we need to get back. What do you want to talk about?" I guessed but didn't want to say anything until I heard from her.

"I just went through my witch's test. Before I say anything else, know that I love you and miss you. I wanted to talk to you about magic for a while now but was afraid because you had lost your powers. I have so many questions, but I just didn't know when I could bring the topic up. I didn't want to upset you." Phoebe glanced down at the ground, looking embarrassed.

"No, it's my fault. I should have been there more for you." I let out how I truly felt and did not hide from the truth. "I've treated both you and Jeremiah horribly for far too long. I let my fear and anger at losing my magic overrun me. I shouldn't have done that. I should have been there for you."

Phoebe smiled and said, "It's not too late. We still have time to talk and get to know each other. I still have so many questions about magic. I could use your help."

I gave her another hug and breathed deep, taking in the scent of her hair. "I remember when you were a baby and I could hold you in my arms. But now you're nearly fully grown, and soon you'll be on your own and, I hope, will one day start your own family. I just can't believe how much time has gone by, and I've wasted most of it lately. Magic or no magic, I am your mother, and I promise you that you can talk to me any time you might have questions about magic. I'll be here for you. I promise."

Phoebe kissed me on the cheek and replied, "I love you. Thank you. We should go back now and help them."

"If the attack overruns the castle, I want you to be ready and by my side. I'll get us all out of there, and we'll go someplace safe." I waved my left hand at the crack in the dreamline, and it widened enough so that we could walk through. "Are you ready?"

"Yes, I am."

She held my hand, and I went first, walking through the opening in the air before us, and Phoebe followed me. We dropped down, fell like the floor had bottomed out below us, and then popped up and out onto the field surrounding the castle.

Jeremiah noticed us first and ran to us. "Where did you go?"

"It's okay. We're back now and we're ready…" I did a double take and stopped talking, staring at Ignatius and a second Ignatius standing in front of us. "How?"

The Ignatius closest to me said, "I told you that there were three of us." He pointed to his chest. "There's me."

"Myself," the second Ignatius, identical in every detail, including the clothing he wore, said and then pointed up at the sky.

Both of them pointed to the same spot and said in unison, "And I."

Jessica stared up at the clouds, looking for the approaching attacking Cryshada. "There's three of you?"

The Ignatius we had first met stood closest to us and replied, "Yes, there are. Unfortunately, he's the Crystal Prince, and he wants to overrun this castle to gain all of the magic that's here."

"But we'll stop him." The second Ignatius stood tall and turned just in time for a portal to open in the dreamline.

Charley came tumbling out and was caught by Ignatius. The only difference that I could see between him and the other Ignatius were dirt stains on his white pants.

"Hey!" Charley stopped from tumbling forward and held tightly onto Ignatius' arm to steady himself. "I thought I had gotten lost."

"You took the long way to get here." Ignatius patted him on the back and pointed over at his twin. "Let me introduce you to my other self."

Charley nodded politely but rushed over to Jeremiah and gave him an embrace. "Finally, we've found each other again." He glanced over at Jessica and said, "My name is Charley and you are?"

"I'm Jessica. I don't live too far from your farm. Ginny comes to me sometimes for medicine when your kids get sick."

"Oh, yes, you're the doctor she always talks about."

Jessica shook her head. "I haven't studied to be a doctor. I'm just a witch who knows her herbs and medicines very well."

"Nice to meet—"

Charley was cut off by the original Ignatius. "We can talk later, but we only have a few minutes before they arrive and we need to be ready." He reached out with both hands, looking to grasp hands with Phoebe and me. "We need to form a circle."

The second Ignatius stood in the center, ready to help if needed.

I took his right hand in mine and gave my left to Jessica, and she held Phoebe's hand. Our rough circle formed, Jeremiah and Charley stepped away from us, unsure what to do. When I looked up into the sky, I could now count near a dozen glowing points of light. The Cryshada were close. They would be on us soon.

"I am going to open a channel and share my magic with all of you. When it passes through you, push it to the person next to you. When it returns to me, I'll cycle it through again. Then I will take the north, Jessica the south, Phoebe the west, and Cinderella the east. We'll release the magic and cover the entire castle with my protective spell." He stared at me and squeezed my hand tight. "Does everyone understand?"

"Yes." The rush of magic poured into me, and I clenched my teeth, overwhelmed by the surge of power that coursed through my veins. I channeled the power through me and added my own, passing it on to Jessica, releasing it and letting my strength go on to her.

All else vanished for me. The power passed out of me, all of it into Jessica, and she funneled the magic into Phoebe who then passed it back to Ignatius. He held it for but a moment, but I watched him, and he turned his face upward, letting out the power he held within him. A ruby-red beam of light shot forth from every pore in his body, and he directed the energy to the northern part of the castle in the sky. Jessica followed next with a blast of violet energy that flew toward the south, Phoebe covered the west with her orange-colored magic, and I let out my own source of energy. The cobalt blue, deep and resonant, surged around my heart and flew up high in the sky, and our magic blended together, covering the entire castle.

When the first Cryshada hit the shield, they were vaporized instantly. The remaining Cryshada held back as the magic coursed through, me and I drank in the power and became it. I lost track of who I was, where the magic began, and how it had all come together. A living conduit, I funneled the power from depth within and let the energy flow out of me, giving more and more until I feared there would be no more to give.

The spell held and I woke many minutes later. The shield still shimmered above us.

"Are they are gone?" I know I spoke louder than I needed, but the energy that zipped through my body hummed, and I had a difficult time concentrating.

Ignatius nodded and let the shield down. He slumped forward and Charley caught him. "Only I remain. Look." He turned his head toward the west, and a solitary figure floated down from the sky like a living god lit with a pulsing red light that surrounded and protected him.

The second Ignatius went to the first and helped him up. "He comes for us now, and we need to be ready. He has become strong with his hate and jealousy."

"I am spent. I need to rest." Ignatius lowered his head onto his chest and closed his eyes.

Charley led him gently onto the field and let him rest on his back.

"I guess it's up to me now." The second Ignatius fixed his shirt and adjusted his hat. "Here we go."

Jeremiah came next to me and whispered, "Should we go before it's too late to escape?"

I had not thought about running, but he made a good point. "I think we should stay. I don't know what will happen if this new Ignatius gains control of this castle. Whatever magic is here is strong, and it's probably best now to let him have it."

Phoebe barely seemed phased by the magic she had released, but Jessica crouched down and sat on the grass. "Are you okay?" Phoebe went to her side.

"Yes, I'm fine. I need to rest a bit. I'm not young like you. Using that much magic took a lot out of me." Jessica wiped her brow, and Charley stood by her.

"I'd feel a lot better if I had a rifle in my hands." He stood in front of Jessica to protect her from any attack.

"That wouldn't do much good. I don't think guns will harm him."

The third Ignatius landed on the grass a few feet from us. He had crossed his arms and looked ready to spring forward, but I doubted any physical attack Jeremiah might attempt would harm a faerie.

"Myself, it's good to see you after so much time." The third Ignatius wore all white clothing like his other two selves but had a red rose pinned to the lapel of his jacket.

"Why are you here?" The second Ignatius stood in front of the first who still lay on his back in the grass with his eyes closed.

"So the others here don't lose their minds, you all may call me Prince Ignatius of the Crystal Realm." He adjusted the rose on his lapel, straightening it. "I am here because I only want what is mine. I want the magic of this place so that I can channel it and bring our world to its rightful place of ruling the world of men."

"We have told you time after time that we will not allow that." Our Ignatius held out his hand. "I may not be strong enough to beat you, but I can stop you from getting what you want."

Taking a handkerchief out of his pocket, the prince dusted off his white jacket and rolled his eyes. "Please, do you really think that I came here for more mindless banter? I know that you will never change your mind." He turned to face Phoebe and said, "But you are different. You know why I'm here, don't you?"

Phoebe looked to me for help, but I did not know how to respond. "I don't know what you're talking about."

He leaned forward toward her and said, "Really? We all want the same thing. We want to stop the automatons in the future from winning. They desperately want to travel through the dreamline and know that their best chance to do that is through you. Your mother will never agree to help them."

Charley stood close to Phoebe and asked her, "Do you have any idea what he's talking about?"

"No." She responded so quickly that I was certain she told the truth.

The prince clucked his tongue and shook his head. "Why do you waste all of our time by hiding the truth? I know that you've been in contact with your future self. That is how my Cryshada found you back on your home plane. If we join forces, we can work together and protect ourselves from the automatons before it's too late."

I took a step forward. My patience had run out. I had had enough of talking megalomaniacs. "My daughter has told you the truth. She doesn't know anything. Whatever happens in the future, she's not aware of it yet."

Phoebe took a few steps past me and confronted the prince. "I did have contact with a future version of myself, but she didn't tell me much. I only know that I need to have my mother help Napoleon escape from his exile. There are some automatons in the future that are trying to destroy the world, and they're stronger than faeries." She shrugged and folded her hands in front of her. "None of it doesn't make any sense to me."

The prince rubbed his chin, thinking.

Jeremiah came to stand by Phoebe and said, "And there's the camera obscura. I know about that as well."

Charley pointed at Phoebe and nodded. "That's where the Golden Fox, Phoebe, and I were headed before we were sent here. We were going to talk to the inventor of the camera obscura and use it to capture Napoleon's soul." He raised his eyes up to the heavens and crossed himself. "If Ginny were here, she'd be blessing me with some holy water. All of this speaks of dark magic to me and it worries me. I've seen what such magic can do before, and it can kill at whim."

Prince Ignatius glanced over to his other self and asked, "Will you help me?"

The original Ignatius shook his head. "Every time we have this conversation, it all comes down to the same point. You want to control and rule everything. If we could work together, it would be different."

"We do not have much time, and my patience is growing short." The prince rose to his full height. "If you do not come with me to help, then I'll be forced to declare war on—"

I lashed out at him, quick and fast, surrounding him with a binding spell. "Listen, I've had enough of you." I intensified my spell and locked him tight within. A bubble of blue light enveloped him. "We don't have time to play these games. Leave us."

He tried to cancel my spell but could not. He banged on the inside of the bubble and yelled, but we could not hear what he said.

With a flick of my wrist, I cast him out of the castle and sent him far, far away.

Ignatius' mouth dropped open and he asked, "How did you do that?"

"I told you that I'm tired of these games. I needed to find my daughter and now I have. We'll be going back soon to our world, and then I'll agree to go free Napoleon." I glanced around to the others. "Anyone want to come with me?"

The second Ignatius fretted with his hands. "But he'll come back soon, with an even larger army. What are we going to do?"

I shrugged. "Fight him. Resist. Build up your army to stand up and combine your powers." I turned away from him and added over my shoulder. "Do what you have to do, but I'm leaving."

"I'll come with you." Jeremiah came by my side. He nodded at me, but I could read his body language well. He would never say it in front of everyone, but I knew he was concerned and wanted to talk with me. We had a lot to discuss, but we didn't have the time.

Phoebe glanced over at me. "Charley and I need to go back and help free the Golden Fox. Why don't you come help us, and then we can all go together to help Napoleon escape?"

Ignatius turned away from looking at the sky, trying to see where the other part of him had been banished to, and said to me, "You can't leave."

"Why?" Phoebe asked.

I walked up to her and put my arm on her shoulder. "Because I'm pretty certain that when I leave here that I'll lose my magic again."

Ignatius nodded. "You're correct."

Phoebe pulled me close to her and spoke directly to me. "What are you going to do then?"

I laughed and smiled at her. "I'm going to leave, of course!"

"But your magic…"

I shook my head and took her in my arms, hugging her tight. I then put her at arm's length to look her directly in the eye. "I have been a fool. I've allowed my lack of magic to nearly ruin my life. I've been miserable and have felt incomplete." I glanced away a moment, working to gather the right words, and then faced her again. "And if I'm honest, I've been jealous of you. That's wrong of me. I want you to know that, and I'm working really hard to find my place in the world without magic."

"I wish the two of us could get away and talk, but I know now isn't the time." She motioned over to Jeremiah, Charley, and the others waiting for us. "Thank you for saying that to me. I thought you felt that way but didn't want to bring it up to you. I thought you would get angry."

"I've made a lot of mistakes in my life, but eventually I come around and admit to what I've done wrong. Don't worry about me. I'll head back and I'll help Napoleon escape. You do your part with the camera obscura, and we'll meet in Paris. Deal?"

I put my hand out to her, and like we used to do when she was a little kid, we shook on it. "Deal."

I hugged her again, and we both joined the rest of the group.

Ignatius gathered us around and said, "I can't stop the prince from coming after you. I'm using all of my magic to maintain this castle and keep what's left of faerie power alive." He looked over at his other self still in a deep sleep in the field by him. "We'll be able to hold him off from coming here for a little while longer, but the time is coming soon when we'll fail."

"Once we rescue the Golden Fox, we'll send him back here. He'll help you." Phoebe dropped the matter and turned away.

All of us were anxious to leave. I turned to Jessica. "You can stay, you know. If you stay, you'll keep your magic and can help protect the castle."

Jessica put her hand on my arm and said, "I think I would like to stay. Would that bother you? I know how hard it will be to lose your powers again. I don't want to desert you."

"Thank you for being so thoughtful, but please, stay and help Ignatius. Once the Golden Fox is freed and can come here, you could always come home then if you'd like. Please, don't make your decision based off of how I might feel."

She let go of my arm and walked over to Ignatius. "If you'll have me, then I'd like to stay."

"We could use the help, and it would be nice to have some company." He waved to us and asked, "Do you need me to call forth a portal to send you back home?"

I held my left hand up and a deep blue arc of fire shot forth from my palm and I opened the dreamline. "No, we're fine. If I don't see you again, thank you for watching over Phoebe."

"You are welcome." Ignatius stepped back as did Jessica, and I unreleased my full power. Swirls of energy crackled in the air, opening up a doorway into the dreamline.

"Phoebe and Charley, you two go first." I hugged Phoebe one last time as she passed me and then let her go. "Be careful. I love you."

"I love you, too." She kissed me on the cheek and said, "You be careful too. See you soon."

Charley stopped before me and said, "I promise that I'll watch over her. I know she thinks she's old enough, but I'll have my eye on her. I'll protect her like she's one of my own."

"I know you will. Thank you. We'll see each other soon. Good luck."

After Charley and Phoebe disappeared into the dreamline, I altered its course and closed my eyes, focusing on the island of Elba. I had never seen it, but my power here on the Other side was formidable. If I had more time, I could explore it, learn what my limits were. I opened my eyes and Jeremiah stood before me. "Ready?"

The lines around his eyes and his weathered look caused me to realize how tired he truly was. We would have a lot to discuss, and without Jessica as a buffer, I expected the conversations to be difficult. His patience had been great and yet he was like any person with limits.

"I almost have it." I imagined the tide, reaching out through the sea, and I sought for Napoleon. Born out of faerie magic as I had been, though he had also lost his powers, here on the Other side I could still sense his presence. His spirit glowed bright like the sun. I could sense him worlds away. There would be no one like him in all of history. I twisted my wrist to the left, funneled in my magic, and the dreamline shifted. "There. Just go on through. I'll be right there."

Jeremiah nodded without a word and gave one last wave to Ignatius and Jessica. He vanished into the dreamline and Jessica came over. "Good luck." She hugged me and kissed me on the forehead. "May your journey be clear and true."

"Thank you."

I watched her go and she pulled Ignatius with her. Unsure of the proper social niceties, he awkwardly waved at me and then stood over his unconscious double in the field. With a twirl of his hand, the three of them vanished.

I stood alone looking up at the blue sky and the green field that stretched out around me, and off in the distance, the castle's white spires gleamed from the brilliant sunlight. I could just make out several faeries, maybe one of them was Snap, flitting around the castle's tallest point. Everything around me looked to be at peace. Once I stepped through the dreamline, I knew all would change. My magic would be gone, I'd be powerless again, and I had a long and complicated road ahead.

I clenched my left fist, and without thinking, I opened it and just let it all go. The worry, my fears, and the heaviness within my heart. I dropped my hand to my side, took one last look around me, and then stepped through the dreamline into the unknown.

Chapter 9

I exited the dreamline and stepped forward into the surf. The sun had risen with several clouds, orange and dark gray, and hung on the horizon. The sea, a beautiful deep blue, turned a translucent green on the shore's edge. I could see directly into the water to the ocean floor. Shells and rocks littered the shoreline, and a gentle wave crashed against the beach, covering my boots.

"It's beautiful here, isn't it?" Jeremiah had taken off his winter coat and rolled up his shirt sleeves.

I shivered from the chill of the morning air and pulled my coat around me. "Yes, it is. For a moment, I just want to imagine that we're relaxing and on holiday, enjoying the sights."

"We've never taken a holiday. All we've done since we met is struggle…" He put his hands in his pockets and stood next to me.

Without speaking for a few moments, we watched as the next set of waves came up on the beach. I closed my eyes and let the sun's rays warm me, go into my heart, and give me the courage to say what needed to be said.

"I'm sorry for how I have treated you." I let the words out and then opened my eyes, turning to face Jeremiah as the wind blew his long dark hair salted with gray wild around his head. His unshaven face and the glare from the sun hid what he felt. I could not tell.

He took a step forward and went to speak, but I held up my hand to stop him.

"Please, let me say what I need to say." I held up my left hand and called forth my magic. My heart beat fast for a moment in anticipation and—nothing happened. My smile faded from my face and I tried hard to not frown but failed. "I have thought only of my magic since you rescued me from the stone throne. I have not been there for Phoebe when she needed me, and I certainly haven't been there for you. I let all of it get in the way of our marriage, and that was wrong of me. I'm sorry."

The waves lapped against the beach, and far off I could hear, but not see, a seagull. The morning wind blew at me, and the scent of the beach gave me much needed strength. Jeremiah kept his hands in his pockets and faced me full on. "I didn't rescue you from the stone throne. I simply pointed out a choice. You saved yourself."

"But did I really? I have obsessed about getting my magic back. I know that I have been difficult to live with and I've not allowed myself to let my guard down. I haven't really given us a chance. I've been trapped inside my own head, worrying, fretting, and trying everything I could to get my powers back."

"I know and you're right." He took a step closer to me. "I am frustrated with you. I expect Phoebe is too, but I haven't really talked to her about this. I've kept my distance between the two of you. It's been hard because I can see that she has needed someone to help train and guide her." He paused a long moment and said, "I know she was seeing Jessica. She came to me and asked for my advice on what she should do."

"You knew about Jessica and didn't tell me?" Anger rose up fast within me, and I bit my tongue for a moment and let it subside. "What did you advise her to do?"

"I told her to talk to you, but she was afraid." He took another step forward, but we were still miles apart. "When she decided not to, she let me know that she'd be seeing Jessica on a regular basis and I agreed."

"You agreed to let my daughter be trained by another witch and didn't have the courtesy to tell me?" I tried hard to remain calm but couldn't. "Is everyone out to get me?" Even to me, my words sounded exaggerated.

"I'm sorry. I didn't mean that. I'm just surprised and hurt that you didn't talk to me about this." I turned away from him to watch the sun. Better to stare at a ball of fire in the sky than to face all that bubbled up inside me.

"You have been depressed and in darkness for longer than I can remember. I had hoped that our getting married and settling in our new home would help heal your wounds, but it didn't. Nothing seemed to help." He stared up at the blue sky above him. "I haven't known what to do. I know you're not happy, and there isn't anything that I could do to help."

"Look, I know you tried, and I appreciate everything that you've done, but it's like a part of me has been ripped out and I've been left damaged and broken." The words tumbled out faster. "I feel like I'm sinking sometimes, and there isn't anything I can do to stop it. The loss has been greater than I ever thought."

"But do you have to do it alone?" he asked.

"I don't want to bother anyone with what I'm going through. I have tried to hide it, to bury it down deep within me, but that didn't work. Then I tried to shake it off, think about it, but I couldn't stop obsessing about the power I had." I turned back to where the dreamline had recently closed. "Do you see what I did back there? I have the ability to travel through time and across the world. I'm a chronicler and that feeling of energy through me excites me and lit up my life. It's all I can ever think about sometimes."

"I can understand that. I do, but you've let yourself go." He said the words and fidgeted with his hands. "I didn't mean it that way."

"Yes, you did." I glanced down at my body. My disheveled look, the extra weight I had gained, and my hair had knots and tangles in it. "What do you want me to do?"

"I want you to stop beating yourself up so much. I want you to start working to help yourself." He came closer to me and reached out. "I want you to learn to accept that you're still loved even though you don't have any magic. I didn't fall in love with you because you had magic powers. I fell in love with you because of how spirited you were, how you'd stand up to any king or queen for what you believed in. But you've let that all go. You chase after dreams that no longer exist, and now I'm standing here wondering what the hell I'm going to do."

I had not seen him this animated and fired up with emotion in a long time. His hand shook as he held it out to me.

"I've tried everything I could think of, but none of it has been enough. It's as though you enjoy being stuck in your little hole of darkness and want people to pity you."

I turned on him in a flash. "I do not want your pity. I want..."

"What? What do you want?" He pointed at me in frustration. "Your magic back? I want things back too. I lost a lot in my life, but I had to get over them. Yes, it takes time, but I had to work at it. I needed to fight and fight hard. I realized that if I didn't then I was truly lost."

"I want you to leave me alone," I said, but I didn't really mean it.

"Why? Because I speak the truth? Or because I bring up difficult topics and questions? Are you going to waste your life away chasing after something that you may never have again?"

"But I had my magic on the Other side. I can't tell you how good it felt to have the magic back, coursing through me."

"You don't have to tell me. I saw it on your face. It's like you've just taken laudanum. I've seen expressions like that before, trust me." He kicked the sand. "And I want nothing to do with it."

"You're just jealous because you never had that type of power." I spat the words at him. "You're so high and mighty up there in the clouds where you never do wrong. Please!"

"You know nothing of what you speak. Nothing!" He raised his voice at me, and his full anger rumbled out like a ferocious lion. "I was a witch hunter. I traveled the world, chasing down your kind because I can sense where magic is. I have had magic going through my veins as well, but I gave that up after I left Queen Mab. I have my own cross to bear for things that I have done, and it's not been easy. You are not the only one to have suffered and gone through loss. I have as well, but I don't wear my pains on my shirt as a badge of honor."

"No, you scamper about thinking you're better than anyone and then go around on your high horse. You withdraw and back away, dropping out when I need someone the most." The words came faster to me now. I just let them out, releasing them without worry or concern. I needed to say what I felt.

"Need me? If I followed you down your spiral, I'd be lost too." He pounded his chest with his fist. "But what about me? Me! I have been patient and kind with you, trying to listen, offer assistance, be there when you needed me, but you've shut me out, shut Phoebe out, hell, you've shut all the world out except for wanting that damn magic of yours. I need more than that. Don't you see? I deserve more!"

His face was flushed with emotion, and a red splotchy mark had appeared on his neck. I watched him, pulled back, and shook my head in condescension. "And that's what it all comes down to? I need to solve my problems how you would, in your time, for you." I shook my head and gave a sarcastic laugh. "Well, the world doesn't work that way for me. I need to figure this out in my own way and time. I need space."

"Space? Time? I'm not saying that you need to have everything all tied up in a bow. But you don't even try!" He pointed at my left hand. "All I see is you sitting alone, when you think no one is watching, trying to ignite that spark of magic. You try incessantly for hours. Why don't you just let it go? You've lost your powers, it's over, just let it go. It's not the end of the world. Life is still moving and the world still turning."

"I just can't." He closed his eyes and a rush of sorrow mixed with anger rose up within me. I lashed out at him and said, "I've used my magic to save so many, and I'm afraid that without magic my enemies will come hunt us, find us, and we'll all die. I can't let that happen. I must be ready for when it does. You saw what the Cryshada did to our house. They're already coming for us. We have to be ready."

Jeremiah lowered his voice and reached out to me. "But it doesn't have to be you, or for that matter, me, who saves the world. The world can save itself. Maybe it's time we really focus on saving each other."

The conversation had taken a turn. We had argued many times over this same topic, using the same points, defenses that I had become so familiar with and knew that we would go round and round until one of us tired of fighting. But this was different. "What do you mean?" I had broken out of the script, and I feared what he would say.

"I can't save you. You know that, I know that, but maybe it's time we both admit that." His hands fell to his sides, and he hung his head down in defeat. "I need to leave. This isn't healthy for me."

A surge of fear came up within me, and stupidly, I said the first thing that came to mind. "Are you giving up and are afraid that I'm too damaged for you? As soon as things get tough, you run?" I flung the accusation at him.

"No, I am not running. I have decided to take care of myself. My world does not have to be wrapped up in your problems. I am and have always been my own man."

"So you're going to run? You made a lifelong promise to me, an unbreakable bond, and now you're going to cut your losses and run at the first sign of trouble?" I shook my head and pointed at him. "Are you serious?"

"What would you have me do? Stay and just watch you destroy yourself slowly over time?" He came up to me, close, and asked, "What would you have me do? Truly. What would you do if you were me?"

I closed my eyes and pushed out the fear and my anger. I cleared my head for a moment and said, "I just want you to listen, understand, and be supportive. I don't want you to tell me what you would do to solve my problems. What works for you doesn't work for me. Don't you understand?"

Touched by my words, he put his hand on mine. "I just want to see you find peace. I don't care if you use what would work for me or not. I truly don't care. I just want to see you get out of this prison that you're in. I can see it, but I can't help you. I want to, but it looks to me that you don't want that. You enjoy being stuck. It gives you something to talk about."

I started to interrupt him, but he cut me off.

"No, please. Listen to me. I don't say these words to hurt you. Look at Ginny and Charley. They lost a child and went through the most difficult of times, but they're still together. They work hard at their marriage and are raising their kids the best they can. Ginny isn't held up in a room for hours on end lamenting the loss of their daughter. And Charley isn't doing that either. They've found a way to work together on their grief. I want that same thing for us. I do, but I don't know how to get there."

I squeezed his hand. "I've tried everything that I know how to do, but it doesn't work. And I'm not Ginny. She has her faith that helped her during their dark time. I don't have that. I have—" I stopped and shook my head. "No, you're right. I hear you. I just don't know what will work for me. I feel lost."

"I would stand by you through anything to the moon and back." He let go of my hand. "But I need to go. I need some time to think and see where I need to be."

"Are you going now?" I looked around at the beach. "We're on Elba and I need your help with Napoleon. I can't do that alone. I need to convince him to come back to Paris with us so we can have him do whatever the future Phoebe thinks is necessary…"

My words failed me. I had no idea what we needed to do and simply trusted in my daughter. All of it made no sense, but I had to try.

"I'm not leaving you on this island." He came two steps closer to me. "When this is all over, I then will need some time to think. We can talk through it some more, but I want you to know that I need to go."

"For good?" I spat the words at him, barely a question. "Because if you're unsure, let me make it clear for you. I don't need someone to be with me only when times are good. I need someone who will help me when I'm sick as well. Can you understand that? That's the promise that we made."

"I'm not going for good. I just need time to think. I need some clarity to figure out what I want to do."

I took a risk and told him the truth. "Do you know how I feel when I hear you say those words? My mother left me for the Silver Fox, my father went on his worldly adventures, and my stepmother brutalized me. All my life I've had people abandon me and I'm tired of it. I can make it on my own, but I trusted you. I love you. This isn't how it's supposed to be."

Jeremiah looked me right in the eye and said, "I'm sorry. This isn't what I want to do either. I don't know what's going to happen. I just need some time to figure out what I want to do with my life."

"Then go now. Seriously, just go." I pointed out at the sea. "I don't want you to stay here with me out of pity. I will find Napoleon and convince him myself to go back to Paris. I can do this on my own. I don't need your help. Go!"

He folded his arms over his chest. "You're angry and I understand that. But I'm not going to leave you here. When we get back, we can talk more. I'm not deserting you. I simply need time to take care of myself for a bit. For now, let's just agree to drop this conversation. It's not helping either of us. We're going round and round in circles. Can you agree to that?"

I didn't want to, but I knew that we had to move on. If we kept talking, we would simply argue more, and the circle would go on and on. "Fine."

I could not keep the resignation out of my voice.

Jeremiah crossed the divide between us. "I know this isn't what you want to hear right now. But I love you. I do."

He went to hug me, and at first, I backed away, but then I changed my mind and put my arms around him. We held each other for a moment, and I let the truth out. "I love you, too. I do. All of this is so much harder than I thought. I'm sorry."

"You don't need to be sorry. We just need to find a way to get through this all." He put the palm of his hand on my back and pulled me closer. "Now we just need to figure out where to find Napoleon."

"I'm right here." A voice far off the beach called to us.

We disengaged from our embrace and turned to see Napoleon, walking out from behind a large rock. He pointed a walking stick at us and said, "And as touching as this private moment is between you, I want to know why are you on my island?"

I turned to Jeremiah and said, "Well, at least we found him."

We both smiled at each other, a rare event these days, and then turned to face the emperor.

Redemption: Cinderella's Secret Witch Diaries (Book 4)

Chapter 10

Phoebe fell out of the dreamline, stumbled, and caught herself on the side of a building. Disoriented for a moment, she clung to the wall in front of her and caught her breath. Night had fallen and the cold crept in on her, numbing her hands after a few seconds.

"Charley?" She whispered to try to stay as inconspicuous as possible.

From behind her, she heard a rush of wind and turned around. Charley stumbled out of the dreamline next to her and knocked his head against the wall behind them. He groaned and rubbed his head. "Ouch."

"Are you okay?" Phoebe looked up at him.

He rubbed his forehead and said, "Just bumped my head. I'm okay. Those last few steps were a bit steeper than I had expected."

From inside the building, one man called out in celebration, and several others cried out in frustration.

Charley pointed inside. "Do you think he's in there?"

She closed her eyes and reached out with her magic. She imagined the night darker, more solitary, until only the presence of the Golden Fox remained in her mind. She focused on what he looked like, imagined the tone of his voice, and reached out, searching for him. A building across the way lit up for her. "No, he's in that house over there."

"How long do you think we were gone?" Charley lowered his voice and glanced up at the sky. "It was daytime when we left. Do you think it's the same day?"

"I think it is, but I'm not sure." Phoebe walked through a small garden toward the other structure. She waved to Charley and said, "Come on, let's go rescue him."

"Wait a minute!" He hurried to catch up after her and was cautious not to move the rusty gate in front of him. Clouds hung heavy in the sky, and the chilly cold air would not produce any snow, but a fine mist hung in the air. Just enough to make the night more miserable.

Phoebe slowed and waited for Charley to catch up.

He leaned in to her and asked, "What's the plan? We can't just go rushing in without a plan."

Light from several lanterns lit her face, and her teeth shone white in the night as she smiled. "I was going to rush in, use some sort of magic spell on any guards, and you'd break the Golden Fox out."

"What if they have guns?" He held up his hands. "I don't have anything but my hands to fight them off with. You could get hurt or killed if they have guns and we don't."

Phoebe closed her eyes and pointed toward the small building in front of them. "There's only one guard and he's sleeping. The Golden Fox is resting in the right corner of the cell he's in."

"Oh, that makes a big difference on things." Charley led the way and made it to the door. He peeked inside. An old man had his rifle propped up against the wall, had crossed his legs, and now leaned back in his chair fast asleep. He took in a deep breath, and when he would exhale, his snoring became louder until all the air had left his lungs. "How about you zap him with some of your magic and keep him in a deep sleep. Can you do that?"

Phoebe walked past him through the doorway. "Yes, I'll keep him fast asleep, and you look for the key to open up the cell."

Charley followed in after her, and he rushed up to the sleeping man, searching his pockets.

The Golden Fox sat up and held up his shackled hands. "You both came back for me!"

"Did you think we were going to leave you here?" Phoebe asked.

"Honestly, I wasn't sure if you'd be able to get back from the Other side. It's not the easiest of places to return from." The Golden Fox pointed at the guard. "The keys are in his left pocket. I saw him put them in there before they locked me up."

"Are you okay?" Phoebe stood away from the cell door, and Charley unlocked it.

The Golden Fox put out his wrists toward Charley. "The sooner you can get this silver off of me, the better. I can't even use the simplest of magic when locked in these."

Charley fumbled with the keys, tried one that didn't work, and finally found the one that opened the shackles. "There you go. That should be better for you."

The Golden Fox rubbed his wrists and let out a deep sigh. "That does feel much better. I hate the feel of iron on me. Messes with my complexion. He smiled and lit his right hand with an orange glow of power. Satisfied that his magic had returned, he doused the light. "What's the plan?"

Phoebe shrugged and looked to Charley. "We hadn't thought that far, but I think getting out of this town would make the most sense. What do you say?"

"I think we find some horses and head out of town as quickly as we can." Charley kept his voice low and asked the Golden Fox, "Is that marshal here?"

"You mean me? You can call me Marshal Jacques MacDonald." He stepped out of the shadows with two pistols raised. "I knew that it would only be a matter of time before you came back to rescue him."

Phoebe reacted on instinct and waved her hand, throwing up a protective spell on them. "We only want go get our friend out of here and mean no harm to anyone."

Charley stood beside Phoebe and looked around in desperation for some sort of weapon. The best he could find were the shackles at his feet. He held them in his hand like a mace, ready to pounce. "Stay back!"

Jacques relaxed and asked, "Why are you all here? What do you truly want?"

The Golden Fox pointed at him. "I've heard about you. You're the witch hunter, aren't you?"

"I'm Emperor Napoleon's marshal and most loyal supporter. I will serve him till the end of my days." He took another step into the room and waved his pistols to the right. "All of you, get into the cell."

Phoebe glanced over at the Golden Fox and relaxed. He had a huge grin on his face. She had seen that smile of his before and knew he had a plan.

"No, I'd rather not do that." The Golden Fox rubbed his wrists and showed the red marks where the iron had hurt him. "Your hospitality is something that I'd rather not have to experience again."

"Guards, to me!" Jacques shouted at the top of his voice, turning his head for a moment back toward the front door. "They'll be here in a moment, and all of you will regret ever coming here."

Charley moved closer to Phoebe, putting himself in front of her to protect her.

"You, if you take another step in front of her, I will shoot you. Do you understand?" Jacques pointed both of his pistols at Charley.

Freezing in his place, Charley put up his hands and stood still. "Yes, I do understand and I'll stay here."

Walking forward, the Golden Fox ignored the warning. "Your guards can't hear you. You understand that, don't you?" He raised his right hand and pointed at Jacques. "If you want to live, then you are going to come right over to me in this cell here."

"Guards!" Jacques called again, but no one responded. "What did you do?"

"Oh, I'm just getting started with you." The Golden Fox flicked his hand, and both of Jacques' pistols crumbled to pieces in his hands. The weapons were no longer even recognizable on the ground. "Come over to me now!"

His right hand glowed a brilliant yellow and Charley turned away from the bright light. Phoebe moved off to the side of the room as Jacques tried to fight the spell, but his legs were compelled to move him forward into the jail cell. He fought but could not stop himself.

"What are you doing to me?" Jacques finished his forced walk and turned around to the Golden Fox who now stood right outside the cell.

"Put the shackles on him." The Golden Fox kept his glowing hand raised and called over to Charley.

Moving quickly, Charley locked Jacques up with the restraints and left the cell in haste. "Let's get going before anyone else finds us."

Phoebe pulled at the Golden Fox's jacket and said, "Come on, enough. Let's lock him in the cell and leave."

"I'll be right there." He turned back toward the marshal and said, "If you and your men follow us, I will not be so forgiving next time. I will unleash my magic on you, warping the insides of your brain so that you'll have wished that you had stayed away. Do you understand?"

"I will come after you like a thousand hounds from hell." He spat the words at the Golden Fox.

Phoebe pulled the door closed and the last image she had of him was his angry face in the shadows. "Now, let's go. We don't have time for revenge. Come on."

She pulled the Golden Fox along with her, and they followed Charley outside as he led them toward a barn. Once inside, Charley closed the door behind them and said, "We need to work together and come up with a plan." He addressed the Golden Fox directly. "I understand that you weren't happy being imprisoned, but we can't have any of us doing something rash. We need to get safely out of here."

The Golden Fox brushed back a lock of hair from his face. "I apologize for losing my temper. I wasn't too pleased that a witch hunter locked me up with iron chains. He planned for far worse for all of us, and when a snake is about to strike, well, I like to cut off the head."

"We need to complete our mission." Phoebe grabbed the Golden Fox's hands. "We met my mother and Jeremiah on the Other side. They're now headed to free Napoleon from his exile, and we need to meet them in Paris with the camera obscura. We don't have much time."

Charley scratched his head. "Where exactly are we, and how far is that to Paris?" He turned to pat the nearest horse that stuck its head out of the stall.

"Nicéphore Niépce lives only a short way from here. On horseback, we can probably make it by morning. The horses will be tired, as will you both, but we can do it. But for getting from Chalon-sur-Saône to Paris is beyond my powers." The Golden Fox snapped his fingers. "I can't get us around like that."

Charley let the horse out of the stall and put a saddle on it. "But you transported us all the way to the Other side. That's a whole different plane than our world here. Can't you just use your magic and get us there?"

"No, I can't do that. I had saved up my powers for months and had laid out the spell to transport you both to the Other side. That's my home and I can, when I have time to prepare, send people there, but I can't travel through the dreamline."

"But I can." Phoebe interrupted him and lit her hand. Like her troubled mood, the color of her hand switched from blue, to red, and then to purple. "I still haven't perfected using the dreamline, but I'll try."

The Golden Fox stood before her and put his hands on her shoulder. "No, you won't try. You'll do it. I believe that you can." Before she could say a word, he rushed on. "You are a powerful witch. More powerful than your mother, and I know that you can do this."

"I don't know…" Phoebe lowered her hand and her magic faded.

"Somehow you have traveled far into the future and have the power to communicate back to people here now in our present. I don't know of any witch who has such power. You may not believe it, but you can do this. I believe in you and so does Charley. Right?" The Golden Fox turned to Charley to back him up.

"I wouldn't be here except for you." He realized what he said and went on. "I didn't mean it that way. I meant that you've saved me a few times, and I know that you'll be able to open the dreamline and get us to Paris."

"What if I fail?" Phoebe turned away from the Golden Fox and her magic went out.

"Then you'll be mortal like the rest of us." He took her left hand in his own. "We all fail from time to time, but it's what we do after that makes us." He lowered his voice and said, "Before you were born, I was selfish and wanted your grandmother only to myself. I even tried to use your mother's powers to feed my obsession. I failed and caused great harm to people. But I paid for what I did, and then I had a choice to make. Either I would remain possessive and selfish or I could change. I decided to change, and now look at me."

He smiled and showed off his golden-colored skin that lit up from the magic in his hand.

Phoebe let a small smile break out on her face, but it quickly faded. "Thank you. Let's get going before we're found."

The Golden Fox held her hand, keeping her in place. "I'm serious. You are no longer a child. Now you need to decide for yourself what you want in your life and what you stand for. If you don't believe in yourself, it won't matter what Charley and I say."

She squeezed his hand back. "I know. I'm just tired. It's been a long day."

"And it's going to be a cold and long night." Charley walked the first horse over to Phoebe and gave her the reins. "You won't be alone though. I'll be with you every step of the way."

Phoebe held the reins in her hand. "Thank you. Now let's ride."

Charley held up his hand in protest. "I need a few more minutes. I have to get the saddle on my own horse."

The Golden Fox walked over to the third stall and let a beautiful white mare out of her stall. With ease, he mounted her with a quick hop up and rode her bareback. "Well, hurry up, we have a long way to go tonight!"

Charley rolled his eyes and shook his head, keeping a sarcastic thought to himself. Phoebe mounted her black stallion and listened to the howling wind outside. They had a long way yet to go, but together they had a chance. And a chance, even a small one, was better than none.

***

Napoleon cocked his head at me. "I don't have much time. Why are you on my island?"

I turned away from Jeremiah and faced the emperor. "We're here to rescue you from exile."

He threw his head back and laughed long and loud.

Jeremiah came close to me and said, "Maybe he didn't understand your English?"

I shrugged and Napoleon slapped his hand on his thigh and fought to control his laughter.

"No, I understand what you said perfectly." He coughed into his hand to clear his throat. "I am in utter awe of your complete idiocy."

If I had magic, I would have burned him to the spot. Unfortunately, for him, I did not have my powers. "If you do not need our assistance, then why were we sent here?"

"I don't know who sent you, but you've been sent on a fool's errand." He pointed his index finger back at the city behind him. "The people here love me, and I'm their emperor. I rule everything on this island."

"But we were told to help rescue—"

He cut me off with a wave of his hand and spoke over me. "Enough of this nonsense. I do not need your help in being rescued. I have heard the rumors about the Allies cutting off my funds, and the tide is turning. My spies have informed me that I'm to be banished to a remote island in the Atlantic. I think they see what I've done here on this little island and still fear me." He took his hat off and smoothed back his thinning hair. "I've developed the iron mines here, fixed the roads, and even overhauled the educational and legal systems. I've brought progress and prosperity, but still the Allies fear me."

Jeremiah waited for him to finish and said, "My little spies tell me that you've also built a small navy and army here…"

Napoleon clicked his tongue to the roof of his mouth and made a dismissive gesture with his hand. "That's nonsense. The few ships I've amassed are only to protect me from those who might come to take my life." His eyes glazed over for a moment. "I've overseen hundreds of thousands of men in battle, and the few hundreds I have here is nothing. But I've had enough. Tonight, I'm leaving with my men on the *Inconstant*."

"Are you headed back to France?" I asked with more politeness than I wanted.

"Oui, bien sûr!" He shook his head in frustration and stomped his foot. "Where else do think I would go? Of course, I'll return to France and eventually to Paris. Always for la France. Toujours."

I headed toward him on the sand and stood across from him. He wore his ceremonial sword but had no other weapons I could see. "I tire of your attitude." I placed my hand on his chest. I stood slightly taller than him and said, "For what you tried to do to my daughter, I will never forgive you, but I've been asked to help rescue you off this island. It's against my better judgment, but I'll do what I was asked because it's for the better good."

He grabbed my wrist and moved my hand off his chest. He did not act out of violence but kept his eye on me and then let go of me once clear of him. "We are relics both you and I. Our magic is gone, our powers depleted, and yet we both still fight. Why is that?"

Jeremiah stood behind me. I could just see him to the right of me. Ready to pounce, he had balled his fists but remained put, respecting my decision to confront the Emperor. "I often wonder that myself. Why do we still fight?"

He shook his head in disgust. "The world is in decay. All is in entropy and the years of reform I've instituted in the laws and codes will fall away. I gave all to my beloved France. Everything that I am and wanted to be will fade away in time." He smiled and looked deep into my eyes. "But still I fight and will not give up. Even when the fools rise up to oppress me. Do you want to know why I still fight for France?"

"Not really." The words left my mouth but I did not truly mean them. I softened and humored him. "I'll play along with you. Tell me, why do you?"

"For the people. All of the people. I've seen the future and I know what's coming…" He looked past me at something I could not see.

I almost turned around to check. "What's coming?"

He returned his attention on me. "The death of everything around us. It's coming like a wave. The sun will eat up the Earth, and we will all burn." He let the words settle into me and leaned closer to me, so much so, that our noses almost touched. "I despise you more than anything and had vowed to fight you till my last breath. When we last met, you took everything away from me. Everything."

I did not flinch from him. I steeled my gaze on him and replied, "No, I didn't. I left you your life. A chance to begin again. You have that chance now."

He sneered. "A life? My Joséphine is gone, my son in exile, and all I have built has been taken away."

I interrupted him. "But you still breathe. You still have a chance to right all that you have done."

"What are you saying?" He cocked his head to the right to listen better.

"If we work together, maybe we can stop the vision that you've seen. Maybe we can save everyone." I just started speaking because I didn't know what else to do. I had not seen the vision of the Earth being destroyed. I only knew what Jeremiah and Phoebe had told me. "I also no longer have my powers. We have cancelled each other out, and now we have a choice. We can fight and lose any chance we have of finding a way to prevent the vision you had, or we can work together."

"And you want to work together?" He laughed at me and pulled back.

"No, I don't. I would much rather kill you here." I did not back down from him. "My greatest desire would be to see your death. But if I kill you, then a chance to save people will have been lost." I shrugged my shoulders. "So, I will not kill you."

He reached for his ceremonial sword, but before I could react, Jeremiah lunged forward and grabbed his wrist. He held back the emperor's arm but did not advance on him farther. "Let's all be calm." Jeremiah spoke the words to both of us.

I took a step back and looked to my husband. "You're right. Our bickering is not going to help."

Jeremiah held Napoleon's arm away, and they still struggled. Their eyes locked, Napoleon furrowed his brow, and I knew what he tried to do. I had tried time and time again myself with the same test. Nothing could bring my magic back to me here. I could feel the energy within me, but I could not find a way to tap into it no matter how hard I tried.

"You will back away from me now!" Napoleon spat out the words.

Jeremiah refused to move and remained firm with his hold, forcing the emperor's hand down and away from his sword. He leaned his head closer to Napoleon's. "No."

Taking a quick step back, Napoleon dropped back and fell to the ground. Caught off guard, Jeremiah stumbled, and with a simple twist, the emperor slipped out of his hold. He drew his sword, holding it in a defensive posture.

Jeremiah knelt on one knee in the sand and kept his hands raised, waiting for Napoleon to charge him.

"You can't control minds anymore, can you?" I walked to Jeremiah's side and headed toward Napoleon. "And it eats at you. The power is just bubbling beneath the surface, but no matter how much you call it, scratch the surface for it, the magic will not come. Am I right?"

Napoleon kept his eye on Jeremiah but did not advance.

"It's only us here on this lonely beach." I reached out my hand. "Please, we've fought enough. If we need to work together, then let's do so."

He flicked his eyes at me for a moment but returned his attention on Jeremiah. "I will not. My guards will come find me soon, and I'll have you both arrested."

"Or we can work together." I kept my hand out to him but did not step any closer. I had sunk a bit into the sand, and I remained firm in my intention.

"Why should we work together?" He kept his sword pointed at Jeremiah but turned his head to me. "We are enemies and have nothing in common."

"No, that isn't true." I took another step toward him. "You have your son, and I have my daughter. We need to work together for our children's children." Another step and my right foot sank into the sand. "If you live, one day your son may rule France again. All the improvements you've made in your empire will last beyond your death. But you still can make more advancements, and together we can find a way to avoid the destruction you saw. For your son. For my Phoebe."

He kept the sword pointed at Jeremiah still. "All I have left is my anger and need for revenge."

"Think of your son in exile. Think of the future. Please." I leaned forward and offered my hand to him.

He rose to his full height and sheathed his sword, but he did not take my hand. He paused a moment, conflicted on what to do, and then took my hand. "I will work with you, but only because of my son."

"And I will work with you only because of my daughter." We shook on it. "We still hate each other, but for now, we need each other."

"Stand up." He gave the order to Jeremiah, and my husband slowly rose to his feet. I prayed that he would not rush the emperor and try to tackle him to the sand.

He did not and kept a stoic look on his face, saying not a word.

"Why do I need you both?" Napoleon put his hands at his side and relaxed. "Tonight, I leave for France, and in two days, I'll stand on her shores. Then all is set…"

"You need us because you haven't met the Cryshada yet." His confusion upon hearing the unfamiliar word could be read on his face. "There are creatures from another plane who are chasing after those of us trying to change the future."

"Magical creatures?" he asked.

"Yes. They are unlike anything you have ever seen, and now that you are set to leave this island, becoming a target again, then I expect you'll need our help in keeping them from killing you." I held nothing back. "That's why you need us."

He thought a moment and when he reached his decision said, "Come with me. We leave later tonight. I will get you food, clothing, and a place to rest. Once we leave this island, I'm never coming back. And if you stand in my way of reclaiming France and the rest of my empire, then I will stop you both no matter what these creatures are that you speak. Do we understand each other?"

"We do."

He turned and headed away back the way he had come on the beach.

We followed him at a distance, and Jeremiah leaned close to me and said, "Well, that went better than I expected."

I shook my head and quickly looked away, trying hard to stifle the giggle that bubbled up on my lips.

Chapter 11

Phoebe tiptoed across the foyer with her left hand up, ready to release the spell. Darkness filled the area ahead, and she moved forward slowly, and with purpose, ensuring that she did not knock into anything to wake him.

The Golden Fox led the way and walked forward with not a care in the world. At normal speed, he navigated around several obstacles in the dark, careful not to step on three books piled in front of the bed before him, and then folded his hands in front of him. "Well, we made it."

"Shhh!" Charley brought up the rear and had the most difficulty, but he made it halfway without knocking into anything, when Nicéphore Niépce sat up in bed.

He wore his nightclothes, and it took him a moment to orient himself. He ignored the Golden Fox, who stood only a few feet away, but said to Phoebe, "Who are you?"

She froze in her tracks like a thief caught in the night. "Hello." She held back a moment, unsure if she should use her magic.

Nicéphore Niépce threw off his covers and got out of bed. "I'll say again. Who are you?"

Charley reached Phoebe and whispered, "Zap him with your spell!"

The Golden Fox laughed and slapped his hand on his knee, but Nicéphore Niépce paid him no attention at all.

Phoebe still did not cast the spell and then stood up at her normal height, dropping her stealthy position. "My name is Phoebe."

Nicéphore Niépce took a few steps toward her and still did not see the Golden Fox who now was only a few inches away from him. "Why are you in my bedroom in the middle of the night with that man? Have you come to rob me?"

"Well, maybe persuade is a better phrase of words." Phoebe looked over her shoulder to Charley. "Umm, my friend and I would like to borrow your camera obscura."

"You're English spies then. I knew that they would come to try to steal my invention. Too damn slow on their own, they'd rather come and steal it from me in the middle of the night. I tell you that I—"

The Golden Fox touched Nicéphore Niépce's shoulder, and he suddenly stopped talking and froze in mid-sentence.

"There we go. I think that will be the best for everyone. I've had enough of guns and arguments over the last few days, and I'd rather just avoid the whole thing."

Nicéphore Niépce's eyes moved rapidly left and right, signaling that he could hear what was being said, but he could not move or speak.

"I was going to talk with him. I want him to know that we're not English spies who came here to steal his invention. Why couldn't we just tell him the truth?" Phoebe faced the Golden Fox.

"Because I sense that Napoleon and your mother have already met. They'll be headed to Paris soon, and we don't have time to play these games. We need to find the camera obscura and get out of here as quickly as we can." The Golden Fox snapped his fingers, and all the candles in the room ignited. The room slowly filled with a soft glow.

"Where do you think he keeps this thing and how big is it?" Charley had started to look at the desk across from the bed. "I mean is it big enough for a person to fit into, or can I hold it in the palm of my hand?"

"It's a wood box, shaped like a rectangle, and it's almost half your size." The Golden Fox searched around the bed thinking maybe the camera lay on the ground but found nothing.

"That's bigger than I had expected. How are we going to travel with it?" Phoebe searched by the window and then said, "I think I found it."

A muffled response came from Nicéphore Niépce, but none of what he tried to say was intelligible.

The Golden Fox rushed over to her and put his hands on the wooden box. A small cylinder protruded on the one end. "We'll have to be careful because it has a mirror inside."

"How do you know so much about this?" Charley came to join them and put his hand on the box tentatively. "And you say that this thing can suck up my soul?"

"No, no. That's not how it works." The Golden Fox flipped up a flap of wood on the top portion of the device. "It's only reflecting an image off of the mirror and shining it on this photochemical paper."

"I have no idea what you just said, but are you telling me that this device isn't magical?" Phoebe made certain not to put her hand by the front portion where the lens was.

"We're going to put our magic into it, and when we capture the image of Napoleon, then I'll use my magic to enchant it, and it'll be like a voodoo doll. We'll control the emperor if he decides to go rogue and try to take over all of Europe again. We'll have trapped his spirit."

Nicéphore Niépce mumbled and his voice hit a high pitch, but still no words could be understood from his attempt to communicate.

Charley thumbed toward Nicéphore Niépce's direction. "What about him? We can't just leave him like this."

The Golden Fox spun around on his right foot and shot a spell at Nicéphore Niépce. A golden shower of light hit him right in the chest, and he fell backward into bed. A moment later he started to snore. "There we go. He's now in a deep sleep, he'll think he had a dream, and then we'll be gone from here by the time he wakes up."

"But we'll have stolen his camera obscura, and he'll report it missing to the police." Phoebe still refused to touch the camera.

"We'll be long gone by the time he wakes." Gingerly, he lifted up the camera obscura and then placed it on the table. "It's heavier than I thought, but I think Charley can carry it."

"Why do I have to carry it?" Charley crossed his arms and shook his head.

"You are the strongest one here, and you won't be carrying it for long." The Golden Fox turned away from him and came up to Phoebe to talk with her. "What about you? Are you ready?"

Phoebe glanced back at Charley. "He could use some help in carrying the thing. That wasn't very nice of you."

"Ignore him for a moment." The Golden Fox leaned in closer and asked, "Can you bring us through the dreamline?"

"But he needs help. It's a heavy thing to carry." She pointed at the camera obscura but still would not touch it.

"Yes, yes, I can help him carry it. We only need to hold it long enough to get us through the dreamline, and then we'll meet up with your mother and Jeremiah." He took a deep breath and stopped talking, wanting to say more but did not.

Phoebe glanced outside the window and caught a cat walking across the path outside. The cat stopped to turn and look at her and then ran off in the night. "I don't know if I can do this or not. I can open the dreamline, but I don't know about traveling to the exact spot where my mother is…"

The Golden Fox took her hand in his and said, "The wheel goes round and round. That's what my mother used to tell me. We get older day by day, and we learn from our mistakes. We can take everything that we've learned and become afraid to try anymore, or we can keep learning. The challenge is that there are times when we'll need to make a mistake in order to grow. It's hard, but we have to push onward. If we want to keep the wheel going round, there needs to be movement. If we stop, then we don't grow."

Phoebe pulled her left hand from his and lit it up with magic. "She hasn't told me what I need to know. And she's been different the last year. Distant, withdrawn, and extremely unhappy."

"Losing one's magic is a difficult burden to carry. Some carry it different than others." He took her hand again in his. "What she has decided to do with her life is not your fault. You understand that, right?"

"But if I hadn't been captured by Napoleon, then she wouldn't have—"

"Enough of that. That's useless talk." The Golden Fox shook his head.

"I could go back through the dreamline and fix things. I could change it all. I have that power, so why don't I try?" Phoebe said.

"Then go do it. Go back to fix what was broken." The Golden Fox made way for her and backed up to give her space.

"You're not going to stop me?" Phoebe looked past the Golden Fox to Charley.

He came to her and pushed the Golden Fox out of his way. "What's wrong?"

"She wants to go back to fix what was broken." At seeing Charley's confused expression, he continued, "She can go back in the dreamline, stop her mother from giving up her powers, and then she'll get back to us in time for tea."

"Are you mad?" Charley asked. "I promised your mother that I would protect you and stay by your side. We need you to help us get back to Paris with this contraption so that we can stop Napoleon." He held her hand tightly. "Please, don't do this."

"She must do what she thinks is right." The Golden Fox stood back and did interfere. "Or do you want to force her to do something against what she believes will help?"

Charley took a step back and stared at Phoebe. "I'm only telling you what I know to be true. Listen to me. If I had a way to go back in time to save my daughter, I would want to do that, too. But I know it wouldn't solve anything. It would only make me selfish for pulling her spirit back to me. We can't go back and fix what was broken or lost. It's not right."

"A chronicler can do that and more. She can go back, fix what was wrong, then come back, and stop Napoleon. She has the power to do it. She just needs to get over her fear."

"I want to go." Phoebe faced Charley and put her hand on his chest. "Please let me do this. My mother gave up everything for me. She sacrificed all her magical powers, and I have a way of making that right for her again. I can fix this, and then she will be healed."

"Phoebe, please, don't do this. It's not right…" Charley pleaded.

"I'm sorry but I need to go. I've wondered about this for a long time, and I've held it off, but it makes sense to do this now. I've learned so much and know that I can fix this. I know it!" She held up her left hand, and the light from her magic shone bright and clear. White magic encircled her, and the dreamline opened at her command.

"If you won't listen to reason, then at least let me come with you. I can—" She rushed forward and he was too late.

Phoebe stepped through the dreamline and vanished. Charley's last glimpse was of her turning to him and shaking her hand in warning for him not to follow. She vanished in a brilliant display of color, and in a heartbeat, the crack in the dreamline vanished.

Charley spun around with his fists in the air. "Why did you convince her to do this? It makes no sense!"

"I know that and you know that, but she doesn't." The Golden Fox sat down on the nearest chair. "Sometimes people have to learn the hard way. No matter how much you tell them, show them, or try and convince them, they'll still not believe you. She'll be back soon enough."

"But what if she doesn't make it back?" Charley's anger deflated, and he slumped against the windowsill.

"You have known Phoebe much longer than I. Do you think that she will let you down?" The Golden Fox folded his hands in his lap and nodded over to where she had vanished. "When she realizes what she's done and how she's stranded you here, she'll come back for you."

"I have known her a long time, but she's torn up about her mother, and she's not thinking clearly. You and I might have to start thinking about getting a horse and carriage to get us back to Paris." Charley stared at the spot where Phoebe had left. "I don't think she'll be back in time."

The Golden Fox shook his head and winked at Charley. "Trust me, Phoebe will do the right thing. We have nothing to fear. She'll be back before we know it."

"And if you're wrong?"

"I'm not." The Golden Fox folded his arms behind his head and then asked, "Has she ever let you down before?"

"No, she hasn't." Charley walked over to a chair next to the Golden Fox and sat down. "But she's young and everyone makes mistakes. She might choose differently this time."

"I guess we'll see then." He closed his eyes for a moment and then opened them quickly and said, "But what does your heart tell you?"

Charley thought a moment and smiled. "She'll be back."

The Golden Fox nodded and closed his eyes again, resting. "See? I told you so."

Both men sat back and waited, each trying to do his best to count the passage of time, and neither doing it well.

***

The dreamline opened and Phoebe fell through. Barely recognizable due to her youth, Cinderella sat at a desk writing in a book. She tapped the tip of the quill to the page, thinking a moment, and then wrote as quickly as she could.

Phoebe watched in awe. Only a few years older than she was now, her mother glanced out the window to her left and thought a moment. Afraid to move and be heard, Phoebe hung back against the wall in shadow. Lost in thought, Cinderella scribbled furiously, and Phoebe recognized for the first time that her mother wrote left-handed. She could not recall her mother ever writing during her upbringing, and yet here she was writing away.

"Precious, isn't she?"

Jumping in fright, she nearly let out a cry. Phoebe turned around, and Mab, queen of the fey, stood behind her. The wall itself had become rendered and split by the approaching thread of the dreamline.

"What are you doing here?" Phoebe asked. She kept her left fist clenched, ready to defend herself.

"Several minutes from now, an older incarnation of your mother will arrive, and she'll stop her younger self from ever using the journal to discover her magical powers. She'll lock that part of herself away to stop Napoleon from ever gaining her ability to travel the dreamline." Mab exited the wall and the dreamline closed, and as she waved her hand, little color lights drifted in front of them. "Don't worry, I've locked us off from your mother. Though she's so engrossed in her writing that I don't think she'd hear us anyway."

"Are you here to stop me?" Phoebe took her eyes off her mother for a moment to watch Mab's reaction.

"You have traveled from the future to come back to stop your mother from making her sacrifice to stop Napoleon. Do I have that right?" She shook her head and then tapped the side of her head with her index finger. "Think about what you're about to do."

"If I let my mother keep her power, then she would be happy again. She'd have her magic, and all would be okay." Phoebe paused and then said, "I can't even sell the lie to myself."

Mab put her arm around Phoebe to comfort her. "If you did stop your mother and her younger self did discover magic again, then what?"

"I know, I know." Phoebe turned away in shame. "Everything that she fought for would be ruined. Napoleon would get her power, and he'd have the ability to travel the dreamline. All of history could be rewritten to how he chose."

"Exactly." Mab lowered her voice and said, "For what it's worth, I tried to do all sorts of things with my powers and failed. The best thing for me was to realize that I couldn't solve the world's problems or save anyone. I could only take care of myself. I know that won't mean anything to you. No one ever listens to the advice of another. Well, at least it seems that way…" She smiled faintly.

"I just want my mother to be happy. She gave up everything to stop Napoleon and to protect me. She wants her magic back, and I could help her if I could, but that would mean that Napoleon would win." An idea came to Phoebe. "What if I gave my magic to my mother? I don't need it. I could—"

Mab laughed. "You're so young, you know? I can see much of your mother in you. Yes, you could give her your power, but you'd be sacrificing your future for hers."

"But she already sacrificed so much for me. I want to help her."

"Then let her go." Mab flicked her hands out in front of her in the symbolic casting of something away.

"I can't do that. I'm not going to leave her when she needs me the most!" Phoebe lowered her voice for fear that she would disturb Cinderella, who still wrote feverishly in her journal, in the corner.

"She needs to come to terms with her own decision." Mab turned back to look over her shoulder. "She'll be here soon. You can stay if you want, but she needs you in the present and not here in the past."

Phoebe opened her hand and prepared to release her magic. She could rip through the quiet spell and then convince the younger version of her mother to protect her journal. It would be so easy to do, but then…

She lowered her hand and let her magic drain out of her. "I just want her to be happy."

"You can't fix that for her. But if you take care of yourself, as a mother, she'll be glad to see you well." Mab opened a passage through the dreamline behind them and gently pushed Phoebe toward the opening. "Let her go. Take care of yourself, and by doing that, you'll be helping your mother. Trust me."

Phoebe walked through the dreamline and already the room started to fade away into the deep, dark oblivion of the past. "I will."

Queen Mab faded from view and Phoebe's last view of her was her reassuring smile. The floor dropped out beneath her, and she fell into the swirling mass of the dreamline. Colors faded into blackness, and she redirected her thoughts, listening to where she needed to go. Charley. She could sense his presence, and a bright golden ray of energy protected him and stood beside her friend. The Golden Fox had lit her way back home to them. She closed her eyes, focused her power, and flew back to them, knowing that she had chosen wisely.

Chapter 12

I stared out at the sea, thinking. The moonlight reflected on the still water, and barely rocking, the *Inconstant* cut through the sea. I closed my eyes and thought about Phoebe and my life.

"Are you cold?" Jeremiah came behind me, and I turned to see him offering me a heavy blanket.

"Yes, I am." I accepted his gift and placed it on my shoulders, wrapping it around me. The night air still bit at my nose.

We stood there together, side by side, watching the dark ocean. Up above us, thousands of stars filled the sky, and I turned my head upward seeing if I could make out any of the constellations.

"We'll be reaching land soon." Jeremiah spoke half-heartedly, and I could hear the worry in his voice.

"I know. Napoleon is probably speaking to his men in the galley below us, inspiring them to retake France and the empire." I laughed and shook my head. "Where did I go so wrong?"

"What do you mean?" Jeremiah still only stood next to me.

I wanted him to hold me, but he kept his distance. "Sometimes I look at my life and wonder what I could have done differently to have more balance in it." I turned to face him and placed my hand on his coat. "I've squandered away my youth fighting faeries, warlocks, and an emperor. I've left no time for me."

Jeremiah leaned in toward me and our shoulders touched. He took my hand in his, but we both wore gloves. "If you could have anything, what would you want?"

I would have you. I fought back my first response and buried it deep within. Instead I took a moment to think, glanced back up at the sky, and then said, "I'd go back to the prairies of America. I remember holding Phoebe when she was a baby, and the wind would whip through the fields of wheat. I would just stand there, listening to the sound of the wheat bending in the wind and hitting each other. It was a quiet sound, and I spent hours from our hilltop, looking down at the ripples in the waves of wheat. Nothing could harm us then. We just had time to be. What about you?"

"I wish we could truly be together again." He turned me toward him, our bodies pressed up against each other. "How we both felt when we first were together. That joy of being alive and the freedom of being able to do whatever we wanted. I miss that…"

His words trailed off, and then he leaned in to kiss me, and I opened up to him. I let out a slight sigh and pulled him tight against me, kissing him as though it would be our last time. Emotion rose up within me, and I struggled to hold back the tears. I would not let him see me cry. I had rescued myself in the past and did not need him to save me. He had made his decision and I had made mine. If we were to stay together, time would tell.

Our kiss lasted long, and when we pulled apart, he took my face in his hands. "I don't want to lose you."

"Then don't go." I said the words that I had so wanted to say. They had been bottled up within me.

"I'm tempted not to, but I need take some time for myself. I need that." He went to say more but shook his head. "I'm not leaving forever. It's only temporary."

"Do you know how many people have said that to me in my lifetime?" I pulled away from him and watched the bow of the ship cut through the sea. "My parents said that to me, and I lost them for good. Both of them."

"I'm not your parent but your husband." He put his arm around me and said, "Look at me."

His words weren't a command, but a plea.

I turned toward him and the wind caused me eyes to tear up, or at least that's what I told myself. He pulled off the glove and wiped the tear from my eye.

"I'm afraid." I let the words out, closed my eyes, and said what I had hidden for too long. "I don't know if I can make it without my magic. I feel lost and hollow inside. And everything around me is going at their normal pace, but I am stuck. I'm losing you. Phoebe and I aren't grounded. And I can't get these fears out of my head. I'm trying so hard to fight them, but I'm doubting myself. I'm weak and I hate that. I despise that about myself."

"You're not weak." He said no more.

"Yes, I am. I'm nothing without my magic, and I've tried to get along, but it's not working. I'm broken inside and there isn't anything I can do to fill up that hole within me. No matter what I do, it's never enough. Never." I opened my eyes and let him really see me. My face crinkled and I let loose a sob.

He held me close and rubbed the small of my back. He said no words but comforted me by giving me the space to be, and I appreciated that.

The moon shone up above, the sea rocked us gently on the boat, and the stars paid witness to my downfall. I could not keep out the hurt and the pain any longer.

"I can't pretend anymore. My heart is broken and I'm afraid of who I have become." I raised my left hand and shook it violently. "Everything is gone from me. The magic is sealed off, and I regret the decision that I made to get rid of my power. I hate that I sacrificed it all to save everyone, and that's so selfish of me. I should be thankful that Phoebe survived and Napoleon was stopped. But now all that we worked on together is being undone. He's free again and headed back to his home. It's tearing me apart inside that I risked it all, for what?"

"You are not weak or selfish." Jeremiah took my left hand, pulled off my glove, and kissed my palm. "I know that you are beautiful and wonderful, but do you really see that? Do you really know that?" His curly hair blew in the wind and the moonlight lit up his face.

I blocked out the hurt, disappointment, and frustration that swirled around me. I had fought hard in life to get to where I was, but I still struggled at times with the simplest of things. I squeezed his hand, and both our fingers were cold. "I do, but it's not that simple." I took a deep breath and faced him. He could see all the way into my soul if he wanted. I opened for him and stripped away the mask I wore most the time, pretending I was okay. "There are times when I'm okay, but then I'm pulled back. I think of my mother, how she left me, and then I fight against wondering why I wasn't good enough for her. I know that I could do nothing to have made her stay and it wasn't my fault that she died, but there's still a part of me that struggles with this. Now I'm a parent and I look at Phoebe, and I've done the same thing. I've distanced myself from her. I've not let her know the struggle I go through. She's not dumb, I know she sees it, but instead I have hidden it away from her and you, thinking that I was fine all this time."

The words came out of me like weights, but as soon as I spoke them, my heart ached a little less.

"I have always been at your side, but you want to go places that I cannot." He did not pull back and spoke his mind. "I cannot spend the rest of my life chasing after magic that may or may not come back to you. I need to be present here and for me to spend time with all that's around me. I have my own demons to fight and need to be grounded. That is why I must go."

"But I don't want you to go. I want you to stay. I love you." I had been afraid to share this before.

"And I love you. But I need to be certain that if I stay it's because I want to and not because of some other reason. I need some time to think this all through and my distance will also give you a chance to decide whether you want to live with me or not." He squeezed my hand and then let me go.

"Where else would I go?" I laughed.

"Do not pretend with me." He shook his head and pointed up at the moon. "I saw your face when we were on the Other side. When you had your magic back, you became a different person. I know it was hard for you to come back here, but you have to decide on whether you want to go back there and stay. You'll have your powers there, but you'd also have to leave everything else behind."

"I won't lie to you. I have thought about going there once this is all done. But there is so much I would miss here." I stared up at the inconstant moon. Its face changed so often through the course of the month, and I would leave all I knew to live in the land of the fey. Could I do that and would I want that just to have my powers back?

"I cannot go there. It reminds me too much of Mab and of the time I had with her. I don't ever wish to go back there and I want to remain here. I'm tired of fighting and just want some time to settle down and rest. I'm exhausted from all of this." He pointed down below deck. "And there's Napoleon and his troops. There will be war again, and I want nothing of it, but again we're pulled back into the maelstrom. I only have so much to give. Let other people step up and be the heroes. My time is nearly done."

I had never heard him speak so freely before of how he felt. I watched him, truly listened to what he said and how he acted, and then folded my hands on the rail in front of me. "Then you must do what you think is right. I looked right at him, through him to his core, and said, "You do not have to stay here and help me. I am fine on my own. I can see this through to the end. But I will do what is necessary to save—"

"Save what? And how many times? We keep sacrificing ourselves for the greater good for what? Let someone else fight these battles. I'm tired and have had enough."

"You and Phoebe both told me that there is great danger. You convinced me to do this, and now you want to back away?"

"Maybe I was wrong." He thought a moment and said, "Being on the Other side changed all that for me. Seeing Ignatius and the Crystal Prince, there are powers beyond what I can understand, and I'm tired of seeing everyone I love caught in the middle. I want all of us out. Let someone else fight for us."

"And who's going to do that?"

He raised his voice, gesturing down below. "Let Napoleon on his damn quest to take his empire back over do it. He still wants to fight. He'll waste his life, and we can go back to living a normal lie."

I caught him in the slip of a tongue. "You mean a normal life, don't you?"

He shook his head. "Yes, that's what I meant."

I stepped back from him and the words tumbled out of me before I could stop them. "Then if you're too afraid to be here, you should go. Leave us once we hit land and go back home. Find that peace that you want, and I'll handle it from here. I don't need you."

"Yes, I know that. You don't need anything except that damn magic of yours. You crave it like laudanum." He pointed his finger at me, shaking it. "And no matter what happens, you still don't let it go. The only reason why you fight so hard is that you hope there could be a way to bring your magical abilities back here from the Other side. I'm right, aren't I?"

As foolish as it sounded, that was my secret wish. I kept quiet and lowered my head, ashamed.

He shook his head and laughed. "I knew it. You'll do anything to get your magic back."

"No, I won't. If anything, I've done the opposite. I gave it all away by shutting myself off from it. I sacrificed it all."

Jeremiah scoffed at my words. "Really? Or is that what you tell yourself? I'm tired of arguing with you. I will stay with you until we get to Paris and meet up with Phoebe and Charley. After that, I'm leaving."

He did not even wait for me to say another word but stormed off, anger swirling around him like a storm brewing, and left me standing out in the cold winter night. I gathered the blanket he had given me and wrapped myself up in it and fought back a mixture of tears and a swell of anger. The two fused into one, and I cursed up at the stars not knowing what else to do.

***

Phoebe fell into Charley's waiting arms, stumbling out of the dreamline. He propped her up on her feet but said nothing.

The Golden Fox had his hand on the camera obscura and asked, "Well?"

Sheepishly, she glanced away from both of them. "I was wrong. I couldn't change the past. I didn't realize what would happen if I did selfishly make things go the way I wanted."

"Lesson learned then." The Golden Fox waved his hand in the air. "There is no time to dwell on that. We need to leave." He turned his head up and sniffed. "I can smell him. He's almost back in France."

Charley ignored the Golden Fox, lowered his voice, and asked, "Are you okay? Really?"

She met his gaze and let out a smile. "I am. I was a fool…"

"Enough of that sort of talk." He shook his head. "There is enough guilt to go around for things we have all done wrong. Time to let it go. We need to leave, and I'm worried that you might be tired."

"I am tired." Phoebe nodded over to the Golden Fox who continued to sniff the air. "Looks like we all could use some rest soon, but I need to get us to Paris."

The Golden Fox raised his voice and smacked his hand down on his thigh. "And that does it. The emperor is officially back in France." He put out his hands and closed his eyes. "Can you not feel the ripple going through the ground?"

Phoebe closed her eyes and reached out her senses, listening, and held her hands out. "No, I can't. We must get going then."

She spun her hand in the air, and effortlessly the dreamline opened for her. The magic tendrils of light that danced around her hand had turned blue. Phoebe closed her eyes and reached out, searching for her mother. She could see her face, her wan smile, and the small dimple in her right cheek. Her hair fluttered in the wind, and she reached out to touch her mother's hand. The imagined connection made, Phoebe opened her eyes, startled. "I can sense her now. I don't know if it's remnants of the magic she had from the Other side, but I can see her clear as day. She and Jeremiah are in France."

"Are they in Paris yet?" Charley asked. He glanced over his shoulder, listening for someone to discover them in Nicéphore Niépce's house, but no one came. The night, silent and dark, brought no curious neighbors to them. They were alone.

"No, but they're on their way." Phoebe turned her head, as if listening, and she went still, a worried look crossed her face. "Something is wrong though."

The Golden Fox rushed over to her. "What is it that you see?"

"I don't see anything, but I sense there's danger—a lot of it." Phoebe crinkled her nose and squeezed her eyes shut. "I can't see any more. But we should go now before I lose them."

Charley went over to the camera obscura and lifted the one end. "I think I can carry this by my—"

The glass window in front of him shattered, and an explosion right outside the house ripped through the surrounding area. Charley stumbled and fell to his knees, covering the camera obscura with his body. The Golden Fox threw himself in front of Phoebe to shield her from the blast. He crumbled to his knees, taking the brunt of the force. Though night, a red pulsing glow lit up the room, and they all heard the unmistakable sound of a crystal whirlwind coming to life.

A loud bellow quickly followed, and the wall nearest the window buckled and exploded inward.

"It's a Cryshada. Run!" The Golden Fox threw up his hands and cast forth the first protective spell that came to mind. A golden shield of light formed over them like an umbrella. Swirling pieces from the Cryshada's breathing atmosphere bounced off the shield and flew across the room embedding themselves into the nearest wall.

Phoebe twisted the dreamline in an open and locked position and then turned her attention on the Cryshada. She dipped into her magic, digging deep into the recesses of her soul, and found a spring of untapped energy. Their need fueled her power, and she pointed at the Cryshada and let loose a stream of blue energy that crackled as it ripped through the air, tearing through the creature's shield and hitting it in its side.

Smashing its two fists together in rage, the Cryshada roared in pain and stumbled back into the opening it had created in the wall.

Charley took the moment to gather the camera obscura in his arms and rushed forward, carrying the instrument awkwardly in his arms. "I need help!"

The Golden Fox grabbed the other end of the camera obscura, and together they brought it to the dreamline.

"Just go! I'll be right there." Phoebe turned around and rocked back on her heels. The Cryshada had stumbled forward and raised its arm to attack.

A crystal javelin flew toward Phoebe. It pierced the Golden Fox's shield, shattering the protective spell with ease, and Phoebe let loose a blue bolt of pure energy. When her magic hit the javelin, it shattered into millions of pieces.

Charley handed the camera obscura to the Golden Fox and pushed him in. "I have her. Just go!"

The Golden Fox nodded and rushed through the dreamline, disappearing from the room. Charley ran toward Phoebe, and the Cryshada released its second javelin at Phoebe. Sweat had formed on her forehead, and she raised her arm, trying to fire off another spell but failed. Charley lunged at her, knocking her to the floor, and the javelin hit him and passed straight through his chest.

"Got you!" He hit the floor hard and quickly pulled them both to their feet. Blood streamed down his chest. He could feel his life leaving him quickly. "Go and finish what we started."

Phoebe pulled him with her, and the Cryshada, out of weapons, rushed toward them with its head down. It bellowed again, a deep rumbling sound in its chest that would wake anyone in the house, and headed directly at them.

Charley grimaced in pain and held his chest, trying to stop the wound from bleeding. He stumbled the last few steps and pushed Phoebe into the dreamline. She desperately clutched onto him, and they both fell through the dreamline, traveling in the in-between. Brilliantly bright red, purple, and blue lights swirled around them, and a whoosh of sound enveloped them. The journey ended fast, and they stumbled out of the portal onto a countryside dirt road. Charley collapsed to his knees, and Phoebe rushed to hold him.

"No, no, no! Please." She did not know what else to say, and she tried to stop his blood from pouring out of his wound.

Charley, white as a sheet, sweat covering his face, held Phoebe's hand. "Tell Ginny and the girls that I love them. Tell them I don't regret a thing. Tell them not to be angry at me for not coming back. I will always love them..."

He closed his eyes and squeezed Phoebe's hand and fell back to the floor. The Golden Fox placed the camera obscura on the frost-covered ground and ran over to Phoebe. "What happened?"

"He pushed me out of the way and was hit." She put her hand on his chest and screamed. Her hand turned white-hot and she focused her power into Charley's lifeless body. "He can't die. I must save him. He has a family to be with and raise."

She placed her right hand on her left and released all of her magic into Charley. Every bit of energy coursed through every vein and artery, filling him up with light and strength. The Golden Fox held Charley's hand for a few moments and then, with reverence, folded both hands on his chest. He stood back with his head bowed and kept quiet.

Phoebe's magic burned through all of Charley's body, and she fell back, tired and spent. She bruised her tailbone and stretched forward to grab Charley's hand. "You can wake up now. I'll take you straight home to Ginny and the girls."

Eyes shut, his face was turned away from her. She shook him, but Charley did not wake.

The Golden Fox put his arm around her. "Phoebe…"

"No, he can't be dead. I can't let that happen." She stood up and pulled away. "I'm a chronicler like my mother. I'll go back in time to save him. I can fix this. I have to."

She took a deep breath and willed the dreamline to open. Her hand blinked out and nothing happened.

"Phoebe, he's gone." The Golden Fox put himself between her and Charley's body. "Trust me, once someone is gone, there is nothing to be done except let them go."

"But I just need to rest. I can go back. I'm a chronicler…" Her words trailed off and she faced the Golden Fox. "You can help me. Together we can do it."

"I tried to do that when I lost your grandmother. I became obsessed with bringing her back. But no matter how much magic you or I have, there is no way to get the person back." He put his hands up and remained blocking Charley from her. "I know you are hurting right now. We need to let him go."

Phoebe's lip trembled and tears streamed down her cheek. She wiped her nose on the back of her hand, and when she exhaled, steam came out of her mouth. Sidestepping the Golden Fox, she knelt beside Charley and placed her hands on his chest. "I'm so sorry. I can't save you. I've failed you and I'm so sorry for that." She paused for a moment to wipe the tears from her eyes. "I will tell Ginny and the girls that you love them. I will share how brave you were saving me and I will never forget what you did."

She reached for his left hand and took off his wedding ring, placing it in her pocket.

The Golden Fox knelt beside Charley and placed his hand on his forehead. He mumbled a few words and a yellow light, like the sun, encased Charley's body. The light disappeared and the Golden Fox looked up. "His body will be protected now. No animal or person will disturb him. I've marked this spot and we can return for him to bring him home when all of this is done."

He stood up and walked to the center of the dirt road. In either direction, he could see nothing. "Are you ready?"

Phoebe kept her head down but walked over to him. "I don't know."

A trumpet blast broke the silence, and from behind them, three riders on horses came toward them. The Golden Fox waved his hand and pointed at the camera obscura. For a moment the instrument glowed and then returned to its normal color. "I've hidden the camera with my magic."

"I'll talk to the soldiers. You stand back." Phoebe met the three men on horseback. They wore uniforms and stopped their horses before her.

The closest soldier pulled his rifle off his back and aimed it at her. "Who are you?"

"We are just traveling on the road and mean no harm." Phoebe kept her hands up in the air. "Who are you?"

"We are the emperor's advance guard. He has returned to France to save his people." The soldier kept his rifle pointed at Phoebe.

Smiling and putting her hands together in prayer, she replied, "Vive l'empereur! Please, we might not have much, but bring us to him, and we'll join his ranks."

The soldiers laughed at her words and their leader shrugged. "Come with us then and we'll bring you to him." He offered him his hand and pulled her up onto his horse.

The Golden Fox glanced over to the camera obscura and said, "We have a gift for the emperor. Can you bring a cart?"

Phoebe kept quiet and held her breath.

"What type of gift?" The soldier she rode with asked.

The Golden Fox stepped away from the camera obscura and smiled pointing at the large box. "It's an instrument that will play music." He pointed at the viewer. "You look in and you'll see a little ballerina dancing to music. We were headed to Grenoble now to share it with the mayor. It's a gift worthy of the emperor."

"He will be pleased with the gift." Phoebe smiled and patted the soldier's arm.

"Where is your horse and cart?" He addressed Phoebe and kept his gun trained on the Golden Fox.

"We had a disagreement with our third partner. He took the other two instruments and left us out on the road with the one left." She smiled again at him and pleaded with her hands together. "Please, we need your help. We've been on this road for the last hour trying to carry the gift to the city but need help. You've saved us both!"

The soldier lowered his gun and said to one of his comrades, "Head back and send up a cart." He slung his rifle on his back and took Phoebe's hand in his. "We'll help you."

She smiled at him and fought back tears. "Thank you. It's been a difficult morning for us being stranded on the road."

The Golden Fox walked up to the nearest soldier and raised his hand. "Here you go, help me up."

The soldier turned his rifle on the Golden Fox and fired. The bullet pierced right through him and he fell back to the ground.

"No!" Phoebe screamed, but the soldier clamped his hand over her mouth and kicked his horse away.

She turned back and could not see much with the horse galloping so fast. She closed her eyes and tried to call forth her magic, but she was spent. She went limp against the soldier and did not fight him. There would be a time and a place for revenge, but for now, she would not resist and needed to rest. Once she had her strength back, she would unleash her magic on him and burn him down to his bones. But for now, she would play along. The horse galloped along the dirt road and she kept her eyes closed listening to the breathing of the horse, biding her time for when she would destroy all of them around her. No one would survive when she was finished with them. No one.

Chapter 13

I shivered from the cold and wrapped my coat tighter around me. Jeremiah marched with the other soldiers, within eyesight, but he kept his distance from me. Days had passed since we had arrived in France, and still we did not talk much. I prayed that Phoebe and Charley were fine and that we would soon meet up with them.

"You look upset. What is wrong?" Napoleon brought his horse next to mine.

"I'm fine." I glanced away from Jeremiah and smiled at Napoleon.

"I might not have my magic any longer, but I can still tell when people are lying." Several of his personal guard rode on horseback by him but gave him enough space to give us a semblance of privacy.

I turned away from him and looked straight ahead at the more than seven hundred soldiers marching on the road ahead. "I would rather not discuss it."

"You and I are both cut from the same cloth. We put up walls between people, ensuring that we have our way." He straightened his hat on his head and, out of habit, placed his hand in his jacket. "My wife is dead, my son exiled to Austria, and there's a king on the throne again. All that I have worked so hard to build has been destroyed, razed, and erased. But I still do not give up. I will see France rise again."

"Do you not tire of hearing yourself talk?" I faced him and made certain that I kept my words low and direct. "Why can you not just agree to live in peace and fade away from history?"

He laughed and shook his head. "Because I'm destined to do great things, and I will always rise to that challenge. Before I lost my powers, I had a vision that I would regain control of France, and I will set everything right again."

"I wish I understood why my daughter wanted me to help you." I shook my head and thoughts of Phoebe came to mind. "Without my magic, I don't know if she is even alive. I have only the hope that she will meet us in Paris. And the sooner that I can be done with you, the better."

Napoleon smiled and nodded. "No one is forcing you or Jeremiah to stay with me. Both of you can leave and go your own ways. I don't need either of you. My destiny will be won by marching on Paris, and the people will claim me as their emperor. I have foreseen it. It is my destiny." He paused and caught himself. "Forgive me, I'm preoccupied with my plans for regaining France. But to help you, I have good news. My advance guards have found Phoebe. They are bringing her to us now and should be here soon."

I kept my eye on Jeremiah. He kept to himself on his horse, riding close to us, but staying out beyond the emperor's personal guards. He had a rifle slung on his back and a pistol at his side.

"That is good news, and I look forward to being reunited with her soon." I tried to keep my voice level and contain my excitement.

Napoleon laughed and shook his head. "You don't trust me and I can understand why. You and I will never fully trust each other, but we do need to work together, and I will honor my word to you."

"What is your word to me? What do you promise?" I confronted him directly and held nothing back.

He was taken somewhat aback by the forcefulness in my response and flinched. "I will not harm Phoebe, Jeremiah, or you."

"What about our friend Charley who was with her?" I could not keep the worry from my voice.

"He was not with them. My advance guards only sent back a message that your daughter was found." He fumbled in his jacket and took out a piece of paper, reading it to ensure he had not missed something. He finished and then said no more.

"You said that they will be here soon?" I asked. By habit, I averted my eyes to Jeremiah. He sat straight in his saddle and had moved his hand to his thigh. He looked prepared to spring into action, expecting danger at any turn.

"Yes, I expect that they'll be here within the hour." He put the paper in his hands away. "You'll be reunited with your daughter, and then we'll head to Grenoble and prepare for our march to Paris. From there, I'll take back my empire."

"And then all of Europe will rise up again to overthrow you. Your reign will not last." I shook my head in disgust.

He shot me an angry glance. "Do not tempt me. I'm agreeing to work with you and ensure that you and your close friends are kept safe. I'd advise you not to push me, or I might renegotiate our truce."

For a moment, I feared that if I had a knife, I would have run my horse into his and stabbed him in the neck. I fought hard to clear away my fantasies and focused on what I could. "My daughter wanted me to help you and I will. I don't fully understand why, but I will trust her message from the future."

He cut me off and added. "And we shall work together. With your daughter under my protection, all of us will head back to Paris, and I will set my plans in motion." He rubbed his hands together to stay warm. "All is coming together according to my vision."

Out of the corner of my eye, Jeremiah stood up in his stirrups and covered his forehead to see something up ahead. A flash of lightning crackled overhead, and the resounding boom shook me in my saddle. The horses became spooked, and each of us tried to control them from galloping off. I pulled the reins tight and then leaned forward rubbing the neck of my horse.

"It's okay. Calm, calm." I stayed low whispering into his ears.

Another flash of lightning materialized overhead, and for a few seconds I was blinded. The loud resounding thunderclap crashed above us as a sudden blast of brilliant red light filled my vision. I could not see from all the light, and the wind whipped up, swirling snow up from the ground into the sky. The sound deafened me, and the ground shook with a tremendous rattle as though a giant had punched the ground in anger.

Covering my eyes, I held tight onto the neck of my horse. Seconds passed and I tried to see, but the red light became too intense. At least a half-dozen spots around me glowed too brightly as though lava had burst out of the ground. I heard men scream as the wind died down, and the unmistakable sound of the swirling wind of the Cryshada rose above the men's shouts.

Six Cryshada surrounded us, their swirling atmospheres of tiny crystals swirling around them. They charged toward us and I willed my horse to the right, out of the direct path of the approaching creatures. Ahead on the dirt road, dozens of men stood up, aimed, and fired off their rifles at the attacking Cryshada. Hundreds of soldiers still fought to regain their purchase from having been knocked to the ground from the earthquake.

Napoleon drew his sword and shouted a command. His personal guards formed around him and fired their rifles at the approaching Cryshada. The bullets pierced through, shattering the crystal creatures, but still they charged.

I had no weapon and no magic. I had never imagined where my death would take place, but I guessed that I no longer had to wonder. I would not last more than a few seconds with any of the creatures. They would tear through me like paper, and I would die alone. I had not only failed myself but also Phoebe in the future.

Kicking the sides of my horse, I urged him onward and headed off the road. Another flash of red light blinded me for a few seconds, and I glanced away to stem off blindness. When I looked back again, hundreds of smaller crystalline creatures had materialized flying in the sky. Before Napoleon's troops could reload, the small faerie-like creatures fired arrows from the bows they carried. Dozens of men fell to the ground, and the rout appeared complete.

I glanced back and tried to find Jeremiah in the chaos. He had swerved around the nearest Cryshada and rushed toward Napoleon. His personal guard had killed four of the charging Cryshada, but the remaining two fired off their javelins killing three of his guard. Napoleon's horse was struck by a fourth javelin, and his horse went down hard. He tumbled off and quickly scampered to his feet, pulling out a pistol he had hidden in his jacket.

Aiming at the nearest Cryshada that rushed toward him with its arms outstretched, he fired. The bullet ripped through the creature's chest, and it fell down, smashing into a pile of dead horses. The creature's atmosphere shredded the carcasses until the Cryshada's glowing globes on its shoulders flickered and went out.

The remaining Cryshada changed direction and lunged toward Napoleon. From all the mayhem, Jeremiah rushed forward on his horse, steadied himself, and took his shot. Firing off his rifle, the bullet pierced through the creature's head, and it fell forward, dead by the time it hit the ground. Still charging toward Napoleon, he slung his rifle on his back and then leaned over with his arm out as he approached the emperor.

Napoleon reached up and leaped in time for Jeremiah to pull him up into the saddle. Nearly falling off, Jeremiah pulled Napoleon back into the center and saved him. I slowed my horse so Jeremiah could catch up, and we rode close together, but at full speed.

"We have to go back!" Napoleon shouted the words in the wind, but neither of us listened to him.

He glanced back over at what remained of his victory force, and for a moment, I felt a twinge of compassion for him. The attacking faeries had decimated hundreds of men. Only about a third of his army still remained. None of the creatures came after us. Instead they remained in an organized pattern in the sky and took turns flying in to release more crystalline arrows at Napoleon's soldiers.

We headed toward a small band of trees and once hidden behind them slowed our horses down.

Napoleon hung his head and then heard me near and looked up. "This wasn't supposed to happen. I saw the future and I was to retake France again. I had it all planned. Everything would go my way."

Jeremiah confronted him and said, "Looks like your plans have been changed."

"What are those creatures?" Napoleon turned back, trying to look through the trees, but we headed down a small hill and could not see the battle behind us.

"They're creatures from the Other side." I kept my voice low and matched my horse's speed to that of Jeremiah's. "It seems that now we see that your future isn't coming to be and I'm better understanding why Phoebe wanted us to help you."

"Where is Phoebe?" Jeremiah stopped his horse and asked Napoleon directly. When the emperor remained silent, Jeremiah kept his voice low and firm. "These creatures have come for all of us. If we don't work together, they'll destroy everything in their path. Tell us where Phoebe is."

Napoleon relented. "We were to meet her and my advance scouts on the road to Grenoble."

I held the reins tightly with my right and then pointed at the road. "Then let's head in that direction on the main road. We might find them before the Cryshada catch up to us."

"Non, I have to go back to my men!" Napoleon struggled to turn around, but Jeremiah held him in place on the horse.

"We can't go back to help them. We'll be killed as well." Jeremiah held the reins of his horse tightly in his left hand and restrained Napoleon with his right. "We have to go or their sacrifice will be in vain."

"Merde!" Napoleon spat and then stopped struggling.

"Now hold on and we're getting out of here as quickly as we can." Jeremiah gently kicked his horse's side to increase the animal's speed.

Napoleon tried to turn back, but there was nothing to see except the hill, trees, and a light coating of snow that covered the ground.

I could hear rifles firing off back at the battle scene, but already the noise became less and less. All of Napoleon's men would be dead soon, and I didn't want us to be anywhere near there after the battle was over.

We rode hard, deeper into the woods, and then turned north headed to Grenoble. My only thought was of Phoebe. I would chase after her no matter the cost to me. I had to find her.

***

Phoebe struggled to release herself from her bonds but could not. The camera obscura was chained to the back of the cart, and she sat next to it unable to free her hands. The soldier who had captured her had used leather rope to tie her up. She had tried to escape for the last hour but could not. And with her hands tied, she couldn't call forth a spell. She didn't know how to call her magic when bound.

Two men manned the front of the cart, and the third man, a soldier who had not given her his name, rode on horseback, leading them onward on the path.

By mid-day, she had rested as best she could, surprised to see they had arrived at a city.

The soldier who had captured her slowed down and matched his horse to the cart's speed. "We're here."

Phoebe kept quiet and did not say a word.

He slowed his horse up and commanded the two men to stop their horse. The cart slowed and eventually came to a halt. The drivers jumped out and one went to relieve himself behind a tree.

The soldier dismounted and then climbed into the cart, facing Phoebe. "My name is Louis." He kept his hands at his side, staying at the far end of the cart.

She prepared to defend herself if he tried to come near her, but the restraints still had cut off her magic. "I'm Phoebe."

"I know who you are," he said with disinterest and pointed at the city. "When we enter there, I need you to behave. Can you do that?"

"What do you mean by behave?" Phoebe watched him, but he kept himself closed off to her.

He wore his military uniform and had a clean-shaven face, but both his cheeks were bright from the cold. "I am going to untie you and trust that you'll not try to escape. Will you do that?"

"Try to escape?" Phoebe played with him on purpose and he rolled his eyes.

"I do not joke and I would rather you be turned over unharmed to the emperor. He is headed here with his army." He tapped the side of the cart and then pointed at her bonds. "Do you agree?"

"Yes." She turned away from him to look at the city ahead. "I'm tired, cold, and hungry. I'm not going to fight you and try to escape. I have nowhere to go."

"Good, then we will be the best of friends." He leaned over and pulled a knife from his pocket. Before he cut her bonds, he held the knife up before him. "If you try to escape, I will find you."

Phoebe showed him her hands and held them apart so that he could more easily free her. "I told you that I'm not going anywhere."

He said no more and then cut through the leather binding her hands. "The emperor has given us explicit instructions on how to treat you." Louis freed her hands and then stepped back. "He warned me about you, and I'll take precaution to protect myself from your powers if you try to use them."

Phoebe laughed and shook her head. "I've given you my word. I'll not run away."

She went to say more but changed her mind and decided to remain quiet.

"There is nothing you have to fear…"

The rest of what he had to say was drowned out by a large clap of thunder. The sky flashed a brilliant pink for a few moments and then the ground shook. Louis' horse spooked and took off away from the city. He held onto the side of the cart and fell to his knees.

Up ahead, a brilliant column of fire sprung up from the center of the city, and tendrils reached up toward the sky. The sound deafened them, and a few seconds later, the force of the explosion hit them and knocked them both backward. Phoebe fell into the camera obscura, and Louis covered his ears with his hands, watching a magical fire spread out over the city, dropping on the city like enormous raindrops.

The ground shook again, and this time the sky opened up, and more fire rained down on Grenoble. Massive columns of fire fell from the clouds, burning right through buildings, people, and anything else in its path.

One of the men who had driven the cart ran away as fast as he could. The second man chased after the first. Louis glanced up at the sky and the clouds dissipated. A massive city floated up above, and the flaming streams shot from cannons aimed down at Grenoble. Louis saw a fireball headed toward them, and he grabbed Phoebe and threw them both off the cart. They hit the hard snow and he pulled her underneath the cart. Around them the snow melted as the ball of fire exploded around them.

Louis covered his ears and shut his eyes to protect himself from the debris that exploded up and out of the ground as additional small fireballs impacted all around them.

Phoebe protected herself as best she could, covering her face and remaining hidden under the cart. After a time, the fire stopped falling from the sky and she could smell the horse's burning flesh.

Louis climbed out from underneath the burning cart and glanced up at the city. "Mon dieu!"

Lost in thought, he did not see the first arrow pierce his chest. He let out a gasp and spun around to see a tall man lowering his bow. Surprised, he tried to speak but fell back and died.

Phoebe pulled herself out from the cart and asked, "Ignatius, what are you doing?"

The faerie lord smiled at her and shook his head. "I have finally defeated my brother Ignatius." A sly grin slowly formed on his face. "And now I'll conquer this world as well."

Phoebe raised her hand to him and fired off a quick blast of magic. He easily deflected her weak spell by waving the energy away from himself and into the ground.

"I don't think so." He pointed his index finger at her, and a red beam of light streamed out at her.

Phoebe dug deep and called forth her magic. The magical ray deflected off of an invisible shield that she had surrounded herself with, and she opened up the dreamline in desperation. Without knowing where she was going, she dove in and closed the portal behind her. The Crystal Prince shouted an obscenity at her, but she fell back and all went dark.

***

I only thought of Phoebe as the winter air chilled me to the bone. We had ridden hard for several hours, pushing our horses hard, but I wanted to be reunited with her as quickly as I could. I tried not to think about the hundreds of men who died in the attack or of the Cryshada that would be scouting the area in an attempt to find us.

Sunset approached and we eased up on our horses. I brought my horse close to Jeremiah's and absently patted the animal's neck. "Are we almost there?"

Napoleon pointed at the hill ahead and said, "Once we rise up and go over that, we'll be able to see the city."

Jeremiah urged his horse onward. "Our horses need food and rest. We can't go much farther."

I took the lead and headed up the hill. When I reached the top, I stopped my horse and shielded my eyes from the setting sun on my left. When my eyes adjusted, I quickly turned around and shouted, "Jeremiah, come here quick!"

About halfway up the hill, he gently kicked the horse's side and came faster. When they arrived at the top, Napoleon dismounted and ran toward the summit. "Non, non, non!"

I came down off my horse as well and rushed over as Jeremiah jumped off his horse in a rush to meet me. "What are we going to do?"

Heavy black smoke rose high in the sky from what was left of Grenoble. The city still burned, and from this vantage point, I could see debris surrounding the populace's limits. Jeremiah squatted down and scanned the entire area. "I don't see any remnants of the army that did this."

"Was it those crystal creatures?" Napoleon asked. He pulled a small spyglass from his pocket and searched the surrounding area. "There's nothing left alive down there."

He said the words and lowered his head, handing me the spyglass.

I could only see smoke from the buildings as they smoldered. Whole buildings had been razed, and with the instrument, I could see overturned carts, wagons, and dead horses that littered the roads. "Anyone that tried to escape was killed."

"Do you think it's those creatures that tried to attack us back there?" He turned away from the city in disgust.

I took one last look through the spyglass and found her. "Oh, my God." I threw the instrument down and ran down the hill as fast as I could in the light covering of snow.

"Wait!" Jeremiah ran after me, but I did not stop for him.

Phoebe trudged up the hill toward me. She waved her arms in the air to let me know that she had seen me. I did not stop to think and kept running until we crashed into each other's arms.

"You found me!" I hugged her close and wanted to keep her at my side forever.

She cried and after a few moments pulled herself from me. "We have to run. The Crystal Prince has killed Ignatius, and the faeries attacked the city. I barely escaped."

Jeremiah reached out and hugged Phoebe. "Are you okay?" He pulled back her hair from her face to make certain she was not wounded.

"I'm fine." She hugged him and said, "But Charley—" Her voice broke and she could not stop her tears. "He's dead."

I grabbed her hand in mine. "We have to go then and get away from here. We have to find a place to hide."

Napoleon heard the last of my words, and he pointed off to the west. "Our best bet is to find a farmer and hide in their barn until we can come up with a plan."

Phoebe ignored Napoleon and grabbed at me. "There's more. The Golden Fox. I think he's dead too." She took a breath and the words tumbled out of her. "Napoleon's men killed him and they captured me."

I turned on Napoleon and slapped him hard across the face. "You promised us that she would be safe!"

He did not react and kept a steely gaze on me. "I needed to ensure that you would not betray me, so I instructed my men to hold Phoebe safe until we arrived at Grenoble."

"You lied to us." I went to slap him again.

Jeremiah moved closer to me and lowered his voice. "Please, calm down."

I don't know what came upon me, but I snapped. "Calm down? I'll do anything but! He took Phoebe against her will and I'm stuck here with my most hated enemy with no weapons, magic, or place to go. Meanwhile, the Crystal Prince has invaded from the Other side, and he's destroyed a city with ease, and you want me to calm down?"

The words rushed out of me, and I lifted my hand, pointing it at Napoleon. I dug deep and willed my magic to come to me in my desperation. Nothing happened.

"Damn you!" I rushed forward and punched Napoleon's chest with my fists.

He stood firm and did not block my blows. I pummeled him and when Jeremiah went to intervene, I turned on him.

"Leave me alone!" I clenched my fists and said, "I've failed and we've lost. There's no need for you to stay any longer. I can see it in your eyes how much you want to leave me. I'm damaged, broken, and you've had enough—so leave!"

"Mother!" Phoebe rushed up to me and pulled me to her. "Please, what has come over you?"

Napoleon turned away and walked toward the edge of the summit. I guessed from his expression that he did not understand my rapid-fire rant. His English was good, but not that good.

Jeremiah waited until Napoleon had given us some space to talk, and he raised his hands to plead with me. "Look, I'm not here to fight you. I'm upset too, but our arguing isn't going to solve our problems. We'll still be stuck here in the cold, and we need a plan to survive. We can deal with Napoleon later, but we need to keep him where we can see him."

My chest heaved and I fought hard not to cry. A complex rush of emotions came over me, and I turned away from him and Phoebe, looking at the embers of Grenoble. "There's only one thing I can think of to save all of us." I faced them and spoke the truth. "It's the only thing left to do."

At the top of the hill, a flash of lightning stretched across the sky, and a dark red hue shone from the other side.

Jeremiah turned around and stared up at the eerie light. He pulled his rifle from his back and readied himself for the approaching onslaught. "What's your plan?"

I faced both Jeremiah and Phoebe, showing them the palms of my hands. "I have been lying to both of you."

Phoebe turned her head sideways and looked at me out of the corner of her eye. Even from a young age, she had looked at me this way when she did not know if someone told her the truth or lied. "What do you mean?"

The urge to show them both rushed on within me, but I still fought it back. I had been resisting for a long time, but each day I felt weaker and I gave in more and more to the need. I held up my left hand and showed it to them. "I can use magic if I want." I released the magic within me, and a dark tendril of power crawled out from under my skin and swirled around my fingers like living tar. "I can use all the dark magic that I want."

Phoebe shook her head and yelled, "No, please don't!" She released her own magic, and it was the brightest white light that I had ever seen. The light floated around her, making her look like an angel.

Jeremiah held his hands up to me, pleading. "This isn't the way."

"It's the only way that we can survive this." I pointed at the red lights up in the sky. "They'll be here in moments, and I can destroy them with the dark magic. I know I can."

Napoleon had come close to Jeremiah and Phoebe, but he said not a word. He had crossed his arms over his chest and waited to see what I would do.

The ground shook beneath our feet, and on top of the hill, more Cryshada than I could count appeared ready to rush down toward us.

A flash of red light blinded me for a moment, and the Crystal Prince materialized in front of his army. He unsheathed a longsword from its scabbard and pointed the weapon at us. "Give me Phoebe and I will let you all live."

I knew what would happen if I acted. I could feel it within me. The anger and hatred had been growing, and I had suppressed it for too long. I turned toward Phoebe and said, "Whatever happens, I love you."

"No!" Phoebe came to stop me, but it was too late.

I ran forward and pointed at the Crystal Prince. Inside I tapped into the dark and murderous part of my soul. The darkness that had always lived there but I had tamed over the years, allowing people to abuse and use me. I had tried to regain my magic the right way. Now I needed it to save us, and I would release my hate to the world.

The Crystal Prince hovered in the sky above the hill, and I pointed at him. The black tendrils of magic that covered my arm shot forth, flying in the air to wrap themselves around the Crystal Prince. I fed off of the pain, my hate, and anger. I released it and a sound came up from deep within my soul, and at my bidding, I let it live.

An explosion of dark energy emanated from within me, and the blackness came out as a living mass. Dark jet-black, the blob shot out of my mouth, eyes, and every orifice, coalescing into a breathing sphere of blackness. I screamed wordlessly, and the sphere exploded into thousands of pieces, flying down at the marching Cryshada. The black energy turned into a living tar and covered over my enemies. I twirled my hand and pulled the energy to do my bidding, and it did, eating away, like an acid, anything in its path.

The onslaught of my hate made me feel strong. I stood firm and let all of my power out. I held nothing back. The darkness grew in scope and size, covering me with its beauty, and I smiled as my enemies faded away.

Out of the corner of my eye, I saw Jeremiah grab Napoleon and pull him away from me. The black energy mass grew and nearly covered every part of my body. I thrived in its energy, allowing it to strengthen me.

Phoebe had thrown up a protective shield around her, Jeremiah, and Napoleon. She stood frozen, unsure what to do. She still yelled at me, but I ignored her.

"Leave us be!" I fired off a fresh glob of dark energy at the Crystal Prince, but he dispelled it with his sword.

He flew down to face me, and when he hit the ground, he raised his right hand and fired an intense red beam of light that hit my dark energy, causing it to become crystallized and shatter into a million tiny pieces.

"Give me Phoebe or I will kill you all." He pointed his sword at me.

"Never!" I clenched both my fists and then roared at him like a madwoman. I lost sight of who I was, what I wanted, and the power devoured me and I it. I let it all go, the reasoning, my fear, hate, anger, and I just let the power stream out of me. I would wash away the world and make it new again. Nothing could stop me.

My dark energy surrounded the Crystal prince but he simply waved his hand and all the energy tendrils I had sent at him turned to red crystal and shattered to the ground.

"You cannot stop me." He smiled and pointed at me with his sword. The tip glowed hot, and a pulse of red light, brighter than the sun, shot forth, and on hitting me, my breath stopped. My magic cut off and I fell to the ground.

I put my hands to my throat and gasped for air. When I exhaled, tiny red crystals spewed from my mouth. They glowed and tumbled down like snow to the ground. I could not talk or breathe, and the Crystal Prince walked past me toward Phoebe. My heart beat faster in my chest. I had only seconds left and needed to act. I had no time.

The prince pointed his sword at Phoebe, and her magical shield shattered, leaving her vulnerable to him.

Jeremiah rushed forward and aimed his rifle, but the prince pulled Jeremiah into the air with his magic and threw him away like a toy. Napoleon had his sword drawn, but the prince swung his blade, cutting the emperor's weapon in half, and then knocked him aside as well.

"Finally, I have you." The Crystal Prince reached forward to put his hands on Phoebe.

No!" I didn't care about the pain in my throat, how my body ached, or anything. I pointed toward Phoebe and released all my magic at her. The dreamline ripped open behind her. "Phoebe, go!"

The darkness around me ate me up and I liked it. Phoebe and I locked eyes, and we stared at each other. My daughter saw me for who I truly had become. I thrived on the hate and anger within me and unleashed the darkest parts of myself. I recalled the time I had cursed Henri and how powerful it had made me feel. So righteous and strong up on my high hill, surveying those below me. I let Phoebe see me for who I had truly become. The person I had hid from everyone for a long time. I chose the dark because it fixed the broken parts of me, and I looked at my daughter for the last time and pushed.

Phoebe shook her head and trembled in fear. But she could not stop me. I was too strong for her. She fell back into the dreamline and was gone. I had cast her farther than anyone had ever traveled. The Crystal Prince would never find her.

Once the portal to the dreamline shut, an explosion of dark energy knocked me backward, and I fell hard to the ground. My hands hit first and the cold snow shocked me. For a moment, I still couldn't breathe, and then a great weight lifted off me, and the prince's magic vanished.

I crawled over onto my side. The Crystal Prince had fallen to his knees. He tried to use his sword to balance himself but fell over into a snowdrift. Wisps of my dark magic swirled around him still, leaving a kiss of death on anything it touched. Struggling to his feet, he faced me and could barely talk. "I will kill you for what you've done."

He stumbled over to me with his sword raised high, and I tried to call on any magic to help me but could not get up. My energy was spent. Death would take me, but Phoebe would be forever safe. Maybe she would start over and find a way to live in peace. I hoped so as I had failed miserably.

The Crystal Prince gathered his strength and raised his sword high in the air, preparing to impale me to the spot I had fallen. I raised my hand, and then the prince's chest burst open. Crystal pieces shattered in all direction and his eyes opened wide. Jeremiah's rifle shot echoed across the land, and he stood eyeing his perfect shot through the prince's heart.

No blood, only tiny crystals that tumbled out of him like sand on a beach flowed out onto the white snow. The crystals hit the snow and melted it, and the prince fell to his knees. He fought against his fading life and spat at me. "My father will come for you all. He will and I will be—"

The light went out from his eyes, and he fell sideways into the snow.

A silence came over me, and his magic dissipated, and I could breathe. I took in a gulp of fresh air and could only hear the beating of my heart. Napoleon rushed toward me as did Jeremiah, and a nagging feeling came over me. I faded back into the darkness and I reveled in it. I did not feel ashamed for what I had done. The darkness saved me and I would do it again. I knew that and looked forward to the next time. Nothing would ever stop me again for using magic. Nothing.

Epilogue

Phoebe squeezed her eyes shut and spun forward through the dreamline. Her stomach churned as she rode the wave of time. Textures of soft silk, jagged walls and the brush of sand came in contact with her hands. Like it was a slide that her mother had made for her as a kid, she slid down, unable to control her speed or direction.

A cacophony of sound washed over her. At first it was the roar of a crowd of people, screaming, yelling in anger. She could not make out the words but opened her eyes to see tens of thousands of people, shoulder to shoulder, marching through the street. Many held signs that whizzed past her in the blink of an eye. The speed of her trip through the dreamline went faster, and the dark energy that propelled her forward cast her off across the ocean, and behemoth ships floated on the water like small cities.

Streaks of light coursed through the air from a particular point south of her. The light transversed the sky like an arch whose tip touched the sky. Up above, the lights all stretched to an invisible point above, but some flew higher toward the moon that was so far away. Time sped faster and the Earth changed, while parts stayed the same, until the journey ended with a loud pop. She fell forward out of the dreamline that then closed in on itself and, with a sucking sound, vanished from sight.

Phoebe caught her breath, taking in air quickly. Her heart beat fast and strange lights lit up the alley where she rested. The air smelled funny, an odor she did not recognize and didn't quite like, but it was warm. The building in front of her stretched up high into the sky, and all around her were similar structures that stretched up beyond where she could see. Next to her a loud fan expelled hot air up into the night sky.

Picking herself up off the ground, she tried to clear away the dirt from her coat but smeared it more than cleaned it. Flashing lights from the end of the alley caught her attention, and she walked toward them.

The lights flashed brightly in neon colors, and several translucent women, dressed like ballerinas, danced in the sky. They twirled and then on finishing their dance each held a bottle that they pointed to her. "Revive for when you need to feel re-energized."

Music swelled and the ballerinas stopped and then restarted their dance again. Below the illusionary ballerinas, hundreds of people walked on the city street oblivious to anything around them. Not one person turned to look at her by the side of the road. Instead they looked up and to the right, almost as though they focused on a point on the horizon that she could not see. The lights and noise overwhelmed her. Every direction she looked was something that she did not understand.

"Miss?"

Taken aback, she spun around to see a man made out of metal standing behind her.

"Would you like a program for tonight's shows?" The voice, soothing and calm, came out of the man's head, but its lips did not move.

The metallic man reached for her and she pulled away. "No, I'm fine."

"All shows are listed on the grid with their start and end times." The metallic man turned its head away from her and pointed in the opposite direction. "Tonight's showing of *Cinderella* will start at eight. If you purchase two tickets, I can give you coupons for your dinner afterward."

"No, I said I don't want anything." Phoebe turned away and left the alley to walk on the street.

She kept pace with the people next to her, and they wore such different clothes. The woman directly in front of her looked barely dressed with a short skirt and hair shaded in multiple colors. But no one acknowledged her as she walked among them. Each continued to stare off to a point in the sky, and many mumbled to themselves.

At the end of the block, she followed those around her to a line of stores. People went in and out of the various storefronts, and in the center courtyard, a massive display of exotic flowers rose up out of the ground. She glanced down at her clothing and knew that she stood out among the crowd. People wore exotic clothing, some had lights on their shirts that flashed symbols or words, and everyone appeared distracted.

Closing her left fist, she focused her magic and reached out to the world around her. Available only for her to see, lines of light crisscrossed the city, traveled through the buildings, and into the hearts and minds of the people walking the streets. The tendrils of energy went from person to person to more metallic men wandering in the crowd and then up in the sky. With each connection, she listened and learned.

A loud buzzing sound overhead frightened her, and she watched as a balloon-like device floated over the stores. People pushed past her and she kept her head down until she turned a corner and stopped.

The crowd, like a living stream, parted around her and flowed past her toward each of their destinations. High above, a golden statue appeared to be flying over a fountain. Water shot up behind the golden man, and he reached forward, appearing to be flying in the sky. In his right hand, he held a ball of fire in his hand. His tunic, all made of gold, wrapped around him, fluttered in an imaginary wind. Lights shone on the sculpture, and it balanced on an illusionary small mountain. Lights from below lit the statue while the fountain behind it poured into a pool of water around the base of the small mountain.

"Watch it!" A young man bumped into her and she took a few steps toward the rail in front of her. Down below dozens of people skated on ice. A warm breeze blew Phoebe's hair back, and she marveled at the ice below. Embedded underneath the ice, red arrows lit up, showing the people which direction to skate. A mother held onto her daughter's hand, and they took small steps with their skates, but the little girl's ankles buckled, and she fell to her knees. Unphased, her mother pulled her back up and helped her daughter grab the guardrail to balance herself.

Phoebe took in the lights and sounds all around her. She kept her tendrils of magic still searching the surrounding city that fed her information. Like a monsoon, the flood of information was almost too much for her to take it. In her wildest dreams, she could never have imagined a city so filled with energy and light. Lost in thought, she closed her eyes and concentrated.

Little by little, she built up her power, piling one spell on another until she had amassed all her energy and concentrated it to open the dreamline. She needed to return to her mother and get back immediately. Too much was at stake.

Turning away from the ice rink below, she opened her left hand and willed the dreamline to open for her. And nothing happened. She tried again and failed.

Music from down below distracted her, and she turned watching three musicians materialize above the skaters. A fourth appeared and she wore her hair long in a bright pink. She sang in a language that Phoebe could not understand, but the emotion was universal. Loss, love, and a bit of hope.

Without warning, a light snow began to fall on the skaters, and they raised their hands up and pointed in joy at the sight.

Phoebe let her magic spell feed her as much information as she could take in about her surroundings until she needed to rest. Closing off the spell, she leaned on the rail, listened to the music below, and glanced up at the snow-filled sky. She then closed her eyes tightly and whispered more to herself than anyone, "Mom, I will come back for you. I swear it."

Feeling better that the words had been released out into the wild, she opened her eyes and watched the skaters. She would have to find shelter, food to eat, and learn how to navigate through this new world, but for right now, she needed to rest.

The hologram, the new word came to her from her learning spell, of the musician floated high above the skaters, and she sang her heart out and smiled. A look of pure joy came over her, and she finished the song laughing and waving to the skaters. She turned toward Phoebe and said, "That song goes out to all those who are lost and dreamers. Don't give up hope! If I can make it, so can you."

She bowed and blew a few kisses at the crowd and then twirled to let her long pink hair swirl around her.

Phoebe smiled at the singer's performance. She would not give up. She had a long road ahead of her, but she still had hope. And that would be enough.

Thank you for reading *Redemption*—the fourth book in the *Cinderella's Secret Witch Diaries* series. Want to find out what happens to Phoebe next? Be sure to read *Faith: The Jovian Gate Chronicles* (book 1) that's available now!

To learn more about Ron Vitale and of the other books he has written, visit his website at www.RonVitale.com.

ABOUT THE AUTHOR

Ron Vitale was born and raised in Philadelphia, Pennsylvania. Influenced by the likes of Tolkien, Margaret Atwood, C. S. Lewis, and Philip Pullman, he began writing at an early age, creating short fiction from his early Dungeons & Dragons role-playing sessions.

In the fall of 2008, he published his fantasy novel *Dorothea's Song* as an audiobook on Podiobooks and for sale in the Amazon.com Kindle store, and in 2011 he published *Lost*, the first book in the Cinderella's Secret Diaries series.

Currently, he is keeping himself busy by writing his blog, and on learning how to be a good father to his kids all while working on the next Cinderella's Secret Diaries novel.

Learn more about all of the books written by Ron Vitale at http://books.ronvitale.com

Made in the USA
San Bernardino,
CA